MW00412130

The Servant of Aphrodite

Philip Matyszak

Monashee Mountain Publishing

Philip Matyszak has a doctorate in Roman history from St John's College, Oxford University and is the author of many books on Ancient History, including the best-selling *Ancient Rome on Five Denarii a Day* and *Legionary: The Roman Soldier's (Unofficial) Manual*. He teaches e-learning courses in Ancient History for the Institute of Continuing Education at Cambridge University. *The Servant of Aphrodite* is the sequel to *The Gold of Tolosa* and is his second novel in this series. For more information visit www.matyszakbooks.com

First published in 2015 by Monashee Mountain Publishing Rossland, Canada.

www.monasheemountainpublishing.com.

© Philip & Malgosia Matyszak 2015

ISBN 978-0-9881066-3-5

Cover design by: **Ravastra Design Studio**
adapted from a photograph by Soham Banerjee
https://www.flickr.com/photos/soham_pablo/2252370968/in/album-72157603874136942/
with Creative Commons license 2.0

The Servant of Aphrodite

The author wishes to thank **Jeremy Day** who contributed to this novel in many ways.

Foreword

Notes by the editor and translator

The remains of what appear to have been a shrine to Venus were recently discovered during the restoration of the church of St Donatus of Zadar in Cvinsk, a small town in the Istrian region of Croatia.

The church itself is of considerable antiquity, dating back to the Late Roman period, but it is otherwise unremarkable. Likewise the shrine to Venus is of no great archaeological merit, being largely destroyed and the remains incorporated into the structure of the church which was later built upon the site. Therefore the finding of the shrine might have been a minor footnote in a local archaeological journal were it not for the mummified corpse discovered at the same time.

By 'mummified' in this case we mean properly turned into a mummy, as were corpses in ancient Egypt. The body was properly cleansed, stuffed and wrapped into a container. This makes it an unusual burial, but not exceptional. There are a number of other examples of Croatian mummies – for instance the church of St Blaise in Vodnjan houses a fine collection of such mummified bodies.

What made the Donatus find particularly interesting is that it appears to be of an earlier date than most other Croatian mummies discovered thus far. Furthermore, if the remains of a nearby inscription are related to this corpse, the burial was of a Roman citizen some time in the late second century AD.

The salvageable part of inscription reads

H.S.E

Q. Vet __ Turp__anus P

and a related fragment contains the abbreviation H.F.C.

From this we have attempted the following reconstruction:

'Here lies [Hic Situs Est] Quintus Vettius Turpillianus Panderius
... this [tomb] was constructed by his heirs. [Heredes Faciendum
Curavit].'

While contentious, this reconstruction has been given considerable weight by the content of the papyrus cartonnage. (For non-
technical readers, the 'cartonnage' is the material in which the
mummy has been wrapped.) As was often the case, the papyrus
wrappings were not constructed from fresh paper but rather
recycled from existing material for which those constructing the
mummy casing had no further use.

The practice of removing the cartonnage and restoring it to a
readable condition is highly controversial, for the mummy casing
is destroyed in the process. In this case the question was whether
to destroy a museum-grade mummy in the hope of retrieving
historically valuable texts. The decision to do so with the Donatus
Mummy was taken by Dr E.M. Anouela, Curator of Antiquities at
the Archaeological Museum.

Dr Anouela later confided to me that she had taken the
gamble in the hope of discovering a valuable text, such as the
earliest ever Gospel of St John which has been also recently discovered as a mummy cartonnage. However, after processing, the
papyri proved to be scraps of a personal memoir written in the
first century BC. Dr Anouela is currently preparing her findings in
an eagerly-awaited paper entitled 'The Taphonomy of Desiccation
and the implications of Cartonnage' which is to be submitted to
the *International Journal of Osteoarchaeology*

The actual text of the cartonnage was revealed to be col-
loquial Latin written in a highly individual style. The task of
deciphering this text was undertaken by Cambridge University. At
the university, it was immediately recognized that this MS was a
further installment of what the popular press has taken to calling
'the Panderius Papers'.

As an acknowledged expert in idiosyncratic and informal

Latin constructions, I had already been asked to translate the first of these texts (now in print as *The Gold of Tolosa*), and was therefore the natural choice to continue the work.

This translation is my best rendering of the lively prose of the author, one Lucius Panderius. Panderius had little regard for Ciceronian style, and rather than writing for posterity, it seems he simply wanted to get things off his chest. It is unlikely that this memoir was intended for circulation. Consequently it is written informally, with occasional profanities and military jargon well leavened with first-century Latin slang.

Here, I have endeavoured to give the feel of the text rather than an exact translation, occasionally substituting modern slang for ancient equivalents incomprehensible to the modern reader. While disreputable deeds in the back streets of Rome were necessarily secret, much of what the author has to say of other events of his day are corroborated elsewhere. Where ancient texts describe the events also related in this account, I have linked to these in the appendix.

Panderius lived in a brutal age, long before modern conventions of chivalry had developed. The nearest definition he could give of a 'fair fight' would be 'a fight which I might lose', and for him, the whole point of kicking a man when he was down was to ensure he would never get up again.

Panderius was a man of his times, and they were rough times. The man himself remarks, 'If I am not one of the good guys, I am at least one of the less bad guys'. This, in the city of Rome in 104 BC, was about the best one could hope for.

P. Matyszak, B.A. (hons), M.A., D.Phil, Lit.Hum. (oxon.)
Rossland, British Columbia, AD 2015

Glossary

Adlection When members of a body such as the Roman Senate choose further members

Amorges cloth A fine-woven cloth so thin as to be almost transparent, often used for revealing clothing

As One sixteenth of a *denarius*

Calanthus A large beaker with gently sloping sides and no stem

Caput Commission The head of a Board of Inquiry

Chiton A simple dress favoured by girls and Greek women

Contio A public meeting in which the Roman people are consulted about proposed legislation

Denarius A coin equal to about a day's wages for a skilled workman

Fetiales The priests charged with carrying out the ritual of a Roman declaration of war

Frater Brother (as in the word 'fraternal')

Gracchus Either of two politicians whose reforms were suppressed by the senate to the accompaniment of rioting and bloodshed

Optimate Member of the aristocratic and generally reactionary faction in the Senate

Praefectus Castrorum The officer charged with the proper running of a Roman military base

Quirites People of Rome

Salii An order of priests often associated with spring fertility rites

Sestertius Four *sestertii* made a *denarius*. Many Roman prices were given in HS (the usual abbreviation)

Silphium A plant grown only in Cyrene in North Africa, famous for its medical and culinary usages

Stola A long dress worn over a slip. The most famous modern stola is worn by the Statue of Liberty

Talent A measurement of weight equal to 71 lbs or 32.2kg

Vica puellarum Literally the 'Manager of the Girls', making her role in a brothel self-explanatory

Ranks of the Roman Magistracy

Quaestor A junior official who had mainly financial duties in the service of a more senior magistrate

Tribune The representative of the Roman people. He could propose laws and veto them and even arrest other magistrates. There were usually ten tribunes. (Not to be confused with military tribunes, who were junior officers.)

Aedile A magistrate charged with the buildings and other aspects of the running of Rome, including the licensing of taverns and brothels

Praetor A higher magistracy with diverse responsibilities, including legal duties and provincial administration
Praetor Peregrinus The Praetor responsible for foreigners in Rome
Praetor Urbanus The praetor concerned with litigation and prosecutions in Rome

Consul One of two magistrates in charge of armies. Consuls often also proposed legislation. The top Roman magistracy, the years were named after the consuls of that year.

Censor Magistrate in charge of state contracts, the census and deciding who was eligible for membership of the Senate

When Rome needed more Consuls and Praetors than were currently available, previous holders of those ranks might serve as *propraetors* and *proconsuls*.

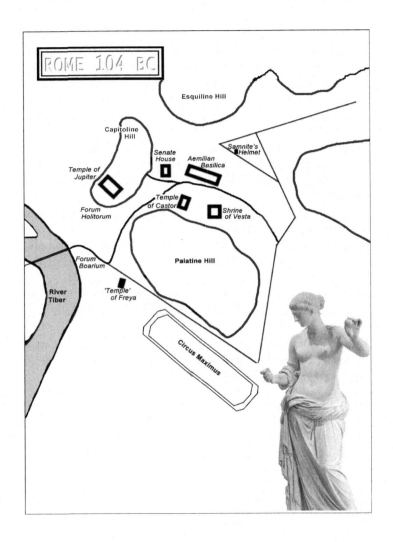

ROME 104 BC

Esquiline Hill

Capitoline
Hill

Samnite's
Helmet

Senate
House
Aemilian
Basilica

Temple of
Jupiter

Temple
of Castor
Shrine
of Vesta

Forum
Holitorum

Forum
Boarium

Palatine Hill

River
Tiber

'Temple'
of Freya

Circus Maximus

Liber I

Spring 104 B.C.

'What did your last master call you?' enquired my owner.

'Marcus Afer, Sir,' I replied stolidly.

'Marcus Afer? That's too long. Where did they tell me you come from? Somewhere in the north wasn't it? And call me Master'.

'From Pisarum, Master. It's in north Italy.'

'Well, I can't call you Piso, can I? So you'll be just Afer.'

Indeed. The Pisones were a wealthy family who counted themselves among the cream of the nobility in Rome, so Piso was hardly a suitable name for Afer (Marcus, deleted), who was a slave and therefore among the dregs of society in provincial Faventia.

As had just been demonstrated, I didn't even own my own name, which would be whatever my owner was pleased to call me. Calling slaves after their place of origin is common practice. If a slave becomes just the talking tool from wherever, this saves the owners from having to think about that slave as an actual person. It was some consolation that, despite my official status as someone else's property, the current situation could be worse - but then, can't it always? At least the job for which I had been purchased involved light work of a kind which I rather enjoyed, and my new owner seemed only mildly interested in my existence.

'So, how long were you with old Asconius?' inquired aforesaid owner.

'Eight years, Master. His death distressed me greatly.'

'Yes, it probably did. I'd guess that working in his household was a comfortable enough billet for you. Now, I'll have you know that things here are run more tightly - you keep the place in order, we'll get along just fine. You screw up, and I'll slice you to pieces with a whip. No doubt you've heard that your predecessor in the job here ran off?'

'It was mentioned, Master.'

'Can't understand why. He got his last whipping months ago. They tell me he found some tavern floozy and the love-birds made a bolt for the hills. Well, it's the mines for him when he's found, and a brothel for her. Do you have any romantic urges, Afer?'

'None that I can't control, Master.'

Caius Vidacilius regarded me indolently. He was a mildly corpulent individual, balding and somewhere in his mid-forties. In self-defence, I had already researched his background comprehensively. No-one knows another human being like slaves know their master. I had questioned the slaves of Vidacilius at great length and now knew a great deal more about Vidacilius than he was ever likely to know about me.

I knew his wife had died in childbirth five years ago, that his family was from the nearby town of Asculum, that he made a good living supplying pack-mules to the army, that he was a restless sleeper and suffered from regular bouts of constipation. I knew that the threats which he had made so half-heartedly were seldom carried out. The household slaves, so deferential to his face, were mildly contemptuous of their master behind his back. Already I was eyeing a stain on Vidacilius' poorly-washed tunic and resolving to have a word with the maid responsible for the laundry.

My job was to be the *maior domus* – the majordomo. In most Roman households that role is performed by the *materfamilias*, the lady of the house, but Vidacilius was a widower. It would be my task to make sure that the place was kept clean, that meals were served punctually and at reasonable cost, that the wine cellar was maintained. When Vidacilius invited guests to dinner, I must ensure that well-brushed couches and good silverware were ready at a moment's notice. It was also my responsibility to keep the other slaves in the house in order, to stop them idling or thieving, and to sort out any petty domestic disputes.

That was the tricky part. For example, the maid responsible for the laundry also shared Vidacilius' bed most nights and was happy to abuse the privileges this gave her. The doorman was partly out of my control, being a freedman and an employee, and he was very annoyed that he had not been promoted to my post. In our only brief conversation to date, he had as much as told me he intended to be as awkward and obstructive as possible. And so on.

In a way, I was rather looking forward to the challenge. From my research and our brief acquaintance, Caius Vidacilius did not seem a bad sort. I was reminded of when that old Greek rascal Diogenes was captured by slave-trading pirates. Before he was sold, the philosopher informed his captors that his only skill lay in managing men. Therefore he should go to a man who needed a master. Fair enough. If Vidacilius did not need an actual master, it was my considered opinion that he certainly needed managing, and his humble servant was prepared to take on the job

That was two months ago. It took a while, but the *domus Vidacilius* was now a rather congenial place to live. Vidacilius had given me a free hand to organize the household, and displayed only mild curiosity at the cane-striped rump which the laundry maid had indignantly presented to him at their next meeting. This comeuppance not only improved morale among the other slaves (for the concubine had been rather queening it over them) but the laundry and linens were now a lot whiter.

My predecessor had been in the habit of assigning whoever was free to tasks on hand, which meant that everyone took longer than necessary to do anything, and never did it well. Under my new regime, everyone had clear responsibilities, and a system of rewards and punishments to ensure that those responsibilities were completed as well as possible. I took care to do more rewarding than punishing, because the best work is done by those who actually want to do it.

Apart from instilling a sense of duty in the laundry maid, there was the matter of the doorman, who was commonly known as Nasone ('Snouty') because of the huge proboscis dominating his face. After tense negotiations, Snouty eventually promised to stop harassing the household staff and interfering with their duties. In a spirit of give-and-take, I had in return agreed to desist with my attempts to cram his head through the small window set into the large door leading to the street. This was something of a sacrifice, as I had almost managed it last time, and was sure that with a little extra effort the feat could be achieved.

My master Vidacilius was another ongoing project. I'd gradually weaned him off the watery, acidic local wines of Picenum, and introduced him instead to the full-bodied vintages of Umbria. Mellow Arratine wines with their semi-sweet, earthy flavours went well with the new diet I had chosen for him. After my second meal on the premises I had got rid of the cook - a surly Gaul - and picked up a Greek slave who could do things with a fish that would make it glad to have been caught. His grilled venison steaks with butter remain my fondest memory of Faventia.

The cook and I would spend hours with our heads together over recipes, and naturally I got to taste-test each meal. In fact I taste-tested my waistline to alarming proportions. An open-minded fellow in his culinary tastes, the new cook was fascinated by North African cuisine, and together we would haunt the markets in a hunt for exotic ingredients. While I was at it, I found a harpist for hire who knew most of the works of Sappho and other erotic poets. Suddenly there was no shortage of guests seeking dinner party invitations to my master's household, and I made sure that every servant afterwards shared the spoils of a successful evening. After all, if you are preparing a meal for ten in the kitchens, it's not hard to cook for thirteen and share the 'leftovers'. We had some memorable banquets of our own, below stairs.

'I'm even crapping regularly thanks to the salads and fresh vegetables you've got me eating,' Vidacilius informed me happily at one of our regular morning meetings. These meetings happened regularly just before dawn when my master and I briefly discussed household affairs before I scurried to the door where the first of Vidacilius' clients was waiting to greet his patron. Then, after a hurried breakfast, I would help Vidacilius into his toga and send him off to meet with *his* patron (we Romans are very hierarchical) while I sorted out the household affairs for the day.

It was at one such occasion that I informed Vidacilius that the drainage from the roof into the atrium pool was faulty. Water had been running over one of the roof beams for years, and that beam was almost rotted through. The thing needed replacing, preferably without taking off the entire roof. Distracted by forthcoming business meetings, Vidacilius did as he so often did those days, and simply told me to sort it out.

'You are making yourself at home here,' remarked the builder's agent once we had settled into the privacy of my absent master's study. 'Sure you ever want to leave?'

'Well,' I agreed, 'north-east Italy lacks the culture and sophistication of Rome; but it has disadvantages too. Even so, the past few months have gone easier than I expected.'

'Did you find it?' The agent leaned forward eagerly.

'In the first week. It's a silver box inlaid with ivory. About one-and-a-half feet by two. Vidacilius keeps it in his bedchamber separate from the rest of his documents. There are letters from his brother in there, and the occasional communication from a character called Pompaedius Silo. All the usual letters I file in his study, but these other letters come by special courier and I'm not supposed to know they even exist. Knowing what's actually written in them would be a death sentence.'

'And you know that because ...?'

'Well, naturally I've read them.'

The agent regarded me sardonically, which I interpreted as a demand to continue.

'The secret letters are treasonous as Hades. Vidacilius' brother and this Silo are real firebrands. They call Rome 'the wolf' and reckon the only way Italy will be free of Roman domination is when the last house and temple on the seven hills have been flattened into the ground. If you believe the letters, the rebellion has support from most of southern and eastern Italy, from Picenum in the north-east to Lucania in the south-west. Vidacilius *frater*, the rat, is using his brother as a sort of archive to store documents he doesn't want to get caught with himself.'

'Do you have a date?'

'For the uprising? No. It's still a work in progress. It's a tough job getting the people of Italy united on anything, let alone something as major as a rebellion against Rome. Umbrians and Etruscans don't have a lot in common with Greek Campanians on the coast, or with the native Samnites in the interior. Most of them were fighting each other until Rome came along and gave them a single enemy to hate.'

'This lack of trust means that agreements and understanding must be reached. Hostages have to be exchanged as tokens of good faith, and so on. It all takes time. I've been monitoring the conversation for weeks, and there's going to be no resolution soon. Everyone understands that Romans and Italians have to work together right now, even if the Italians hate our guts. So the revolution is on hold.'

'The Cimbri?'

Almost of its own accord, my finger ran along the scar between my ear and chin. That scar had come courtesy of the Cimbri. Or at least from trying to get away from the Cimbri. To escape from the doomed battlefield at Arausio I had been forced to jump into a rain-swollen river, where my face had been slashed open by a broken branch as I was tumbled along by the waters. This was a lot better than the alternative would have been if I'd stayed on dry land, so I was prepared to be stoical about the scar. Things could have gone much worse for me, although not much worse for Rome, on that awful day.

I briefly closed my eyes and replied, 'Yes, the Cimbri. Our would-be rebels understand that the invading hordes don't discriminate. To the Germans, Romans and Italians are all short men in chain mail who have to be chopped down before the Cimbri help themselves to our women and farms. So it's Roman and Italian, shoulder-to-shoulder in a fraternal effort to keep the barbarian host at bay - for now. Beating back the Cimbri is the first priority. What happens afterwards is what Silo and friends are plotting about. That is, assuming Marius and Catulus actually avoid getting themselves and their armies slaughtered. If the Cimbri win, Italy gets flushed into the sewers and there will be no 'afterwards' for either Italians or Romans.'

'So, what was it like at Arausio?' asked the agent curiously.

My face went slowly blank. Arausio. They called it the worse Roman defeat in a century, and probably in the top three of all time. What was it like to be there? How to answer that question? How do you explain a war-cry from tens of thousands of throats that hits you like a physical blow? Or the very ground thrumming under your feet as the charge hits home, and the battle lines crash together? How do you explain the half-glimpsed grotesques that two pounds of razor-edged steel can slice into a human body, or describe the sick sense of horror as you see the banners of your broken army falling? How do you start to explain, to someone who wasn't there, the grim comradeship of the doomed as we built barriers from human corpses to slow the final attacks we couldn't stop? What was it like?

'It was ... unpleasant. It rained all day. Now, moving on, what are the orders for Vidacilius' letters?'

'They're originals?'

'Confirmed.'

'Giving real names with verifiable seals on the documents?'

'Confirmed.'

'We'll want them. The whole boxful.'

I nodded. 'So some people can be quietly discouraged, others blackmailed, and a few will just quietly disappear. Oh, and talking of which, make sure that my Vidacilius falls into category one. He's to be discouraged without any lasting physical damage. I feel rather proprietorial about him. Apart from having a brother who is a hot-headed idiot, he's actually harmless. And talking of harm, how did you dispose of my predecessor and old Asconius' major-domo, the man I'm supposed to be?'

The agent looked mildly contemptuous. 'You know, for some-one who was knee-deep in corpses a few months ago, you're remarkably squeamish about a bit of judicious killing. They're slaves. It's not even murder. Vidacilius could have you crucified for breaking his favourite chamber-pot, and the law wouldn't do a thing. Why the bother keeping these two liabilities alive?'

'Well, I've been a slave myself these past two months. It gives one a new perspective. Killing don't pay, sonny boy. Knife the wrong person and it always comes back to bite you. Also, here's an odd thing about human nature. When Vidacilius finds out that he's survived the loss of his little box, we'll have a friend for life, because Vidacilius knows he should die though he doesn't deserve to. On the other hand, don't kill someone - like the brother who does so richly deserve to die - and he'll forever hate you for your mercy. People are funny that way.'

The agent shrugged. 'I'm not much for philosophy, myself.'

'It's called studying human nature. Either get good at it, or get into another line of work. Or be a messenger boy for the rest of your career. Which will be a short one, since before long your corpse will get stuffed into the drains by someone who thinks the same way as you do. And you didn't answer my question.'

'What question?'

'Keeping track of conversations is another necessary skill in this job. Try to learn it. I'll repeat, what happened to the other two majordomos?'

I got a sullen glare along with the answer. 'Both happy and healthy, as you recommended.'

'Demanded. It was one of the conditions on which I agreed to do this job.'

'Hmm. So what were the other conditions? I can't think of much that would make me risk my dignity and my neck as a slave. Was it a huge carrot or a bigger stick that brought you here?'

'Focus on the question. The majordomos.'

'Okay, okay. Your predecessor is back in Bruttium. As your owner suspected, he's with his new girlfriend. They're running a tavern together. He has family down there, though personally I'd not want much to do with them. They sold him into slavery in the first place, back when he was a kid. Money troubles. Oh, and talking of that, apparently he had a small bag of coins stashed behind a loose brick in his - now your - cubicle. He'd like that back when you get the chance, since you didn't give him the opportunity to retrieve it before you hustled him away.'

'Tell him freedom comes at a price.' I'd found the loose brick and the bag. Snouty had beaten me to the contents. 'The other slave ...?'

'Is running the manor on one of our employer's Sicilian farms. He's still a slave since he was part of the late Asconius' estate, and we purchased him fair and square. But as far as I

9

know he's as contented as a pig in the proverbial. Happy?'

'Content enough. Well, it looks as though Vidacilius is going to lose another majordomo. I'll skip while he is away visiting a widow lady he has been courting. She's set on becoming a wife again, and will be happy to have me out of the way so she can take over here. So, in three days time. Hopefully there will be one last courier delivery before then. Make sure there's transport waiting in the side street alongside the Twisted Pig tavern, and have that transport ready to move at short notice. I'll be along just before moonrise.'

'Why so late?'

'Because whenever I leave, the doorman is sure to challenge me about the box I'll be carrying. Things will get physical, and there's this small window in the street door ... it's a personal project, that's all.'

'Oh, and one other thing, ' I said as the agent rose to depart.

'Yes?'

'You wouldn't actually happen to know anything about fixing roof beams, would you?'

There were torches on brackets outside the Twisted Pig, though these did not so much illuminate the street as set a demon's circus of contorted, flickering images dancing across the boarded-up kiosks over the road. On my side of the pavement a drunk was bent over and noisily throwing up cheap wine into the gutter. I flinched as a waft of the vomit reached me, and turned to where the dark alleyway gaped like the mouth of Hades.

Normally the drunk would do his vomiting in that alley, where he could be mugged quietly at leisure by the footpads who lurk there for just that reason. But tonight the food scraps and broken pots shared the alleyway with a different class of litter. This litter was a two-seater sedan with heavy black drapes, no more than a deeper patch of darkness in the shadows. The drapes ensured the occupant total privacy within. Whatever privacy the drapes did not bestow was guaranteed by the eight Nubian litter-bearers who stood impassively beside the carrying poles. It occurred to me that a swift blow to the stomach would cause a man with a skinful of wine to puke in the street outside, and I therefore approached the Nubians with appropriate wariness.

However, I was expected. No movement other than that of white eyeballs in ebony faces followed me to the litter. I parted the heavy curtains and stooped within, screwing up my eyes at the sudden brightness of oil lamps. One seat was already taken, so I dropped into the other and blinked owlishly at the leonine man in a white robe who sat opposite. Apart from a swift glance he ignored me, and returned to carefully annotating a scroll with an ink-dark stylus.

'Ah, the *Caput Commission*! The head of the Inquiry himself,' I exclaimed, and received in reply a blank look from pale blue eyes - the means by which Cornelius Sulla indicated that he did not like what he was hearing. 'Er ... greetings, anonymous stranger,' I amended. A gentle rocking movement told me that the litter had already been picked up, and the Nubians were carrying it through the dark streets, moving as smoothly as oil across water. 'These guys are good.'

In reply, Sulla put his scroll aside and held out pale, manicured hands. I fumbled under my robe to produce the bulky ivory-and-silver box and passed it over.

'There's blood on it,' Sulla observed in the same tone that others might use to remark on a mild evening. He dabbed fastidiously at the lid with a linen kerchief.

'A nosebleed. Not mine.'

Sulla paid no attention. He was flipping through the contents of the box and every now and then holding a particular document up to the light and uttering a gruntle of satisfaction.

'Got what you wanted?'

Sulla ignored me for a few more minutes, and I leaned back against the soft cushions, mentally shedding the persona of Afer the slave from Faventia. Overall, now that it was over, being Afer had been rather fun. Certainly it was a lot less stressful than being me. At least, as a parting gift, Afer had arranged to get that cursed roof-beam fixed before it caused any serious structural damage to the house. Right now, he would have been making dinner arrangements for the following night and organizing a substitute for a servant away visiting a sick mother. Instead I was back to being Lucius Panderius, brothel owner, reluctant war hero, and even more reluctant agent at large for the nefarious, aristocratic and highly dangerous Cornelius Sulla.

Have you noticed that when life starts getting difficult, the only solutions either make things more complicated still, or you have to chuck it all in and go live in a peasant's hut in the mountains? Since Sulla would have tracked me down in even the most isolated Alpine valley, I had been stuck with complexity. Having only one option is no option at all, so Sulla had offered me an alternative to doing some spying for him. This second option involved certain misdeeds on my part becoming public knowledge, with the inevitable scandal followed by a trial, condemnation, and death in the arena or a slower but equally certain death in the mines. These were not usually punishments inflicted on a Roman citizen, but Sulla had assured me that he could persuade the judges to make an exception in my case.

So I had gone for Option A and become Afer from Pisarum. Hopefully Afer's success in finding and making off with that ivory box would make at least some of Lucius Panderius' problems finally go away. I felt hopeful about the short term. All going well, there would be a comfortable supper awaiting me in some secluded villa well out of town, and on the following morning horses would be waiting to take us down the via Aemilia to

Rome. Faventia was in the past, and I could focus my attention on the life which I could now resume.

Sulla looked up from his papers. 'This is good stuff, Lucius.' He recalled my earlier question. 'It seems that in fact that *you* have got what you wanted.'

'Exoneration?'

'Total.'

That was a weight off my mind. Six months ago, I had raised eyebrows in Rome by apparently returning from the dead - well at least from the river Rhone. Escaping alive from the carnage at Arausio made me one of the few survivors of the ill-fated battle of the previous autumn. No-one blamed me for not going down fighting. The Romans already knew whom to hold responsible for Rome's latest and most spectacular military débâcle, and that blame fell squarely, and very fairly, on the piggy rolls of fat adorning the shoulders of Servilius Caepio. In fact it rather helped my reputation that my last recorded act on the battlefield had been to throw a javelin with murderous intent at the fleeing Caepio. One wit in the Senate had gone so far as to suggest that I repeat the attempt in the Campus Martius and this time make a better job of it. Thanks in large part to the testimony of Caepio's aide-de-camp, a man who had no intention of going down with his former commander, my position as the survivor of a creditable last stand on the doomed battlefield was secure.

More problematic was my involvement in the disappearance of a truly massive amount of gold that had gone missing at about the same time as Rome's army. The Romans might not like it, but at least they knew what had happened to their legions. The gold, on the other hand, had vanished into thin air. Certainly the treasure had been there when Caepio looted it from the city of Tolosa before the battle. But when the ships carrying the treasure docked at Massalia a month later, they were found to be carrying nothing but urns full of seawater. A a huge uproar had followed, and over a year later the furore was only slowly dying down. There was a public enquiry of course – whenever something goes horribly wrong in Rome there is a public enquiry; with 'public enquiry' defined as the Good and Great of Rome meeting to decide which version of the 'truth' should be fed to the unwashed masses.

The *Caput Commission* who headed this the public enquiry was chosen because he had been away in Africa at the time, and so could not possibly have been involved in the theft. He was also both a popular hero and a confidante of the ruling cliques in the Roman Senate. This paragon was Cornelius Sulla, my patron and friend.

At least, I called Sulla a friend because I didn't want him to think of me as an enemy. Some people are incapable of keeping their friends, but Sulla was incapable of keeping his enemies. It was unfortunate. Before they could be won over by his charm and charisma, Sulla's enemies suffered catastrophic business failures, their health collapsed, or they fell tragic victim to un-resolved crimes and/or a freak javelin accident. Sulla was never at all implicated in these misfortunes, not least because no-one was suicidal enough to investigate to that depth. So I called Sulla a friend, and kept my health. Now it seemed I was also to keep my business.

'You haven't told me what the public enquiry discovered,' I remarked.

Sulla raised an eyebrow. 'Wouldn't you prefer me to forget what was discovered?'

'Of course not. You have discovered that there is absolutely nothing to connect me to the missing gold.'

Sulla hefted the ivory box in his hands. 'That is now the case,' he agreed. 'I would have lent you the money, you know,' he added reproachfully.

While I had been away, large sums of money had been spread

like a soothing balm around Rome in the name of Lucius Panderius. It had cost a fortune, but part of the expenditure had paid off a massive fine for running a business enterprise with irregular plumbing (okay, for running a brothel which was stealing water from the Marcian Aqueduct). Likewise an even larger fortune had been quietly paid out to atone for a degree of embarrassment plus wear and tear on the City Praetor who had discovered the theft. Fortunately, as the saying goes, *omnia romae venalia sunt* [the whole of Rome is for sale], and I'd purchased forgiveness and forgetfulness by the sack-load, albeit with borrowed money. Up to now Sulla had been running my bawdy house through a manager, and I was eager to re-take up the reins personally.

'I know you would have shown your usual generosity, but it's not just that the loan from Metellus was the better offer, even though his loan was gigantic and interest-free. More importantly, Metellus needs to be shown that he is forgiven.'

Sulla nodded. 'That one has always had a conscience. He'd leap at the chance to make up for what happened in Africa.'

'No, he's paying interest on that. It's not something you can atone for with cash. We both know that.'

'Of course. Metellus is going to be Censor this year. It's a shrewd move to let everyone know he trusts you with so much money.'

Indeed. A Roman Censor has the power to award the contracts for the maintenance and building of roads and temples. The Censor can make a senator of a man who deserves it, and strip the rank from anyone considered unsuitable. So I owed a Censor a huge sum of money, and this was a good thing. If any of my various well-placed enemies tried to destroy me, they would in the process destroy my ability to repay Metellus. An annoyed Censor could make life very difficult for all involved. Ask Lucius Manlius, the man who annoyed Cato the Censor. He was expelled from the Senate for a trivial offence, namely that he had kissed his wife in front of his daughter. Such an un-Roman display of conjugal affection had doubtless rotted the poor girl's mind, and was deemed by Cato to have sufficiently breached social norms to warrant expulsion from the Senate.

Our Censor-to-be, Metellus Numidicus, was a stolid, thorough type. Anyone he expelled would find the case for removal more solid. In Faventia, rumour had it that Metellus was already taking aim at a greasy demagogue called Saturninus whom he intended to expel from the Senate because he had unsuitable friends. To which the jurist should say a hearty 'proven beyond doubt' as one of the friends in question was that amoral, unconscionable oaf, our Consul and leader, Caius Marius.

'Barbarian invaders and seditious rebels notwithstanding,' I remarked aloud, 'the snake-pit of Roman politics roils on'.

'Are you hoping that the political process will eliminate Metellus and free you from your debt?' asked Sulla, 'Or is re-payment of all that money not a problem for you?'

It was a nagging worry. How much did Sulla know? Guilt and annoyance prompted me to respond, 'You never know. I might get a legacy or two. Someone might remember me in her will.'

That was a low blow. Less than a decade back, Sulla had been just another bankrupt aristocrat passing his time with low-life types in theatres and taverns. Then his lover, a wealthy com-moner called Nicopolis, died suddenly and unexpectedly - just after leaving her fortune to Sulla. That fortune was the bedrock upon which Sulla had rebuilt himself as a power in the Roman Senate. He did not like to be reminded of the fact, however indirectly.

I got one of those blank looks in reply, and silence fell. Sulla was sulking, and I was mentally kicking myself for having hinted that there was indeed enough money in my private treasury to repay the loan from Metellus many dozens of times over - if only there was a legitimate way to explain where the gold had come from.

Gradually, and despite everything, a smile that was unconscionably close to a smirk slid across my face. I had escaped my feigned slavery and was again obscenely (though secretly) wealthy. Furthermore, I was about to be officially cleared of stealing the money that had made me so very rich in the first place. Since I now knew that my name would not even appear in the official report, it would be fun hearing the conclusions of the Inquiry (which was, in fact, such an epic whitewash that my whiny young friend Cicero later referred to it as among the great cover-ups of Roman history. [Cicero *On the Nature of the Gods* 3.75 – ed.]).

Afer from Pisarum had come through. As Lucius Panderius, my reputation was intact, all charges were dropped, nay, had never been laid; my brothel was back in business, freedom, good friends, great girls and bucketfuls of vintage wine awaited my return to Rome. All was well in the world.

Liber II

A month after I got back to Rome, people started trying to kill me.

At first I didn't notice. For example, there was an incident one April morning, just two days past the Ides. It was a market day, and I was going grocery shopping with Ava, one of the girls from the Temple of Freya (as my brothel is known). In the business it is always a good idea for the management to feed the patrons. Not only does a full stomach make a man more relaxed and generous, it also absorbs some of the wine in his system. This in turn reduces drunkenness and the number of regrettable incidents which are among the less pleasant aspects of my job. So our Ava was in the process of becoming the resident cook for my little enterprise. As a prostitute, she was somewhat under-employed. This had a lot to do with her being short and chubby with curly black hair - a marked difference from the statuesque blonde Teutons who were the trademark of our institution which was, after all, named after the German Goddess of Love. But as a cook, little Ava had great potential.

As with all Rome's top bawdy-houses, our premises were south of the Palatine Hill on the via Patricus. From here, there are two routes to the Forum Holitorum, which is Rome's vegetable market. There is the usual route past the Portus Tiberinus, which involves shoving through the throng in the Forum Boarium and swatting away those who prey on market day crowds; the cut-purses, the beggars and the sellers of dodgy amulets and similar tat. It is easier to avoid this aggravation by taking a slightly longer route and ducking around the back of the temple of Venus Fortuna. (A real temple, this one, not another love goddess-themed whorehouse.) From there one walks down the narrow alley alongside the fancy new residences that have sprung up on the lower slopes of the Palatine, and then cuts in through another side-street alongside the Velabrum to arrive at the Forum Holitorum from the Tiber side. Today, even this little-known short cut was thronged with pedestrians.

'We're looking for the stall of a farmer from a smallholding in the Alban hills,' I explained to Ava. 'He manages to cultivate beets most of the year round. Fat, juicy beets, bursting with flavour. Why beets, I don't know. You could use his carrots as stone chisels, and the worms usually eat those bits of his cabbages that aren't rotten. But his beets! The man is an artist.'

'We'll need honey,' Ava put in, 'and really fresh yoghurt'.

'Honey is easy enough. There's a bee-keeper who brings his wares from near the Pomptine marshes. The orchards there have just been in bloom, and the flowers give the honey that ... ,' I waved a hand for emphasis, '... that light, tangy flavour with just a hint of apple in the scent. Oh yes, um ... if wine vinegar is not available, we'll marinate the beets in cheap red wine from the Janiculum hill. It tastes pretty much the same anyway. Then we'll go around the stalls tasting yoghurt till we find a blend that you like, and we'll get some dill that you can chop into the mix when preparing the beet leaves. Serve with pine nuts, and ecco! That's the appetizer for our guests tonight.'

'With Thedda, Calriaca, Adalhid and Biltwin as the main course,' giggled Ava. 'It's going to be a great party.'

'The wine will be tricky. I'm thinking of starting with mustum, flavoured with a bit of honey. Mustum is made like wine, but it is unfermented. Our guests can drink an urnful and get nothing worse than loose bowels the next day. Then for afters, we'll break out one of those syrupy wines from Tunis, the ones with the raisin flavour. They'll go well with the date cakes - which reminds me, look out for North African figs. Fresh ones should be arriving any day now. Careful here.'

'Here' was an ox-cart being pulled across the road by its driver, a surly-looking thug whose evident indifference to the rights of pedestrians could not be plainer. The intention was evidently to back the cartful of dressed stone to where a block-and-tackle arrangement was waiting on the kerbside. A pair of workmen loafing on a balcony two stories up idly watched our attempts to squeeze by before the road was fully blocked.

'They're so big, these buildings,' marvelled Ava, craning her neck to look up at the storied ranks of luxury houses marching up the flanks of the Palatine. 'Every one of them is bigger than the biggest hall back home'. Ava's father was among the minor retainers of some Germanic noble exiled to Rome after a tribal squabble. The girl was still new to the big city, despite having taken to its cosmopolitan ways like a duck to water.

'Can't cross here,' growled the crane operator. 'We're winching up the stone.' He stepped right up to me, forcing me back a pace.

'Give us a moment, and we'll be past,' I responded, looking past the man for a way through. It was impossible. The builder's bulk occupied all the space between the wall and the ox-cart. Short of picking him up and actually carrying him with me, there was no way past. Nor would carrying the man be easy. He was a well-set and very bulky individual. He and I glared at each other for a few seconds until he finally took two careful steps back.

'Look out!' screamed Ava and simultaneously grabbed the neck of my tunic. She yanked it so hard that I almost went over backwards as something blurred an inch from my nose, brushed my groin and smashed into the cobbles between my feet.

'Wha ...?'

'Everyone okay down there?' yelled one of the builders cheerfully.

Massaging my throat where the hem of the tunic had dug in, I glared up at the balcony. 'You nearly stove my head in, you ignorant lout! Why don't you watch what you're doing?'

'It's a building site, magistrate. Keep your wits about you, or don't be here in the first place.'

Ava was white-faced. 'You okay?' I asked, and got a quick bob of the head in reply. The crane operator was looking at the smashed brick. It had not missed him by that much either. I took the man gently by the throat. 'Either we get by right now, or you can try operating your little winch with broken fingers. You may want to know that the way I feel at present, I'd just as soon you stayed in the way.'

Some of the other pedestrians on the street joined in the discussion, crowding forward indignantly. Someone shouted, 'Bloody builders. You think you own the city. I saw that - you couldn't have done different if you'd tried to kill him.'

No-one much likes builders to start with, and the blocked alley was causing resentment. 'How about you shift that cart before we shift it for you?' demanded another passer-by. Some public-minded individual shied a mouldy cauliflower at the builders on the balcony. It missed and bounced off the wall, but the prevailing sentiment was clear. The builders ducked out of sight, and the ox-cart driver resentfully began to pull his beast back. Man and ox were rudely shouldered aside by pedestrians who shoved into the gap as soon as it opened.

'Just another bit of street theatre in the great city of Rome,' I muttered to Ava as we proceeded towards the market. She remained shaken. 'If I hadn't looked up, seen it start to fall ...'

'Media vita in morte sumus,' I agreed. In the midst of life we are in death. It had been a close shave, and I tipped Ava an extra week's wages after the party that night, but otherwise thought nothing of it. Not even after the incident two days later.

The Samnite's Helmet tavern has, exactly as the name says, a Samnite's helmet. It sits by itself on the shelf next to the barrel from which the owner serves his wine. The wine is invariably an acerbic red from Biturican grapes which mine host gets from his family vineyard near Volterrae in Etruscan country. It's rough stuff, but I don't go there for the drinks. The place is a legionary pub, and the helmet was honestly acquired as spoils of war. In fact that helmet was formerly occupied by the grinning skull of its original owner until the Aediles made the tavern get rid of it,.

As a drinking hole, the Helmet is a congenial place. It's on the edge of the Subura, close enough to share some of the louche atmosphere of the Esquiline Hill's infamous slum, but also generally safe and accessible thanks to its proximity to the Forum Romanum (which is Rome's main forum, and therefore generally called 'the Forum'). Not many people cause trouble in a tavern full of ex-soldiers. Not twice, anyway. One-Eye Hirtius is there after the ninth hour, almost any day of the week, and he runs a straight dice game. So I like to drop in occasionally, try my luck, swap a bit of army gossip and sample the house's signature dish of smoked thrush and pickled mushrooms. The thrush comes all the way from Spain, and one day I'll get the importer to supply my Temple of Freya directly.

'What's he doing here?'

Since the comment was evidently aimed at me, I looked up rather irritably from the game. There was two day's wages on the table, and my predecessor with the dice had rolled a vulture with threes (a 'vulture' is four dice all with the same value). Beating that took a Venus, which means all four dice showing a different value. It was my firm opinion that this could be achieved only with a resolute mind and a precise wrist action in tipping the leather cup holding the dice. At such a point any distraction was unwelcome.

'And you are ...?'

'We're real soldiers, legionaries. Not turd-kicking officers who sip wine and watch the other ranks do the fighting. We thought this was a proper soldier's place.' Three men, each thirty-something and unshaven glared at me truculently. They had been in the tavern when I arrived, and had apparently soaked up a fair bit of wine since.

'Ex-officer,' I said mildly.

'Eh?'

'I'm retired.'

'Anyway, watch your mouth, sonny,' growled One-Eye Hirtius. 'If you know he's an officer, you know that's Lucius Panderius. He killed more Germans at Arausio than you've ever met. Did no-one tell you how he swam the Rhone in flood, spent three days living rough and finally joined a cavalry unit to spend a month seeing those hairy Cimbric bastards off to Spain? What have you done that you can talk?'

'I had a brother at Arausio,' interrupted one of the legionaries. 'He was a foot-slogger. The commanding officers, Caepio and Manlius, and also this perfumed dandy saved their own backsides - but how many legionaries got out alive? My brother didn't.'

One-Eye stood up. This took a while, as there is a lot of One-Eye Hirtius to get vertical. He's got a massive stomach on him, but he has the height to carry it well, especially as his shoulders are even wider than his substantial waistline. My fellow dice-players got up too, and there was a general realignment of the tavern's patrons. Those looking to join any action edged forward, and the others shuffled back to watch the show. The barkeep gently eased back his shoulders, reaching behind for the cudgel he kept leaning against the wall for occasions as such as these.

'Sorry about your brother,' One-Eye said quietly. 'Rome lost a lot of good people that day. But don't go blaming Lucius. He's okay. Now you've had your drinks, and said what you have to say. It's time you went on your way, don't you think?'

There was a general murmur of agreement, and the three

legionaries turned their heads this way and that, assessing the odds. They didn't like the way it added up. One of them twisted his face and leaned forward, evidently intending to spit on the dice table. I held up one finger, and raised my eyebrows warningly. One-Eye raised a forearm larger than most men's thighs and this was considerably more convincing. Without a word the three turned, and shoved their way out of the tavern.

'Pleasant fellows,' I remarked, and we returned to our game. But my mood was spoiled. It was a dank, drizzly afternoon which reminded me all too strongly of that autumn day just over six months ago when sixty thousand Romans had lost their lives on the battlefield. Only by the grace of the Gods had I not been among them to make it sixty thousand and one. Eventually I pushed back my stool, and scooped my winnings into my purse.

'I'm done, boys. Till next time.'

Outside, the light was starting to fade and the air smelled of wood-smoke as the evening's cooking fires were lit. With my cloak wrapped warmly about me, I turned to walk downhill towards the Circus Maximus and home. It was getting misty, so it was almost a hundred paces before the trap became obvious. There was a man some thirty steps ahead, walking with a measured pace, and another shadowy figure keeping level with me on the other side of the road. Loosening the clasp on my cloak and patting my side where my purse should be, I made a loud sound of irritation and turned back as though I'd forgotten something. Sure enough, there were two men closing in from behind. There was something familiar about these beauties, and walking back toward them revealed two of the roughnecks from the pub.

Come to think of it, there was also something naggingly familiar about the man who had been walking ahead, but I couldn't place him, and at that moment there were other things to think about.

One of the legionaries gave an unpleasant grin, and slipped back his cloak to reveal a short sword in a crude leather scabbard. It was a sight to stop a man in his tracks, which was exactly what it was intended to do. A flicker of movement in the corner of my eye told me that the man at my side was moving in, and undoubtedly the man behind was too. The trap was closing.

It is not intuitive to run straight at a man with a sword, but as a legionary the man should have been expecting it. When caught in an ambush, standard army procedure is to charge straight through the killing zone and get among the ambushers before they can spring any more nasty surprises. So that's what I did. A half-second before our bodies collided, I let out an ear-splitting yell with every ounce of wind my lungs could muster, and faked a two-fingered stab at one man's eyes while slamming my left forearm hard against the other's wrist as he drew his sword.

Sheer surprise on their part and the strength of blind panic on mine combined to carry me through. Frantic hands grabbed my cloak as I went by, but with the clasp already loosened the cloak dropped off as easily as a lizard drops its tail. Fortunately the dank weather meant that I was wearing a pair of snug Gallic boots. My pursuers were hampered by their own cloaks and legionary caligae. The hobnails on those leather sandals give great traction on a battlefield, but they are less than optimal on slippery urban cobblestones. There was a clatter and a grunt as someone went over behind me, but this was not the moment to turn to look. I simply belted up the street towards the Helmet, hollering like a madman. Some kindly soul flung open the door at my approach, and a curious heads turned in my direction.

'Cudgel,' I gasped at the barman, and he grasped the club and flicked it across the room at me with in single motion. I caught the spinning weapon cleanly by the hand-grip, which afforded a moment of grim satisfaction as I whirled to face the four men skidding to a halt at the doorway. Only one man could fit through at a time, and facing a red-faced Lucius with a club in hand and homicide in mind made each man very polite about letting the others go first. This was especially true as the patrons recognized my attackers, saw that one carried a sword, and quickly put two and two together.

There was a general roar of outrage, and half the tavern's occupants surged to their feet and charged the door. The hunters became the hunted as the four thugs turned and fled. At this point the case for wider tavern doors became clear. Had a dozen men not tried to exit the pub at the same moment, my attackers would never have escaped before the crush at the door sorted itself out. As it was, by the time an orderly exit had been arranged the chase was fruitless. Those first out of the tavern went off hopefully scouting anyway, but I was not among them. My desperate sprint to safety had left me breathless.

'Wine - a full beaker,' I gasped at the barman while passing back his club.

'Seriously? You only ever have a half, and then you drink like it was medicine.'

'Shut up and pour. And yes, it's medicine.'

The scouting party was not a complete failure. Someone found my cloak (which I had completely forgotten) and so earned himself a tab at my expense for the evening. Since I was back at the Helmet, there seemed no reason not to have a few more rounds of dice, so I rejoined the game.

'Rome is getting dangerous,' I mused aloud. 'There was something familiar about those legionaries. I've seen them before.'

'One of them looked liked something-or-the-other Vulso,' chipped in a voice from a nearby table. 'He was in my legion in Sicily. But he wouldn't be in Rome - that lot have been posted north to face the Cimbri.'

'Whoever they were, they meant you no good,' rumbled One-Eye Hirtius. 'You bring knuckledusters if you want to beat someone, and a man can break a few bones with a lead pipe. But a sword? That's for killing.'

'I can't think of any legionaries I've upset that much. I'd have remembered. Maybe they really do just hate officers. They were pretty drunk.'

The barman was nearby, sweeping up clumped sawdust from the floor. Overhearing my comment he looked over. 'Those three? In the whole afternoon, they ordered just a beaker of wine each, and left most of that untouched.'

'Well, with your wine, what do you expect? The stuff is an acquired taste. Like arsenic. You've got to take small doses till you become immune.'

Amid the general laughter, a thought struck me and I sat up straight. 'That's it! That's why the big thug looked familiar. He reminds me of a builder I had a run-in with the other day. Okay, I'm glad I got that sorted out. It was nagging at me.'

Perhaps it was just as well I was retired from the intelligence business. Given my current inability to recognize the blindingly obvious, I would probably have bivouacked in the middle of an enemy army without noticing it was there. In retrospect it was clear that someone was getting impatient for my death. The first attempt on my life might have seemed an accident. The second could have been put down to disgruntled soldiery in a pub brawl. The third try came a week afterwards and at the time I missed it altogether. However, the fourth attempt later that same evening was such an out-and-out attempt at murder that even I finally got the message.

It came as a stutter-step. The sound was enough to propel me out of both my bed and a languorous doze. This still left me with enough energy to twist so that my shoulders hit the floor with a jarring thud. Landing that way allowed me to kick my bent legs hard against the bed-frame, driving it solidly into the knees of the shadowy figure stooped over it.

A stutter-step is about timing. It's when you rush to embrace someone and discover that you'll either bowl the person over or end up half a step short. That's when you do a stutter-step, a hurried half pace that brings you right against the person you wish to embrace, or as may be, the person into whom you wish to drive a dagger. I'd spent the earlier part of the evening making lazy love to an elegant lady who was unlikely to get out of bed just to rush at me. Therefore that part of my mind that never sleeps had immediately and correctly translated the stutter-step into immediate danger.

The bed frame hit my assailant with a thud, but I'd also been hoping to hear the clatter of a dropped knife. That didn't happen. Instead, my opponent recovered with a speed and sureness which told me that this was not the first time he had been to the dance. He was both strong and quick, and clearly unconcerned about inflicting violent death on a stranger. My only salvation was that his eyes had not adjusted from the moonlight outside to the darkness of the room - and that advantage was draining away every second. Using my kick against the bed-frame as a spring-board I rolled to my feet, even as the assassin started feeling his way around the edge of the bed. Reaching over, I lifted a handful of bedclothes up at his face, and was rewarded by a literally wild stab in the dark that ruined a perfectly good bed-sheet.

That stab let me inside the assassin's reach. Cupping my hand, I whacked him firmly on the side of the head. Once, back at my family's home on the island of Pandateria, a man who had ruptured an eardrum while diving for sponges assured me that the sensation was like getting a red-hot skewer shoved into his skull. The pain was instant and so blinding that for several seconds he could do nothing, and after that all he wanted was to make it stop. For those seconds I had a free pass to do as I wished, and I used the time to deadly effect. The assassin had clapped his hands to his ear and thrown his head back, so I folded my fingers to let the tips rest against the calluses at the top of my palm. Then I drove the stiffened knuckles of my middle finger joints hard into his throat. There was a sound of gristle tearing, and the little wet crunch which signifies a crushed larynx.

Having no need to do anything further about the thrashing man, I ignored him as he fell and instead turned my attention to stirring the charcoal in a brazier back to life. My blow had caused massive swelling around the broken larynx which would quickly close the assassin's airway. For all practical purposes the man was dead already, though desperate gasps and wheezes indicated that he was fighting for breath to the last.

With the room lit, I looked around hurriedly for Fadia, the lady who had been sharing my bed. She was huddled in a corner, dark hair awry and a night-gown pulled around her. She looked at me with wide, startled eyes, and appeared not to hear my query asking if she was all right.

'How in Hades did he get in here?' I wondered aloud, and slowly turned my gaze to the door where the wooden bar that secured the entryway had been lifted carefully off its brackets. I looked at Fadia as she struggled to her feet. Noticing my attention, Fadia made a dash for the door. I caught her by the elbow and swung her around to face me.

'You let him in? Why?' Even with his purple face and bulging eyes, I recognized the dying man. 'Hey, you're the builder ... and you were with the legionaries ... .' there was a long silence as I belatedly put things together. Turning to Fadia, I asked with some bewilderment, 'You wanted him to kill me. Why?'

'Why?' Fadia gave me the coldest grin I have ever seen on a living face. 'Why? Because you wouldn't drink your accursed wine. That's why.' She grabbed the goblet of wine which still stood on a side table, and mimicked my actions of earlier that evening, delicately sniffing the bouquet, swirling a swig around in her mouth, and then spitting it back into the cup.

In an appalling take-off of an aristocratic accent she proclaimed, 'Mah deah Fadia, ay hate to have to tell you this, but you ah Falernian wine has been adulterated. The taste should be heavy with just a hint of musk, but this has a reallah bitter aftertaste, and a bouquet of almond. Ahm so sorry, but it's quate, quate, undrinkable. Undrinkable! Do you have any idea of how long I spent preparing that wine, you pig?'

'You tried to kill me because I insulted your wine?' I asked in confusion.

Fadia knocked back the wine with a single swallow. 'No, you blathering idiot. Because of what you said before that. Right after you spat the wine back into the cup.'

'So what did you say?' attracted by the ruckus, Helga, my house manager and *vica puellarum*, stood in the doorway. In one hand she held a flaming torch which lit up the room and in the other she held the short cudgel which she used (with remarkable efficiency and ferocity) to sort out the occasional fracas between the girls and their clients. Helga's gaze took in the flushed Fadia and the assassin who lay in a tangle of bedclothes, still occasionally kicking spasmodically. A large wet patch showed that the dying man had emptied his bladder. Helga raised her pale eyebrows.

'You arrange interesting evenings for yourself, boss. This is unusual even by brothel standards. Now I have to wonder what it was you said to the lady.'

'It was a joke!' I protested. 'She can't have taken it seriously.'

Behind, there came a huge, shuddering gasp and the clatter of the wine beaker falling to the floor. We both turned to see Fadia wrap both hands around her throat as though attempting to strangle herself. Her body went as rigid as a board, then broke into a series of sudden, jerky seizures. Her eyes rolled back in her head. Always pale, her skin now seemed white as ashes. One finger pointed at me accusingly, and then Fadia slowly collapsed in a heap on to the floor where she lay, shuddering violently. Shaken, I stepped back and looked at the two twitching bodies in what had been a peaceful bedroom, just minutes before.

Incredulous, I looked at Helga. It was a major effort to form a coherent sentence. 'What I said before, with the wine ... I ... I asked her if she was trying to poison me.'

'Interesting,' said Cornelius Sulla. 'The body has gone cyanic; did you notice that?'

It was hard to tell in the flickering light of the lamps which lit the now rather crowded bedroom, but there did indeed seem a bluish tinge to the late Fadia's skin. Having made this observation, Sulla turned his attention from the corpse to the fallen wine beaker. He sniffed the inside like a connoisseur, and then dipped a finger into the dregs. Licking a drop off his finger, Sulla thoughtfully moved it around his mouth before spitting hard onto my mosaic floor. Then he carefully rinsed out his mouth several times before sniffing the beaker again.

Not everyone can rustle up an expert in poisons with just five minutes notice, but fortunately Sulla was on the premises to practice his German - which is not a polite euphemism for screwing a Germanic prostitute (though he was doing that too). Sulla was interested in anything and everything, and had taken it into his head that since the Germanic tribes were such threat to Italy, he had better learn their language. That he had been assiduously doing all evening, in a typically Sullan way which combined business with the maximum of pleasure.

My patron had acquired his extensive knowledge of toxins while in Anatolia where the poisoning of monarchs is a minor contemporary sport. Few kings in the region die of natural causes, although perhaps death by successor is common enough to count as such. Of course, there were rumours that Sulla was already expert before that, as witnessed by the otherwise inexplicable death of the wealthy lover who had left her fortune to him. Now, dragged from a bedchamber in one of the more exclusive suites in the Temple, my patron seemed to rather enjoy showing off his expertise.

'A blended wine, Lucius! One for the experts. This drink must have cost a fortune.' Sulla tapped the small flask from which Fadia had poured the drink. She had done so slowly and sens-uously, leaning over me in the bed so that her breasts brushed my chest, her body a silhouette against the lamplight.

'This is a special treat for you, Lucius. A rare flask of Falernian wine from the consulship of Mancinus and Serranus. That makes its twice as old as you are, my sweet boy. Enjoy it, because you'll never taste anything like it again.'

I told Sulla, 'At the time, it seemed incredibly generous of her. I was flattered.'

'Oh, you should be. The wine is vintage Falernian all right, but the poison blend ... that was five times the cost of the wine. I'm guessing cherry stones were used as the base.'

'Cherries?'

'You wouldn't have heard of them. It's a fruit that grows in southern Armenia.'

'Ah, very poisonous, are they?'

'No more so than apples, but cherries are smaller and more delicious. The stones in the middle, though ... you don't want to eat the pulp inside them. My guess is that your lady here,' he gestured at Fadia, who had finally stopped twitching and lay still, ' ... had the original wine complete with the cherry stone extract. However, she decided it was not strong enough, which is why ...', he sniffed the wine again, 'I'm getting a definite flavour of apples. She'd have purchased a sack-load of them, just for the pips. You need to separate the pips out, split them, and put a cupful into the wine. Mash and strain, and there you have it - a drink that would kill an ox.'

'Except it would take an ox to drink it. One sip and you could tell the wine was off.'

'Ah yes. She got a bit over-enthusiastic. Still, how many people actually drink enough top-class vintage wine to actually know how it should taste? I could piss in a cup and tell people it was a rare blend. If they believed me, most would praise the flavour to the skies. Not many people are sure enough of themselves to spit out a once-in-a-lifetime drink and complain about the taste. Especially not to a lady friend who has gone to huge trouble to get it. Anyone else would drink down their dose, and be diplomatic and dead. You just happen to be the bloody-minded exception.'

'A bit extreme, isn't it?' I mused. 'For her to drink the wine to hide the evidence?'

Sulla shrugged. 'She didn't have any options. Once you discovered she was in league with that assassin she would be held for questioning. If she is not - er, was not - a Roman citizen that questioning would be extreme and painful. And once we discovered the poisoned wine, she would certainly get a death sentence no matter what her status. So once the assassination had failed, she was dead anyway. She simply took the short route to her inevitable destination.'

'Incidentally,' Sulla went on, 'that taste of wine has rather sparked a craving. Got any Falernian in your cellar? The unadulterated variety? I'll take a beaker or two as my consultant's fee. Join me in my suite?'

'Thanks ... I think. Okay, I'll be along in a bit. Before the night watch take the bodies away, I want to spend a few moments alone with Fadia and her friend here. And Helga,' without turning my head, I addressed my brothel manager who had been lurking in the background, fascinated by the proceedings, 'you can stop raising your eyebrows to the top of your forehead.'

'Working in a brothel might give you a dirty mind, but really, there are limits. Someone will know who this assassin was, and I want to take a death mask to help with identification. Now get oil, wax, and some boiling water, but above all, get out.'

Liber III

'Try again, Sir?'

The wiry little man opposite me hefted his staff and watched politely as I rubbed my skinned knuckles. He stepped back as - with a mixture of trepidation and fury - I stooped to retrieve the sword which he had knocked from my hand with a snake-quick tap of that cursed staff. That tap could have easily broken a metacarpal in my hand, but my opponent had softened his strike. He was playing with me. Scooping up the sword, I tried a sudden low lunge, aiming to get under my opponent's guard before he was set. Yet even before I straightened into the thrust, a whack on the shoulder threw me off balance. Then the little brute wielding the staff suddenly sidestepped and took the legs out from under me with a sweeping strike. As I quite literally bit the dust, a gentle rap from the steel-shod staff tip connected with the back of my neck, just where the spine meets the skull.

'A little harder here ... and it's goodbye mother, farewell father,' mused my tormentor, and he tapped the spot again for emphasis. 'But it was an excellent effort, going for the groin like that, even if a touch unsporting.' The pressure on my neck eased as the man stepped back. 'Would Sir care to try his luck again?'

I twisted my head to see my opponent's stitched-leather sandals and knobbly knees, and beyond that a pair of senator's daughters reclining on a couch and thoroughly enjoying my discomfort. The senator was a friend, Marcus Aulus, and we were in the *palestra* at the back of a villa in the Alban hills just outside Rome. The *palestra* was a sort of exercise yard, this one close enough to the rear of the house for Aulus' gladiators to occasionally put on a show for dinner party guests. I was here auditioning for bodyguards, and it looked as though I had found one. His name was Tancinus; a little bundle of energy apparently constructed entirely of sinew and ox-hide. He had a wrinkled, leathery face that made one think of a philosopher down on his luck, and the slightly startled, sour expression of a man who has unexpectedly swallowed a mouthful of vinegar.

On seeing this beauty hobbling along, his staff almost as tall as himself, the natural impulse was to help the man across the street rather than take urgent defensive action to protect skull and testicles. Apparently Tancinus rather took advantage of his appearance and had on occasion incapacitated an entire street gang in less than a single hectic minute.

'It's the staff, you see Sir. Fire-hardened wood, the length of it, and tempered steel on the ends. When you swing the whole thing like this ... ,' he swung and a practice dummy flew back in an explosion of dust and straw, ' ... then that end which hits, it hits uncommon hard. Don't really matter if you're wearing chain mail Sir, except of course you'd need someone to dig the links out of your flesh afterwards. And hold hold the staff midway, like this, here and here, well, come on Sir ... have a go. Stab me.'

'See? I can lift and block, then hit with this end, no, this end, here, here, here ... and here. Oh, very good, lots of passion in that attack Sir, but you see how a whirling block can parry a sword and come right back for a counter-strike? If I may be so bold, I would suggest you put a cold compress on that forearm. The bruising will go away in no time. Can I help you up?'

Timendi causa est nescire, they say. Ignorance is the cause of fear. Yet when ignorant of the fact that someone wanted me dead I had been merrily getting on with my life for the past ten days. Once enlightenment had arrived in the form of a pair of corpses in my bedroom, this had brought with it not exactly fear, but at least a degree of introspection.

The obvious thing to do was to determine who wished to kill me. So, late last night I'd sat down with a stylus and a wax tablet, and drawn up a list. There were some dozen wealthy young

Romans who had been thrown out of the brothel on their ears after more polite invitations to leave had been declined. Roman pride is a terrible thing and getting evicted from the premises of a bawdy house can injure this pride badly, especially when a group of the evictee's friends are catcalling and whooping in the court-yard while it happens. Threats of horrible vengeance had been made, some drunken, some sincere.

Then there were operations in Africa which might have given leading figures in Mauretania, Numidia and Utica cause to want me dead. And on reflection, the king of Galatia might want the same. I had upset a couple of people in Gaul too, and my recent exposure of Italian rebel correspondence had doubtless led to the gnashing of teeth and sharpening of daggers in certain quarters.

With three tablets filled, I sighed and pulled up another. On this I listed business rivals and a supplier who had been short-changing me with adulterated wine. The latter was now blacklisted throughout Rome and was apparently going out of business. He too had sworn to kill me, and had suggested a death more colourful than anything my recent assassins had attempted. Then there were a pair of prostitutes kicked out for bullying the other girls. Either of them might have found a wealthy paramour to fund repaying a grudge. Also, there was the wife of that wealthy equestrian in the corn trade whose husband had practi-cally abandoned her to take up with one of my German girls. She had sworn revenge as well.

Then something else occurred to me, and this required another tablet. On this I thoughtfully inscribed the names of another two dozen aristocratic Romans, men and women with a taste for sex involving inappropriate persons, species, objects, or a combination of the three. Might one of these persons have suddenly panicked at the thought of their exotic predilections becoming public? Two of the men were standing for office in the coming elections, and I certainly knew enough to ruin their chances. Had someone opted for a pre-emptive strike? Appalled, I considered the tottering pile of names in front of me. Seriously? How did a happy-go-lucky chap who simply wanted to enjoy himself and facilitate the pleasure of others end up with so many enemies? I had only stopped listing them because the wax tablets had run out.

Fortunately Rome is a big city which contained a measurable number of people who did not want to kill me. Diligent research in this latter group had produced Tancinus, the man now apparently determined to prove me wrong. At first I had jocularly pretended to mistake him for the agent, or perhaps an elderly relative of the strapping young gladiator type I'd had in mind. On reflection, perhaps that polite derision had been unwise. There had been something in that last set of whacks to the ribcage which suggested that a few of my barbs had hit home; which was more than my sword had been able to do. I was using a *rudis*, a wooden training sword. It could have been the most finely-honed steel *gladius* or a stick of celery for all the difference it made.

In Rome, laws such as the *lex de sicariis* make it illegal for a butcher to so much as absent-mindedly carry a cleaver more than five paces from his stall. Yet in all their prohibitions of swords, daggers and other sharp-edged weapons within the city, how had the Praetors missed the fact that a common walking staff in the right hands was a lot more lethal than any of these? That Tancinus possessed the right hands was now abundantly clear.

While the senator's giggling daughters made it plain that it was far too late to save my pride, a dignified withdrawal might at least save those patches of skin that would not already be black-and-blue in the morning.

'Okay, you're hired. A denarius a day, plus a room and meals.' Tancinus raised his eyebrows in query. We had discussed his terms earlier. I sighed. 'And yes, all the girls you can bed. May the Gods have mercy on them.'

A thought struck me as I hobbled towards the *palestra's* little wooden gate. 'Oh, and Tancinus? A fifteen denarii bonus if you don't tell anyone you're my bodyguard. We'll call you my spiritual advisor or something.'

Life is basically about tackling problems one at a time. Unable to work out who was trying to kill me, I had organized some protection. This was not a permanent solution, but the best available right now. With that issue out of the way, the next crisis was looming. The Temple had lost Ava, its cook.

'Run through it once more, Helga. I can't believe you'd be so stupid in just one telling. Go through it again so that the full enormity of your idiocy can slowly embrace me.'

A *vica puellarum* is the woman directly responsible for the organization and finances of the girls in a brothel. Helga's current bungle showed why I preferred to do the job myself.

Her reply was offended. 'This is a brothel. She works in a brothel. Ava was finished doing her cooking for the evening, and Lamponius was one short for a threesome. So I told her to join in. All the other girls were busy, and she wasn't. She refused, I insisted, and she walked out. Today she did not come in, and she has emptied her room. So she has gone.'

We were in the kitchens. The dome-shaped clay ovens were fired, and the flames from the grill threw warm shadows across the bare brick walls, but that had been done by the household slaves for their evening chores. The rabbits that were meant to be grilling still lay on the stone counter where I had dropped them that morning. The parsley was wilting on a bench and two chickens clucked in a coop made of twigs and bark strips, unaware that they had missed a date with their executioner.

Forcing myself to patience, I explained again.

'If a girl doesn't want to, or won't, she doesn't. That's the rule here. It's not ethics, but image and cold, hard cash. Look at these people.'

I flung out an arm to indicate our little establishment and the first patrons arriving for the evening. 'They are not here to climb on to some wench who has been coerced into the job. They can do that with any slave girl at home. The girls of the Temple are the most skilled, the most fun, and above all, the most enthusiastic party girls who ever dropped a toga. Their hearts - and other body parts - are really into the job. That's why we all make so much money. You supply some surly lass who really doesn't want to be there, and the customer might as well go home. Or worse, to a rival establishment that hasn't figured out my winning formula. Not surprising they haven't, since even you seem not to have grasped it.'

'See what happens when you try to interfere in management and don't stick to doing the books? Next time, stop trying to be a tribal war-leader and come and get me. No matter what your job title says, I do the managing, you accursed barbarian clod-head. Now Lamponius didn't get his threesome, our guests are not going to get their rabbit, and damn it all, I've got six dozen quail eggs and who's going to put them in aspic?'

I squinted at the flames. 'Let's see ... do we still have some of those baby spinach leaves left over from yesterday? Okay ... you skin the rabbits. Are you sure you can do even that without screwing up? I'll get a pot going. We might as well boil those eggs. Then I'll slice the rabbit thin and sear it over the grill. Serve on platters with pastries and white cheese. Add some liquamen sauce, and it won't be our best dinner, but we'll probably get away with it.'

'Ava has likely gone to her father. He lives in one of those insula apartment blocks on the west side of the Esquiline hill. I'll get the address off one of the other girls and bring her back in the morning. You're coming too. Spend the evening practising your apologies.'

My life has many roles. Five minutes ago, I was a chef. Now I was simultaneously host and parasite. Actually, that last sounds better in its proper form - *parasitos*. Translated literally from the Greek, a *parasitos* is one who 'dines with' a dinner party. A *parasitos* is chosen for his interest value to the other guests; a poet, a playwright, a traveller returned from exotic foreign lands, or someone close to the epicentre of Rome's latest social scandal. Our Consul, Marius the Magnificent, had recently returned from the African war and held a splendid triumph to celebrate his unearned victory over the renegade Numidian king, Jugurtha. So today's menu for our little dinner party featured a war hero from Africa. That was my good self - though I was privately convinced that the honour afforded me was as ill-deserved as the acclaim given to Marius.

'So you did not attend the triumph?' enquired Atilius Serranus. He was the son of that Atilius who was Consul a few years back and thus felt entitled by family rank to ask mildly offensive questions. His query was to kick-start the conversation - he already knew I had boycotted the proceedings. My distaste for Marius and his faction was a matter of record.

'Indeed not. Avoidable business took me elsewhere, so I missed the sight of our leader in his chariot with his face painted purple.'

'It always struck me as odd that we do that to someone being given a triumph. Paint his face, I mean,' mused Glaucia. Glaucia was an up-and-coming young politician currently occupying the couch of honour in the centre. Usually I'd be reclining next to him in my role as host. However, given my secondary role as *parasitos* I had opted for a place on the bottom couch near the door of our *triclinium*. This also allowed me to speedily re-assume my role as chef and dive off to the kitchens in an emergency.

Another of the new generation of politicians, one Octavius, took it on himself to enlighten Glaucia.

'It's to honour Jupiter, our patron god.'

'Well, no-one else honours Jupiter by painting their face purple.'

'That's because the *triumphator* honours Jupiter by actually *being* Jupiter. He becomes a sort of statue dedicated to the God, but living flesh rather than marble.'

Glaucia grunted in slight annoyance, and helped himself to one of the delicacies on a tray set between our three couches. That's what *triclinium* means - three couches. A formal Roman dining room has three couches, and on each couch three or four people can recline and eat in comfort off a central table. The fourth side is open to allow serving boys to bring the food. This particular tray held grilled baby pigeons purchased in haste and at huge expense from an upmarket eatery up the street. In my opinion they had been much too liberal with the garlic, which I'd partly tried to conceal with a spicy mushroom sauce. Fortunately Glaucia was more concerned with defending the slight to his knowledge than in critiquing the cuisine.

'I know that. It's the sort of thing your tutor beats into you when you are five. Indeed, I hope to celebrate a triumph myself one day. Don't we all? But still. Name me one statue of Jove that has a purple face.'

The old statue of Jupiter in the Capitoline temple, I thought. It had been wood and burned up with the rest of the temple when Jupiter hit it with one of his own lightning bolts a few decades back. Rome had been less sophisticated in the antique days when the statue was first carved, and because purple dye was so rare, painting something purple was seen as the classy thing to do. Being solid traditionalists, once the Romans had painted someone to resemble a particular statue, the Romans were not going to change it just because the statue wasn't around any more. I waited for someone to point this out, but the conversation had moved on, or rather back. Atilius was grilling me again.

'I would have thought you would want to see Sulla. He was in the parade too. Your patron did rather well.'

'By actually finishing the war, you mean?'

'Well, the capture of Jugurtha counts as a notable achievement on any scale, especially when done almost single-handed, the way he did it. But I was actually referring to the way it put Marius' nose out of joint.'

There was general laughter around the table. Atilius rewarded himself for his witticism by taking another generous swig of wine. Then he looked at his beaker and remarked, 'Everyone's unnaturally cheerful tonight. I blame this stuff. What are you putting into us, Lucius?'

'Well, I'm compensating for our culinary emergency with a rather special amphora from the cellars. The wine's a Sabine variety. Given that the gathering tonight is drinking Persian-style I thought you gentlemen might like a drink with a kick.'

'Persian style' means undiluted wine. That is the sort of thing young men do when being decadent. Civilized dinner parties mix the wine with water, and the more genteel the occasion the more watery the wine becomes. Fortunately when in a brothel, gentility gets down and dirty along with everyone else, and outré behaviour is the norm. This Sabine wine was for some reason particularly alcoholic, possibly because they ferment it with a more ferocious blend of yeast.

'Now,' I went on pontifically, 'I know that Sabine has a reputation for being heavy, but there's a way around that. Don't water it down - that's like taming a spirited stallion by beating it almost to death. Instead put it into an urn that once held Greek wine. The Greeks like their wine sweet, and after a couple of decades that sweetness leeches back from the clay into the wine and civilizes it. Rather like Greek culture has done with the Sabines themselves in fact.'

There was more laughter, and I held up a warning finger. 'Take note though gentlemen - there's an iron fist within the velvet glove. The wine might be smooth going down, but over-indulge and tomorrow morning it will kick your head like a donkey.'

'Not a bad idea to hitch your star with Sulla's,' remarked the diner beside me. He was a tough-looking youth with a square-jawed face reminiscent of a Molossian hound. While I racked my mind for his name, the young man went on, 'You have heard about his Marsian exploits, I assume?'

This was a reference to Sulla's recent trip to Marsian country, just south-east of Rome. The Marsi are one of those Italian peoples who have done as much for Rome's rise to power as the Romans have done for themselves. The saying 'No victory over the Marsi and no victory without the Marsi' pretty much sums up that nation's military contribution to Rome's greatness.

In gratitude for the Marsic contribution, the Senate had recently pushed up the taxes for goods from Marsic territory and had also channelled those goods through the Roman fortress colonies of Carsoli and Alba Fucens, thus depriving Marsic traders of revenue. These colonies were aggravating reminders to the Marsi that the Romans had expropriated the land from them to build the fortresses in the first place.

Consequently Romano-Marsic relations had recently been so bad that the Marsi were threatening to pull out of the alliance altogether. However, Sulla had stepped up for Rome and his month-long tour through Marsic territories had calmed things down remarkably. Of course, thanks to my stay with Vidacilius, my patron was in possession of a set of treasonous letters by leading Marsic grandees. This had given him considerable leverage to exert behind the scenes, but it was more than that as well. Sulla could change from carefree party animal to cold-blooded schemer and back again in the course of a single sentence. When he wanted to be, he was a superb diplomat. I had no doubt that he had charmed the Marsic aristocracy with sheer force of character, and left not a few Marsic ladies with fond memories of his company.

'Then there's that ring,' sniggered Ledanius. He was a pasty-faced individual barely out of his teens who had shoulder-length hair done up in oily ringlets. Glaucia's hand rested possessively on the lad's buttocks, and if our brothel currently catered for individuals with his inclinations, I would have seriously considered charging him corkage.

'So Sulla has a seal ring showing his capture of Jugurtha,' retorted Octavius. 'So what? It happened, and it ended the Numidian war. Can't see why Marius is complaining. He has his own ring - and a much more pretentious one at that.'

'Trust Marius to break with tradition,' Atilius chimed in. 'Romans have seal rings of iron, a reminder of those days when iron was a rarity. But no, after his triumph Marius has to sport a ring of gold - further proving that the man is a provincial jackanapes with no sense of how things should be done. Sulla's ring provides him an opportunity to flaunt his achievements, Marius' ring does the opposite.'

'Rumour has it that Marius is getting more than somewhat fed up with his over-achieving subordinate,' someone else contributed.

I didn't identify the last speaker because there was a bustle around the doorway as the main course arrived, preceded by what I considered to be a suitably tantalizing aroma. Given the short notice, the meal prepared in haste had not turned out too badly, although there had been something not a little intimidating about the ferocity and skill with which Helga had skinned and filleted the rabbits. The men around the table were accustomed to the finest cuisine in Rome, and I was uneasily aware that the current offering only just met their standards. While mentally skinning and filleting Helga for creating the problem, I realized with some relief that the minds of the diners were more set on politics than the fact that the sauce served with the rabbit was more appropriate for pork. (Which was what it had originally been intended for. A frantic search of the kitchen had failed to turn up the pot where Ava kept the rabbit sauce ingredients.)

'It's shaping up to be a rough old year, and no mistake,' Atilius mused. 'I've never seen the courts so busy.'

'You mean the Fabius Maximus case?'

'That - not every year a leading senator is convicted of having his own son assassinated - but they also reckon there will be a legal challenge to Domitius getting elected to the top priesthood.'

'And Albucinus getting done for extortion after his governorship in Sardinia,' someone else added.

'Then there's the Caepio thing,' remarked Atilius casually, and suddenly everyone was looking at me.

Ah, I thought, the 'Caepio thing'.

'It does not help,' remarked one of Atilius' cronies - Alatus, the man at the table opposite me - 'that relations between Senate and people are so poisonous right now.' He picked delicately at a shred of rabbit flesh.

'Well, when we mismanage the African war through blatant corruption, and then lose army after army to the Germans through incompetence, you can understand the populace getting a bit testy. It's their fathers and sons that are getting killed after all.' This Pug-face contributed from beside me.

I would have expected his contribution to draw black looks

from the others around the table - every one a senator's son - but instead there were a few nods of agreement. This was the new generation, after all. No group of men in their twenties needs reminding how thoroughly the previous generation have cocked things up.

'But the last thing we need now is conflict between the social orders,' responded Atilius, smoothly getting the conversation back on track. 'Not with the Cimbri set to return and Italy under threat of a German invasion once more. Ejecting Caepio from the Senate sets a terrible precedent.'

'Ejection from the Senate will just be the start,' predicted Pug-face. 'He'll be exiled. Manlius probably, him certainly. After all, he not only lost the battle, but also all that gold from Tolosa. There's not a few people who reckon he stole that too.'

I put my face into my spinach and kept silent. Caepio deserved everything the courts could throw at him and then some, but of stealing the gold he was innocent. No-one knew that better than I, who had actually stolen the stuff. Of course, the official enquiry had totally exonerated me, but nevertheless, I felt it was time for a diplomatic exit to check on things in the kitchen. Sadly, I had left it too late. After getting a significant look from Glaucia, Ledanius popped the question that he had been primed to ask - the question I was beginning to realize that this entire dinner party had been about.

'So what are you going to testify, Lucius?'

They might not approve of their elders, and might be certain that they would do a better job when their time came, but these were Roman aristocrats, and Quintus Servilius Caepio, damn his blundering, cowardly hide, was one of them. By any rational count, Caepio was guilty of massive incompetence that had caused the deaths of over 80,000 men on that autumn day at Arausio. In my highly prejudiced opinion, Caepio didn't deserve to be exiled for it - he should have been disembowelled and left to die slowly on the battlefield for it. Were it not for politics, most Roman aristocrats would heartily agree with me. However, the people hounding Caepio were Marians, and so naturally the Optimates - the anti-Marian aristocratic party who called themselves the 'best men' - supported Caepio almost as a reflex action.

This left me in a cleft stick. No dyed-in-the-wool aristocrat despised Marius and his works more than I personally loathed the man. If the Marians wanted something, that alone was sufficient reason for them not to have it. Marius was bad. Not just bad for Rome, but a bad man, without the morality of a gutter hound and fewer scruples. Take an ego so inflated that he considered whatever honours he received as less than his due, and add this to a sneaking sense of (well-justified) inferiority combined with breath-taking pettiness and vindictiveness, and what you got was an over-rated peasant with a chip on his shoulder the size of the Aventine hill; a man who was prepared to stop at nothing to get his way.

On the other hand, well, on the other hand was Caepio. I had been there, and seen what he had wrought. No way in Hades was I going to help him get away with it. Yet to hinder Marius, I would have to support Caepio. Quandary, meet dilemma.

'No-one has called me to testify yet,' I temporized.

'But they will,' Alatus assured me.

Whatever Alatus was going to say next Atilius overrode with that infuriatingly self-entitled attitude of his. 'Come on Lucius. They say that ten men survived that battle.' I nodded. Ten men out of 80,000. And they still wanted me to defend the man who had done that?

'There's Caepio, and two of his aides. There's his fellow general Manlius - his aides died so that he could escape.'

'So did his sons,' observed Pug-face. I was starting to like Pug-face. Atilius ignored him.

'Then there's Quintus Sertorius - he survived by swimming the Rhone, as you did yourself.' My fingers were absently stroking the scar on my face, so I snatched them down again.

'Sertorius was trying to get a cavalry patrol organized, then some Cimbri rode up and took him. He hasn't been seen since.'

Atilius had that wrong, though I was not going to contradict him. The cavalry had been local Gauls loyal to Rome, and Sertorius had joined them with the hare-brained idea that they would all merge with the enemy army and then send regular reports to Rome about what the barbarians were up to.

The idea was so far beyond stupid that I had left the group in disgust and set about organizing my own unit of Gallic cavalry to harass the Germans. Sertorius meanwhile had joined the Cimbric army and spent the past few months sending regular intelligence reports back to Rome. The only explanation for his cockamamie scheme being so successful must be that Sertorius has a patron deity keeping him safe. The man does not even look remotely Gallic or German, nor even speak their language, so his survival testifies that the Germans far out-do the Romans in tolerance, multiculturalism - and naivety.

Since Atilius' betters had not bothered bringing the young ass up to speed on Sertorius or where the Senate was getting its intelligence on the Germans from, I munched spinach and assumed an air of polite attention as Atilius continued, 'There's also three camp followers, and that badly-wounded soldier who was hidden under a pile of corpses.'

That badly-wounded soldier was called Marcus Badicus, and he was currently recovering on a small farm in that same Sabine region that the evening's wine had come from. The farm was his own - purchased for him by an anonymous benefactor with a large amount of stolen gold and a guilty conscience. That anonymous benefactor tried once again to slip off to the kitchens, but Atilius wasn't letting up.

49

'So four of the ten are prejudiced. That's Caepio, Manlius and attendants; another four know nothing relevant, that's the soldier and camp followers; and two are missing ... '.

'Two?' I interjected.

Atilius nodded, and swallowed a mouthful of food. 'Caepio's aide-de-camp. He set off for his country estates two months back, and has not been seen since. Odd, that. Wolves maybe, or bandits. The family are investigating. So anyway, that leaves just one man who saw the opening phases of the battle, fought in the second half, and has the knowledge, wits and training to know exactly what he saw. That one man is you, Lucius. Think they won't want your opinion?'

'Um ... the dessert. I need to make sure the honey-cakes ... '

Atilius suggested doing something messy and anatomically improbable with the honey cakes. 'So what are you going to do, Lucius?'

Everyone at the dinner party regarded me expectantly.

'There's only one thing to do. I am not going to help Marius, and I am not covering for Caepio, not after what he has done. So they will get no opinion from me. What they will get is an account of what I heard and saw. As near as possible, the jurors in any court will know exactly what I know. What they make of that information is up to them. The oath of testimony demands that a witness give the truth, and that's what they'll get. The truth. No more, no less. What those at the hearing make of that truth is up to them.'

The *triclinium* was silent for a few moments, and then Pug-face muttered under his breath, 'Bye-bye Caepio. Have a nice exile.'

Glaucia intervened diplomatically, 'Let's have those honey-cakes now. And given Atilius' intentions for them, I would be obliged if you served mine first.'

The meal went smoothly after that, though the atmosphere

was slightly strained. The young men had been sent by their parents to sound me out, and were not looking forward to reporting their findings. On the other hand, they were young and each - even Glaucia - was cheered by having been singled out by a comely female member of the establishment for personal attention when the meal was over.

To add to the cheer, the generous supplies of wine were being punished just hard enough to ensure a degree of disappointment when the ladies did get their hands on the diners. However, the tipsy gossip of well-placed young men who often did not appreciate the importance of what they were revealing was well worth the ear-chewing my lasses would give me later.

Last to leave was Pug-face, or Mucius Scaevola. I had been saved the embarrassment of asking by a fellow diner who saluted Scaevola by his full name as he departed.

'My Pater will want a word with you soon,' murmured Mucius Scaevola as he said his farewells. 'I'd advise you to listen. The Marians are your enemies, and if you go ahead with your plan to testify, the Optimates will be after your blood as well. That means well-connected men such as Licinius Lucullus and Aemilius Scaurus, Leader of the Senate. Bad things happen to their enemies.'

'I'm caught right in the middle,' I agreed ruefully. 'After this is over, a long holiday somewhere remote might be in order. Maybe Pandateria. Care to visit me at the family villa on our cosy island off the Campanian coast?'

'Don't be frivolous,' Scaevola reproved me. 'This is serious.'

'Indeed,' I told him. 'Tomorrow I plan to order another dozen wax tablets.'

Liber IV

'You broke his nose.' Helga sounded somewhere between astonished and awed. 'Maybe his jaw as well.'

I looked ruefully at my right hand. Blood oozed from a hole above the middle knuckle where my fist had struck an exposed tooth. Apart from my blood-covered fist, there was also a generous splattering of blood across my tunic, very little of it my own.

'Well, he should not have picked up his sword. I was already angry with him, no, make that furious. Him trying to stab me was the last straw. The bastard.'

'If you call a German warrior a bastard, he will try to stab you. And that thing you said about the pig, the latrine, and his mother, that was bad. And the part about the dogs, and those other things ... I blushed to tell him. I blush to think about it even now. You should never, ever call a free German man those things.'

'But you translated accurately?' I asked with concern. It was important to me that I had got my feelings across.

'Of course,' responded Helga somewhat haughtily. 'Why else would he want to stab you?'

We were walking toward the Forum, down the hill of the Esquiline towards the sunny ridge called the Velia. The next item on the morning's agenda was to find a market stall where I could get a clean cloth, some water and a sponge to dab the worst of the blood from my tunic. Passers-by were giving me funny looks.

The interview with Ava's father had not gone well. Given that his daughter was short, chubby and dark-haired, it had been something of a surprise to find that the father was huge, blond and muscular. He had also been thoroughly hung-over and utterly unprepared for the eruption of myself and my translator-manager into his rooms. After a polite start, the conversation had taken a sharp turn for the worse. This had happened at the precise point where I found out that her father had sold Ava into slavery.

'He is her father. She is his daughter. A father can sell his daughter. That is the law. Among my people and yours. You had no right to call him those things.'

'Helga?'

'Yes?'

'Shut up.'

It is called *patria potestas* - the power of the father, and we Romans believe in it to an insane degree. Basically, a father has total power over his children, for as long as they both shall live. He can starve them, beat them to death, (though the neighbours tend to 'tut' over this) and certainly sell them into slavery - though Roman law has unbent to the degree that if a son manages to buy his way out of slavery, the father is only allowed to sell him twice more. That is why, after a bad harvest, slave-dealers do the rounds of the countryside, picking up the daughters of peasants whom their families can no longer afford to feed. And of course a drunken father can sell his daughter off in the pub; just as easily and just as legally as if he were selling a second-hand toga. As far as I could gather, that is exactly what had happened to Ava. Now I had to find her and buy her up. Then I'd have a slave, because sure as nuts, if I freed her that damned father would just sell her again.

Once I had cleaned up, I planned to hurry to the so-called Graecostadium at the back of the Forum. The Graecostadium is where the *mangones*, the slave-traders, exhibit and auction off their human wares. My hope was that Ava would be among them. Our enquiries had established that she had indeed gone home to dear old dad. He was upset to discover that he could no longer stay soused on the salary his daughter had just given up, so he had impetuously traded her off that same evening to a bunch of businessmen he had met in the tavern. Ava had cost forty denarii and an amphora of Etruscan wine. The paperwork was properly written up, signed and witnessed, and still sitting on the dining table where I had discovered it.

'It wasn't even decent wine,' I grumbled. 'Did you see the vendor's mark on that amphora? Fufidius. The only stuff he gets from Etruria is that sour, musty stuff he usually retails to the whores who entertain travellers among the tombs outside the city gates. They buy it by the skinful.'

'I'm hoping that the businessmen who bilked the father into selling Ava cheaply will try to turn a quick profit at the slave-market. So when we get there we split up and start looking. If we don't find her lined up for the auction block, the tavern where she was sold will be open soon. From the slave market we'll head back uphill to cross-examine the staff and see if anyone knows the buyers. At least we got their names from the contract.'

'Why all the fuss?' Helga wanted to know. 'There are other cooks. If you want a slave cook, there will be a dozen on sale at the market. Good ones, experienced. Better than Ava because you had to teach her all the time. She was stubborn. She had left her job, so she is not your concern. She wasn't even that pretty. And now you'll have to pay the father a big fine when he reports you to the magistrates.'

'Forty sestertii,' I muttered. 'By now you should know the standard rates of compensation for minor bodily injury. It's not as if our younger customers never come to blows. Get them to settle up on the spot and there's no bad publicity and no hard feelings.'

'I will make a fuss about this. Do you know why? Not because Ava is hard-working, and happy and good company to be around. Not even because she has real talent as a cook. I'll tell you why. Not that long ago, she saw a falling brick that would have smashed my head in. She couldn't have known exactly where it was going to land, and she was standing right next to me. She didn't jump clear. She pulled me clear instead. Instinctively, because there was no time to think about it. She saved my life, because that's the person she is. Therefore I owe her. You are partly responsible for this mess, so you owe her too. That drunken sot of a father owes her most of all. If we weren't pressed for time it would be worth going back and investing another eighty sestertii in his ribs.'

'Murderer! Murderer! Lucius Panderius the Murderer! Killer! Killer! Yes, you are, Lucius Panderius, murderer! You are a killer - hey, look at all that blood! Everyone, take a look! Look here! It's Panderius the Murderer!'

My accuser was a small fellow, Syrian by his clothing, with an earring gleaming in the sunshine as he danced backward down the street in front of me. I made a grab for him, but he skipped easily out of reach, grinning cheerfully.

'Kill-er! Kill-er!' he chanted, pointing a long bony finger at me. 'Lucius Panderius is a murderer!'

This could go on all day. From his enthusiasm and professional approach, the man was quite clearly a paid accuser. In Rome, court cases are by mutual consent. Both parties have to appear in front of a judge before he will conduct a trial. Without defendant and plaintiff both physically present there is no case to be tried. This causes a problem if the accused does not want to appear, for example, if his guilt is blatantly obvious.

The way a plaintiff gets his man to face charges in court is by hiring an accuser. Or three, so they can work in shifts following their victim through the day, screeching imprecations for the benefit of those nearby as he dines with friends, and sitting under his bedroom window at night, howling his guilt to the stars. The only way to get an accuser off your back is turn up in court. Waiting for whoever is paying the accusers to run out of money is seldom an option. Not only do some accusers only get paid if they force you to judgement, but the longer you delay, the guiltier you are assumed to be and the more your reputation suffers.

In Rome reputation matters. None but other scoundrels want to be associated with a scoundrel, and if you duck a court case too long, it is presumed to be because you are a scoundrel. Then you lose all your friends. Suddenly you can't do business with an honest man. Your patron disowns you, and your clients leave. The landlord chucks you out and the barber on the street corner short-changes you with impunity. This loss of reputation is called *infamia* - and if becomes an official blot on your record, life is barely worth living. Therefore, when an accuser turns up the only real options are either to present yourself in court at once, or to leave town for good.

'Who accuses me?' I demanded loudly, partly for the benefit of the gathering crowd. 'Who do you say is dead?'

'Hee-hee - he's killed so many. Lucius Panderius doesn't know. Which of the people you've killed needs justice? Who? Who? Look at him, in his butcher's clothes. Blood! Blood! Murderer! Murderer!'

'I have killed nobody!' I roared, well aware that the gore splattered over my tunic rather contradicted this thesis. There were mutterings among the people beginning to close in around me, and I realized that this needed stopping right now. The Roman people can be alarmingly arbitrary with supposed wrong-doers. Not every thief - or murderer - lived long enough to face the magistrates. Since returning from the wars I had several times stepped over a corpse in the marketplace, and the only action taken by the authorities had been to throw the alleged shop-lifter's body into the Tiber before it started to smell.

My accuser was capering around me in circles, enjoying the audience. Helga, I noticed, had quietly sidled off somewhere, leaving me alone. Well, almost. Carefully timing the human gadfly's orbit, I side-stepped into his path, forcing him to step back. I followed this up with two quick steps, with the accuser bouncing on his toes before me and easily keeping just out of reach. I looked over his shoulder and nodded.

'Murderer! Now he wants to kill me too! Kill - aargh! Ow! Yow!' The flow of accusations was interrupted because, grinning balefully, Tancinus had reached an arm out of the crowd and seized the accuser firmly by his bejewelled ear. He was now twisting hard. The accuser dropped to his knees, while the crowd moved in closer to appreciate the sudden turn taken by the morning's street theatre. Tancinus was now revealed as a bodyguard shadowing me, but in the circumstances this was a necessary sacrifice.

'Belt up,' I advised the accuser, and then turned to address the growing crowd. 'Some of you know me. I'm Lucius Panderius, of the Temple of Venus. Many people wish to destroy me and my reputation - including the people who have just sold my freeborn cook into slavery. This is the blood of the wretched father who sold her for wine. He is alive, as anyone who visits his house on the Esquiline can discover for himself. This,' - I gestured at the blood on my tunic - 'is merely the wine that dribbled from the drunken sot's nose when I confronted him. The innocent girl's name is Ava. She's Germanic, and has short, curly dark hair. Five denarii to the first person who tells me where she can be found. She was sold for forty. Tell whoever has her that I'll repay that forty and give a hundred more for her safe return.'

'I repeat - I've killed nobody.'

'Liar!' shrieked the accuser before Tancinus could silence him. 'You killed the Lady Fadia!'

The sheer effrontery of the charge silenced me for a moment. My jaw dropped open and I gaped like a fish. To those watching it must have appeared as clear a display of guilty conscience as anything over-acted on the pantomime stage. The crowd became restive once more.

'I ah, you ... .' I paused to rally my thoughts back into their ranks. 'I ... who accuses me?'

'Marcus Laeneas Fadius, brother of the deceased. The grieving kindred of the woman you foully ...unngh!'

'Thank you,' I nodded at Tancinus, and turned again to the accusing faces of the spectators. 'The Praetor sits next in the Basilica Aemilia on the Kalends of this month. Let it be known I shall be there to repudiate all these charges in full. My innocence will be proven, and the guilt of those who seek to blacken my name will shown to all.'

'Who's this Lady Fadia?' Someone in the crowd wanted to know.

'A woman of questionable morality who died at my brothel in the company of a gladiator and an assassin.' (I too could twist the facts.) 'It was I who called the authorities, as my patron Lucius Sulla can attest. This charge is a fabrication by my enemies, and I shall gladly appear before the Praetor to reveal their lies.'

Satisfied with this, the crowd began to disperse. The mention of Sulla's name helped considerably, as I had assumed it would. No-one wanted to suggest Sulla was a liar, or take on the man himself by attacking one of his clients. Sulla, as was well known, stood by his friends and never forgot an enemy. My promise to appear in court had also defused things. As people began to drift away I shouted after them, 'Remember, her name is Ava. There's a reward!'

For all he looked Syrian, my accuser was third-generation Roman. 'Granddaddy was in the army of Antiochus. Taken prisoner in the Seleucid Wars and brought over from Asia Minor to take part in Scipio's triumphal parade,' the man informed me. Officially he was called Septimius Cornelius Alentinus. The 'Cornelius' bit in the name told us that granddaddy had not only been captured by a Scipio but also freed by a Scipio, because freedmen became officially a part of the household of the manumitter, and the

Scipiones were part of the Cornelian clan.

Like me, my accuser was a voter in the Collina tribe, but for reasons that escaped me, he rather liked hamming up his ancestral origins. He was known to his friends as 'Surus', 'the Syrian', though in response to an irritated query from Tancinus, he admitted that he spoke not a word of Syriac.

All this we discovered sitting at a pavement eatery just off the Street of the Sandal-makers on the lower slopes of the Esquiline, where the late-morning sunlight bleached white everything under the filmy awning of *carbasus lina;* a linen-cotton mixture popular for this purpose. From the scents drifting from the clay oven behind the counter, lunch would be roast lamb and rosemary.

'Good stuff, this,' remarked Surus, swallowing his wine in two mouthfuls and wiping his mouth with the back of his hand.

'No, it isn't,' I assured him, and pushed my beaker across the rough wood of the table. 'Have mine too.' Beside me, Tancinus sniffed disapprovingly.

'With pleasure,' said Surus cheerfully 'It's a thirsty job, I have. All that shouting and exercising. Wears a man down. I've got to say, I've never come across a mark with so much blood on his clothing. You looked as though you'd just done the deed. Made my job so much easier.'

He looked concerned for a moment. 'You are going to turn up in front of the Praetor, aren't you? 'Cos if you don't, I'll have to get back on your case again, and we wouldn't want that.' He shot Tancinus a worried glance.

'I'll be there, just as I said. So who hired you?'

'Well now, that's a professional confidence. But seeing as how my job's all done, and you were so gentlemanly as to buy me a drink ... ,' he paused and I smiled encouragingly. The words 'and since Tancinus is still around to break your ankles if our meeting should turn unfriendly', hung unspoken in the air. Surus swallowed and continued. 'You'll be seeing him in court anyway, I expect, so there's no harm in my telling.'

Tancinus tapped a fingernail on the tabletop to suggest there was plenty of harm in not telling, and even in not telling very soon. I'd found Helga lurking by a bread-stall, and after reproaching her for her lack of team spirit, had sent her down to scour the slave-market for Ava while this latest complication got sorted out. While Helga was getting her instructions, Tancinus had taken the captured Surus into a nearby alleyway for a short heart-to-heart conversation. The man did not appear to have taken any physical harm from the discussion, but he had become remarkably co-operative.

He leaned back and watched a bickering couple pass a few yards away. They were looking at something in her basket and arguing. 'A girl should never let her boyfriend buy the vegetables.' Surus advised us. Finger tap from Tancinus. 'Okay, okay. Don't know how much I can help you gentlemen. The client paid cash. No names, no questions.'

'Description?'

'Sun-tanned. Tough-looking. Big guy. Like a slab of beef stood vertical. Very flat nose, like an Ethiopian.' Surus depressed the tip of his own nose with a forefinger to demonstrate. 'Black hair, greying slightly, bristle-cut in army style. Eyes sort of oriental. Didn't say much, but he had a bit of a Samnite accent.'

Surus giggled. 'He'd be a really scary guy, but for his lisp. 'Lucius Pandewius', that's you. I had the devil of a time finding how it's really said. 'Cos, you need it right for the denunciating ... .' Surus' voice trailed off as he looked at my face. 'You know him, don't you?'

'Did he,' I asked with a level voice, 'have the top half of one ear missing? The left?'

'I was coming to that. Yeah, a clean cut. I wasn't going to ask what happened to it though.'

'He ducked away,' I said absent-mindedly. 'I was going for his throat.'

Surus looked decidedly uncomfortable at this turn in the conversation. In retrospect, this was reasonable. He must have wondered what sort of homicidal maniac he was drinking with. When he'd come to accuse me of murdering a woman, my tunic had been covered with another man's blood. Now I'd just admitted to trying to stab someone else as well.

'Well, um, if that's all, I had better move on. *Carpe diem* and all that. Thanks for the wine.' He glanced at Tancinus. 'Our arrangement is still good, right?'

'Nasty little turd-scrape,' remarked Tancinus dispassionately after Surus had vanished into throng of pedestrians in the street.

'Arrangement?' I asked delicately, and signalled the management to bring more wine. Something made from grapes this time.

Tancinus looked embarrassed. 'Sorry about that, Sir. I reckoned that you'd be quite keen on getting the little weevil to open up. So I promised that if he spilled the beans, then later this week one of your girls would visit him for an hour.'

I raised my eyebrows. 'Quite a promise. And which of the girls do you want to go gutter-diving on my behalf?'

'Reva, if you don't mind my saying, Sir. She has a taste for gentlemen of an eastern disposition, if you get my drift, so it won't be any hardship for her. She'd do it as a favour for me anyway, but if you could see your way to a generous tip ...?'

I sighed. 'Consider it done. Don't try that too often though. We've got the Temple's high-class reputation to maintain. It's just fortunate that our source was a randy little sod.'

'Well, that was the carrot so to speak, Sir, a bit of extra encouragement. The main incentive was the stick. And the stick was, well, the stick.' He affectionately patted the staff propped up on the bench beside him.

'Our Surus understands how hard it is to do his job with just one busted kneecap, and I told him if he was withholding toward us, well, I'd do both as a bonus. But we are generous men, sir, and understand that a man must make his living in this hard old world. That's why I told him that if he breathes a word about his visit from Reva, I'll only break an elbow. He might consider it worth the risk just to brag.' Tancinus looked regretful. 'I hope not, for all that I can't stand Syrians.'

'Okay. Good job, overall. If you keep the girls out of it in future, you might be called on to negotiate with some of our suppliers. The laundry people, for instance. They might benefit from your … persuasive negotiating. Now it's time for you to do your blending into the crowd thing, and note that next stop is the Viminal Hill. The picture has suddenly got a bit clearer, and Sulla needs updating. I'll bring you up to speed as well, as soon as I can.'

Tancinus nodded, and moments later he was just another somewhat elderly pedestrian moving slowly down the crowded street. Going to the eatery's counter, I ordered honeyed almonds to go. As mine host bustled off to fill the order I asked quietly of no-one in particular, 'Did you get all that?'

An utterly undistinguished man with nondescript brown hair was sitting with his back to me. He might have nodded fractionally, but I didn't look at him as I took my almonds and headed out into the morning sunlight.

'So now we know who's being trying to kill me. Unless one person is behind this bullshit court case, and someone totally different is behind the assassination attempts. Which is a bit of a stretch. It's more logical to assume that someone wants me out of the way, and if they can't do it by killing me, they plan to drive me into exile. But to accuse me of killing Fadia? That's rich. The cow tried to murder me, and then she drank her own poison.'

'Um ... Certain as I am that it happened just as you say, Sir, did anyone but you see her drink the poison? Witnesses, you'll need witnesses. Who is this brother? Is he the one behind it all? And if you now know who, do you know *why*? Is it revenge, a case of good old vengeance, plain and simple? It's all still a bit confusing for me, Sir.'

Tancinus and I were seated on a comfy couch in Sulla's antechamber. My patron was busy meeting a delegation from some Alpine tribe. His next posting was north, there to use his famous powers of persuasion on the Centrones, Graiocelli, Caturiges, and other denizens of the high valleys. Next spring the Roman armies would be trying to close the mountain passes against the Cimbric invasion, and while the legionaries were fighting to save civilization, Sulla's job was to ensure that they were fed. Being Sulla, he was putting in the preliminary spadework now. While Sulla negotiated prices for beef and cheese, I was taking the chance to fill in Tancinus with the background story.

'Now, as my bodyguard, the main thing you need to worry about is Sabaco. Cassius Olmeda Sabaco. His description is as per the specifications given by that Surus fellow. If you see him, expect that you'll be fighting for your life within the minute. If you don't see him, it might already be too late. He never works alone. As we've already seen, he is a back-room boy. He does the organizing, hires the thugs and the assassins, but seldom gets his own hands dirty. That doesn't mean he can't, if it comes to the crunch. He is unexpectedly fast, utterly unscrupulous and deadly. He's killed a dozen people, and that's just that I know of, and done that with his own hands. The Gods alone know how many he has betrayed, had murdered or is currently blackmailing. He's a fixer. For Marius.'

'Sort of like you are, for, you know... ,' Tancinus jerked his head towards Sulla's room from which sounds of indignant dissent now emanated, '... him.'

I studied Tancinus long enough for him to become uncomfortable. 'No, nothing like that. And I'll thank you not to make the comparison again. Sabaco was even a senator once. Marius got him adlected through his high-ranking connections. As a senator Sabaco bribed, intimidated and gave false testimony on his master's behalf for exactly a year, after which the censors chucked him out of the Senate House on his ear for conduct unbecoming. Then he vanished back into the shadows. They call him 'Sabaco' after his lisp, by the way. There's nothing else 'girly' about him.'

Like most Roman men, Sabaco used the *tria nomina*, the three names. There was the *praenomen*, the name his mother had given him; which was Cassius, and his family name, which was Olmeda, and his *cognomen*, Sabaco, the nickname which others had given him. No-one gets a lot of choice with his *cognomen*, and many *cognomina*, like Sabaco's, are unflattering. I was fortunate to simply be called 'Panderius' after my family home of Pandateria.

'Sabaco resurfaced in Africa during the Numidian war, when Marius was still second-in-command to Metellus. Marius, being the over-ambitious and scheming hound that he is, was already making plans to take over the war and win all the glory for himself. One of the things he did to achieve this was to weaken Metellus by peeling away his clients and supporters.'

'There was a man called Turpillius, a client and a close friend of Metellus. Metellus made him the chief of the engineers in the army, but the poor guy didn't have much aptitude for it. So Turpillius was taken off that job and put in charge of the city of Vaga. This was a large town in a strategic location, and again to be honest, poor old Turpillius wasn't up to the challenge of holding it for Rome. He was a bit of an amiable duffer really, but Metellus liked and trusted him.'

'A number of people, myself included, urged Turpillius to arrest a cabal of the leading men in town, but he refused. We knew, for a stone-cold certainty that these people were in secret communication with the enemy, with Jugurtha, but Turpillius didn't care. He said that with kindness and humanity the conspirators could be brought over from the side of the Numidian king and made loyal allies of Rome. So the fool invited them to dinner so that they could talk things over. Of course, the citizens let Jugurtha's men into the city during the meal, and we lost the stronghold of Vaga. We'd have lost Turpillius too, except that the citizens recognized that he was harmless and his intentions were benign. Anyway, I missed that dinner with the traitors, being otherwise engaged in taking hostage family members of the leading conspirator and smuggling them out of town even as Jugurtha's men were coming in. I offered to return the man's wife and children - in instalments - until Turpillius was returned unharmed. Which he was.'

'That's where Sabaco came in. There was an inquiry of course, as to how Vaga was lost. Marius presided, because even though he was commander-in-chief, Metellus had to recuse himself. A man can't try his own client. At the enquiry Sabaco produced documents showing that Turpillius was not the benevolent dupe he appeared to have been. In fact, Turpillius had conspired with the Numidians to hand over the city of Vaga to the enemy. The letters showed that he had been paid a fortune in gold and precious stones for his treachery.'

'At the end of it, the case was irrefutable, especially as Marius was intent on pushing the case through. He would not allow friendly witnesses to testify, and he steadfastly refused to delay for an investigation as to where the letters had come from. They were forgeries of course. However, proving that involved going back to Vaga and getting the real seal-ring and a handwriting sample from the person who was supposed to have written the incriminating letters. Since Vaga was now in enemy hands, this took some time. Meanwhile, Marius and his cronies put the screws on Metellus. With no evidence to the contrary, Metellus was forced to agree that his client was guilty. So he reluctantly condemned Turpillius to death. Sabaco himself carried out the sentence that very evening.'

'The next morning we got back with the proof that Turpillius was guilty of nothing but having a too trusting nature. By then, of course, he was dead. Metellus was devastated when we showed him the evidence, and not surprisingly so. He had just killed a friend and a client who was completely innocent. Metellus immediately confronted Marius, but Marius vehemently denied knowing that the letters were forged. He claimed that he had acted reasonably on the basis of the facts as they appeared at the time. That was not even the worse of it - for months after that he openly, actually gleefully, claimed that the condemnation was his own work. The swine did not blush to tell anyone who would listen that he had set Nemesis on the trail of Metellus for condemning his own client and friend.'

'And Sabaco?'

'Well, everyone knew he was the forger, so he did not stop to face the charges. As soon as the facts became public, Sabaco became a liability, and Marius promptly disowned him. By then Sabaco was on a fast horse heading for Utica. I caught up with him at a guest house by the docks. That's where he lost part of his ear. Regrettably, he moves a lot faster than I had expected, and he had his bravos on hand. Then the town watch got involved, and I lost the chance to finish the man. He got away and vanished. No-one saw him again, and believe me, I've looked. He disappeared off the face of the earth. Until now.'

Tancinus was putting things together. 'Lucius Panderius. But Panderius is a *cognomen*, and Lucius is your *praenomen*. Your *nomen*, your actual name, that you never use.'

I nodded. 'Mine is the name of a condemned traitor. Turpillius. Marcus Turpillius Panderius was my father.'

Liber V

On returning home I discovered that the Temple had a new cook. Helga was inordinately proud of this, and more than somewhat put out when I impatiently pointed out that the Temple did not need one. Ava was our cook, and it was just a matter of locating the unfortunate girl. However, Helga had not found Ava anywhere in the slave market.

'Yes, we will find her. But until then? How long will you cook and manage, and do all the other things? You don't let me manage the girls even though it is my job, and you interfere with my doing the books, and now you have that silly accuser to deal with as well. This is a good cook. He was very cheap. Yet you complain because I have helped you.'

'He was a real bargain. You wait, it won't be long before his owner comes round. He will be begging to buy him back again and you will make a nice profit. Meanwhile, we look for your Ava girl, and then you can decide whose cooking you like best. He was going to be auctioned this evening. He didn't even get to the auction block before I bought him at the reserve price. You have saved a fortune and got a very good cook. All thanks to me. You can pay me back later.'

After that, there was nothing for it but to go round to the kitchens, with my manager trailing along behind, and interview my latest acquisition. 'Oh, for the God's sake, Helga, unshackle him! Where did you even get the chains from?'

'They came with the slave. He might run away. Let him stay chained up until he sees how stupidly indulgent you are, then after that he won't want to. But you will blame me if he runs off before he even cooks dinner. And you won't have the chance to see how good he is.'

'What's your name?' I enquired of the slave, who was cringing against a sack of flour. Suddenly a powerful memory came back of the very similar interview I had gone through a few months ago with my then master Vidacilius. 'Helga, the shackles ... .'

'My name is Cyrenicus, if it please you, master'.

My interest was piqued. 'From Cyrene? In Africa?' The slave nodded.

'So you know how to cook with silphium?'

Silphium is one of my favourite herbs. It is light, spicy and has a unique flavour. It only grows around Cyrene in Africa, and because it is the town's main export, it has been over-harvested and is becoming rare and ridiculously expensive.

My new cook evidently shared my enthusiasm for his native herb.

'Oh yes, master. Just three days ago I used silphium in a sauce, it was poured over the flesh of wild boar. I boiled the meat and made the sauce with the silphium and some lovage and added fig-dates, mustard and pepper.'

I ran the recipe through my mind. 'H'm. Not bad. What went into the mustard?'

'Well, mustard seeds, obviously ...'.

'Black or brown?'

'Black, they add colour and have a stronger flavour which balances nicely with the richness of the nuts. Ah, thank you master.' Helga had removed the chains, and after giving me a dirty look marched out of the kitchen with them. 'The nuts are pine nuts, chopped with almonds. Add sea salt and some red wine vinegar. Then you have a reserve condiment you can keep chilled in a pot and use on its own or in a sauce, like the silphium sauce.'

'We'll try that, though it seems a touch heavy - have you thought of adding some oregano? Spicy, almost minty, but adds depth to the flavour.'

'I did! But the oregano takes the edge off the taste of the silphium, and that's the luxury ingredient. You don't want to hide that. Marjoram oil, though, that might work. The flavour is less powerful so it will add the lighter, subtle overtones you want without dominating the silphium.'

'So what went wrong? At your last gig, I mean?'

The slave, who had become interested and animated, dropped back into sullenness.

'There's a fresh whip welt on your cheek. Did that have anything to do with it?'

Cyrenicus looked at me, calculating what was safest to say. 'My master, my former master that is, ordered dinner to be ready at the second hour of the night, exactly then, without fail.'

'And ...?'

'I cooked a soufflé. With mushrooms in butter sauce, and sheep's udders marinated in wine.'

'Reasonable enough.'

'Except,' remarked the cook with some bitterness, 'He and his guests came in at the fourth hour.'

'Ah. Well, by then the butter sauce would have congealed, the udders become over-marinated and the soufflé beyond saving.'

Cyrenicus shrugged. 'So I got a whipping, and then this morning with no warning, I was pulled out of my kitchen, shackled, put on the auction block and sold to your manager, all within an hour.' He looked at me with a trace of defiance. 'Because of one soufflé. It was a good one too. At the second hour.'

I nodded thoughtfully. 'And your former master was ...?'

'Marcius, Sir. Not the noble family, one of their freedmen. A former slave himself.'

'Tallish, skinny, but got a paunch that makes him look five months pregnant? That Marcius? The one who's doing rather well in the grain trade?'

'That's him. He only has the best these days.' Cyrenicus' chin lifted. 'Including his cooks.'

'Yet he's like many a freed slave, eh? Beastly to those who

remain in captivity. He's been here at the Temple a few times. As I recall, the girls said he can get a little rough.'

Cyrenicus opened his mouth to add something, but I forestalled him.

'But let's not gossip. We'll find you a room in the basement. We'll have to empty a storage room. Sorry about that, but we're pushed for space right now. What was your *peculium*?'

Slaves generally get a small salary. This is as a matter of convenience as it stops the master from having to bother with shelling out money for every little necessity a slave needs for personal maintenance. You have to watch it though - saving up a *peculium* is a traditional way for a slave to buy his own freedom, but he might starve himself to death in the process.

'Marcius didn't give any slave a *peculium*. He said he knew what we could get up to with it.'

'Okay. We'll start you with three *asses* a week. It's not much, but you can get clothes and other necessities off Helga as required. You'll eat your share of what you cook for the rest of us. And please don't run away. I've lost one cook this week already.'

'Now, let's discuss dinner.'

Returning to my quarters I found I had a guest. The visitor's identity was not immediately discernible, as he had his back to me while he browsed the shelves containing my collection of pornographic oil lamps. Roman oil lamps are little flat clay cups about the size of one's hand. There's a sort of spout on one end where the wick comes out. The top of the cup is covered, but has a hole through which the oil can be topped up. Usually there's a small ornamental picture in bas-relief around the hole.

I informed my guest, 'The reliefs on the top row show mythological themes. Imitating those on the bottom row will necessitate medical attention afterwards. The middle row are all practical, provided one limbers up first. Ask for Brangita - she's been working through that row as a personal project. She's up to lamp number nine, I think.'

My visitor turned. He was one of the dinner party guests from last night. 'Ah, Pugfaa ... er, Mucius Scaevola. Good to see you here again. The rule about ninth-hour girls does not apply in a private establishment, so feel free to indulge as soon as the fancy takes you. Some wine while we discuss your requirements? Or do you want to get straight down to it?' (The ninth hour of the day - about 2pm - is when a Roman prostitute is allowed to begin soliciting for custom.)

Scaevola wrinkled up his nose and smiled. I wondered if he would do this if he realized how much more closely it made him resemble a wolfhound. The same pug nose, short jaw ... but eyebrows not shaggy enough. Did he trim them, I wondered?

'Oil lamp three is, um, intriguing,' my guest commented. 'It might enliven a quiet evening as the winter draws in. Followed perhaps by a restful bout of lamp number ...,' he counted along the row, 'seven.' He paused, and resumed in a different tone of voice.

'But I'm here for business, not pleasure. Sulla has informed me that you face murder charges. He has asked that you consider me to represent you.'

'My word. That's quite an undertaking. As your potential client, let me be sure you know what you are getting into.'

'I think I know.'

'Let's be sure. You know that there have been three attempts to kill me recently?'

'Indeed. Presumably that is why the gentleman by the door is trying unconvincingly to sweep the floor with a bunch of twigs tied to the end of a quarterstaff. Some sort of bodyguard, I take it?'

I sighed and went to lean out of the window. 'It's okay, Tancinus. Bugger off and get a drink or something.'

Young Mucius Scaevola waited patiently while Tancinus removed himself into the atrium. I noted approvingly that my bodyguard settled down in a position from which he could see both the entrance to the temple and my office, while he himself was largely hidden in the shadows.

'Do you know who is behind the assassination attempts?' I asked Scaevola.

My would-be attorney chewed his lip thoughtfully. 'Not sure. I had filled up three wax tablets with possibilities before I realized the point of your comment last night. I would guess you yourself managed to fill more than three tablets, even if you wrote very small?'

'My first thought was that it was one of Caepio's people trying to kill you, but by and large the Optimates don't go in for assassination. They'll bankrupt you, ruin your reputation, get you beaten up, but killing is not usually their thing. It's not that they are nice people, more that a dead man can't feel despair and humiliation, and the Optimates like their enemies to feel both. This lawsuit now, *that's* their style.'

'Um ... I'm pretty sure that a man called Cassius Sabaco is orchestrating the lawsuit, and he's a Marian.'

'*That* Cassius Sabaco? The one that used to fix elections for Marius?'

'I forgot that - of course. It was when Marius was elected as Praetor. Yes, Sabaco was there co-ordinating payouts right next to the voting urns. It was so blatant that Marius was tried for bribery afterwards. It was one of those trials - where the defendant was so guilty that he only got off because he bribed the jury to acquit him of bribery. Ironic, in a way.'

'And worrying. If Sabaco's working on this, you'll have a world-class jury-fixer operating behind the scenes to make sure you're found guilty. Whether Sabaco is working for Marius or Caepio, either man can put massive pressure on a juror. And not just financial.'

Scaevola stopped as a thought struck him. His jowls rippled as he almost literally chewed over the idea. 'You don't think they might be working in tandem on this? Have you managed to pull off a double and got not just one, but both of the most powerful and corrupt factions in Roman politics combined against you? Marius and Caepio together? Oh my!'

'Do you still want to take my case?'

'Oh, more than ever. Jurisprudence runs in my family's blood. Usually a young man makes his name in the courts with a successful prosecution. But if I can get you off despite the fact that both the Marians and the Optimates are after your head ... my word, I'll make my reputation with my first trial.'

'Er, your first trial?'

'Of course, that's if I can get you off. It depends on what sort of case they have, and whether they've managed to fix the judge as well.'

'Can we discuss this 'first trial' thing some more?' I asked urgently, but Scaevola ignored me.

'Now, we need to act fast. I'll move that we have the case tried in the standing court, the *iudicaria de veneficariis*. They can't stop us doing that. The *de veneficariis* is a specialized court dealing with poisoning, and poisoning is exactly what you're alleged to have committed. Mind you, if we fail to get an acquittal in that court, you will get strangled by the executioner rather than just exiled, as is the usual sentence. It's the more dangerous choice, but I'm prepared to risk it. Yes, definitely. The *de veneficariis* it is.'

'Strangled? Seriously?'

'Oh, yes. Exciting isn't it? Look, we are going the poisoning court route because the poisoning court is a standing court, so they can't choose the judge, because the court already has one. In a court where they do choose the judge, you might as well plead guilty now instead of waiting for the judge to rule later that you are guilty, no matter what evidence you produce.'

'That means we have to get it done soon, before they rotate Lutatius Catulus off the bench. Before the end of the month he's the judge sitting in the *iudicaria de veneficariis*, and Lutatius can't be bribed, bullied or blackmailed. Get into April and Dulctito will be your judge. And he's a client of Caepio.'

'They can't do that!' I yelped. 'There's an obvious conflict of interest.'

'Um, no. This is about you poisoning the Lady Fadia, not about you possibly testifying against Caepio later in the year. And anyway, on my way here I had a quick word with Norbanus, the Tribune of the Plebs. He'll veto your being strangled ...'

'Oh, good.'

'... until after your testimony against Caepio. So you get to testify no matter what happens. That removes the conflict of interest thing, unfortunately. Oh, by the way, Norbanus wants to talk to you about your deposition describing events at the battle of Arausio. A few points to clear up.'

'When you say your first trial, you mean your first big trial, yes? You've done some other stuff, surely? An assault, a homicide or two?' I asked pleadingly.

'No, no, it's in at the deep end for me. Now, I've got a list of jurymen here.' Scaevola fished down the neck of his tunic and came up with a scroll. 'These men. They'll all be sitting for the poisoning court until Lutatius steps down. Let's see which of them might be bribed, intimidated or blackmailed. You might as well get to them before Sabaco does. And dig out your toga. We'll go before the Praetor tomorrow and insist on an immediate trial.'

'Tomorrow?'

'Yes. Remember, time is of the essence. That whole Lutatius Catulus thing.' Scaevola gave a worried frown, pushing his jaw forward at the same time. It almost made me want to toss him a marrowbone or some other doggy treat. 'You did follow all that? Sulla gave me the impression that you are quite bright.'

'Why, thank you. However, my about-to-be-imminent trial is not my only problem. Matters keep getting more complex by the hour. For example I've just acquired a new cook in suspicious circumstances, and this makes me wonder if there is not also something suspicious about the disappearance of the previous cook. So tomorrow I want to do some investigating in the spare time I don't have.'

Scaevola looked interested. 'Your previous cook disappeared? Do you think kidnapped to introduce a new cook to your household? An assassin, or merely a spy?'

'Well, if he's an assassin, he's an assassin who can cook. He passed a test on meat sauces and mustard recipes without hesitating once. I have informed him he's eating out of the same pot as me which should stop any attempts at poisoning, and if he's a spy, well, I've put him in a room in the basement which will dramatically limit his chances of snooping around. Tomorrow I need to look at the freedman Marcius, his patron the aristocratic Marcius, and to whom both men owe favours.'

This latter job would involve pulling on a coarse, unbleached tunic of the style often worn by slaves, re-styling my hair and going down the the fortnightly market at the portico of Marcellus. That was on the Caelian hill, and the market was my best chance of meeting and gossiping with slaves from the households of the Marci. This I declined to mention to Mucius Scaevola, as he certainly would not approve. He would also worry that I might be recognized, though the truth is that people see only the tunic. They tend to look right through the slave within.

'What exactly happened to your last cook?' Mucius Scaevola wanted to know.

'Sold,' I looked ruefully at the dried blood crusting into a thick scab on my knuckle and gave a brief summary of events pertaining to the disappearance of Ava. I was surprised by Scaevola's reaction.

To say my attorney was perturbed by the girl's enslavement and disappearance is putting it mildly. The young man came out with a string of remarkably fluent invective largely inspired, I imagine, by oil lamp five (bottom row).

Before I could comment on his superb profanity - his Latin gerunds and accusatives of motion were as perfectly placed as the physical components he was describing - Scaevola asked me, 'Don't you see what this means?'

'It means that you got a scratch meal last night, and ..... Oh. Bugger.'

Mentally I ran through some curses of my own, taking in oil lamps seven to nine, inclusive. Then I used the contents of the next three lamps to take myself to task for excessive stupidity. This took all of ten seconds, during which time Scaevola looked at me sympathetically. At the end of it, I remarked quietly and without any particular emotion, 'I think I'll kill Helga.'

'It explains your new cook, anyway.'

'Yes. Someone got Marcius the aristocrat to get Marcius the freedman to give Helga a cook - so I'd stop looking for the old one. As soon as she was alone this morning Helga probably went straight to her contacts to set up the sale. Then she went round to the slave market, collected her man and brought him here. The whole performance wasn't about getting a new cook into my household after all. It was about getting their hands on the old one.'

'It is almost certain Caepio's minions or that Sabaco fellow have got your Ava,' prompted Scaevola to ensure that our thoughts were running in tandem. They were, and our thoughts were grim.

'She's a slave,' I said bleakly. 'And slaves can be tortured to give evidence.'

'Not can be. Must be. The evidence of slaves is not valid without torture. And if Sabaco has any time to work on your cook - your cook, of all people - then they'll have forced a confession from her. She will tell the court that you've cooked up a witch's brew of poisons in your kitchen.'

'Helga fired her, of course. She didn't walk out. That would have been too convenient a coincidence for them. Helga must have forced Ava out of the Temple, knowing she'd go back home. They probably had the sale fixed up with her father already, and she was delivered to them like a kid to the sacrificial altar. So they - presumably Sabaco and friends - have got to Helga. Oh, and that creates another problem.'

'Oh good. I like a challenge.'

'My main witness, the one who actually heard Fadia confess and saw her knock back the wine she'd poisoned. ... That was Helga.'

'... Furthermore the witness Helga will testify that she heard the Lady Fadia's bodyguard yelling for help. She saw that the Lady Fadia had opened the door to the bedroom. She was attempting to escape while Panderius murdered the bodyguard who had rushed in to protect his client. With her own eyes she saw that man there - Lucius Panderius - force open the Lady Fadia's jaws and then hold her mouth and nose shut until she had swallowed the lethal mixture.'

Servilius Caepio junior, counsel for the prosecution, and son of the Caepio against whom I would be testifying later in the year, was in full flow. As he paused for breath, the Praetor leaned forward.

'Why did the witness not come forward with these facts at once?' he enquired interestedly.

'Fear, Magistrate, pure fear. She knew that her employer was a vicious killer, and he threatened her with death unless she told the authorities the story he had concocted. As if a gentle country noblewoman like the Lady Fadia would know anything about murders and poisons.'

'So vicious a killing troubled my witness' conscience. When she heard that the brother, Fadius here, had come looking for his sister ... ,' at this point Caepio junior nodded at his client, a stocky fellow with curly chestnut hair, 'she could keep quiet no longer, so Helga left her employer, just last night, and threw herself on my protection.'

The Praetor on the bench was Glaucia, father of the young man who had adorned my dining couch earlier in the week. He shot me a sympathetic glance and remarked, 'Together with the evidence you have already presented, I have to say that there is a case for the accused, Lucius Panderius, to answer.'

The watching crowd gave a murmur of agreement. Court cases are a spectator sport in Rome, followed with interest by anyone with time on his hands. As a result, a juicy case did much for an aspiring politician's public exposure. Any ambitious youth aiming for high office made a point of prosecuting or defending cases during his early career. Both Caepio and Scaevola were playing shamelessly to the gallery, and I could hardly disapprove. Roman law forbids counsel to accept payment for their services, so Scaevola was getting his money's worth in other ways.

The Praetor's court was sitting in the Basilica Fulvia, opposite the Senate House in the Forum. The weather had turned cold and cloudy overnight, making me thankful that my warm woollen toga blocked the cold draughts swirling under the gloomy arches of the old building. They were calling it the Basilica Aemilia more often these days, because Aemilius Scaurus and others of his family had been embellishing and refurbishing the place for years, keeping up a tradition begun over a century before, when the Aemilius who had been Consul when Fulvius died had finished the building that his colleague had begun.

The Praetor was sitting with his back to the wall, with a charcoal brazier smouldering by his feet. My own feet, in sandals, were starting to feel uncomfortably chilly. Nor was this just from the weather. Even to me the prosecution case looked strong, and we didn't have that much with which to fight it. Helga's disappearance from the Temple last night had been the last straw. Mucius Scaevola had insisted that we send word immediately to the Praetor that we wanted to go to trial, and had got a reply that same night that we should present ourselves at the basilica first thing in the morning. The fact that other cases and petitions had mysteriously cleared themselves from the Praetor's docket for the day was further proof of the strength and influence of the hidden forces ranged against us. Neither Scaevola nor I had slept last night, and my eyelids felt heavy and grainy.

'Here's my formula,' pronounced the Praetor.

The Praetor does not judge cases himself. He is too busy for that. However, he arranges for the case to be tried elsewhere and gives the 'formula', which stipulates exactly what the prosecution must prove for the accused to be found guilty.

'I rule that as plaintiff, Quintus Fadius through his agents and counsel must prove to the judge - and any jury that judge might appoint - beyond doubt, that on the night in question Lucius Turpillius Panderius did with malice and intention kill with poison the sister of Quintus Fadius, namely the Lady Fadia. Got that?' Glaucia looked at the clerk of the court, who nodded.

'Shall we go on to the selection of judges?'

Usually at this point the Praetor would ask for a list of potential judges for a case. Defence and prosecution would work down the list until they found a judge both could agree upon. If that failed, then the Praetor would reveal the last name on the list, hidden until then, which both parties must perforce accept.

Mucius Scaevola had been listening quietly, occasionally glancing at his clerk who was busily scribbling down details of the hearing, then leaning over to check the clerk's shorthand to make sure he had noted a particularly relevant point. Scaevola himself might be new to the game, but as he said, his family were very, very good at it. I could only hope that some of the experience had rubbed off.

Now my attorney stood. 'No need for the judges' list, Magistrate. We will go to the standing court. As you yourself have just said, the charge is that the decedent was killed by poison.'

The Praetor's eyebrows climbed. 'You must be pretty sure of your defence. You do know what happens if your client is found guilty in that court?'

'He won't be,' Scaevola spoke with a confidence I did not share. 'We are ready to go to trial immediately.'

This caused a some consternation on the prosecution bench. Young Caepio, his advisors and client quickly put their heads together, evidently arguing among themselves. Given the strength of their case, and - without Helga - my lack of anything like a solid defence, the prosecution had been certain we'd opt for a regular trial with the less drastic penalties which a guilty verdict would entail. Caepio and his client were definitely at loggerheads, with the others pitching in for either side. Eventually Caepio pulled his head from the huddle.

'Um, Praetor, we are not laying a criminal charge here - this is an *actio homicidi*, in which we are laying claim for recompense for the killing, not seeking punishment for the killing itself. So there's no need to go to the standing courts.'

'To Hades with that!' Fadius the client jumped to his feet. He glared pugnaciously across the court at me. 'He killed my sister, and damned right I'm seeking punishment. She's dead and I want him dead too!'

'Your turn, Caepio.' The Praetor looked at the prosecutor with evident amusement. Caepio was floundering.

'Maybe the *lex Talionis* then, Magistrate? That law gives the

claimant the right to get compensation in kind for wrongdoing.
Panderius took the Lady Fadia's life, so Fadius should be allowed
to take his. That's what the law says.'

'Allegedly took her life!' called Scaevola loudly. He wasn't
going to see my guilt taken for granted. This interjection earned
Scaevola a disapproving look from the Praetor before he turned
his attention back to Caepio.

'You don't intend teaching me the law, do you?' Glaucia
enquired sweetly, reducing Caepio to stammering incoherence.

'As far as I can see from your deposition, this is a poisoning
case. There exists a standing court which deals with poisoning.
This would seem to be the appropriate court. The defendant,
however foolishly, agrees. His counsel insists on it, and so does
the plaintiff. You seem to be in a minority of one, Caepio, because
I'm going to insist on it too.'

Glaucia looked over at the clerk. 'Let the nature of the action
be changed to a criminal case to be tried before the public court,
the *iudicum populi de veneficariis*, with the defendant Lucius
Turpillius Panderius on trial for his life.'

Beside me, Mucius Scaevola hissed a satisfied 'Yessss!' Somehow I could not match his level of enthusiasm.

'I - I'll need time to amend my case,' protested Caepio. 'We
were not looking to conduct a criminal trial. We need until at
least the end of the month.'

The Praetor smiled grimly, and Scaevola muttered a little
prayer. Fortunately Glaucia was a Servilius, a wealthy aristocrat of
ancient family not currently aligned with his none-too-close
relatives the Caepiones, and not allied closely with Marius. This
changed later, but for the moment Glaucia was a Roman
aristocrat in the prime of his power and he knew it. He too was a
politician, and eager to demonstrate to his audience his complete
independence from even the powerful Caepio clan.

'If you wanted recompense from Panderius for poisoning,

then somewhere along the way you would need to prove he actually did the deed. So presumably you have the evidence and witnesses to hand for the task. Otherwise, what are we doing here?'

'Um, we withdraw the charge,' muttered Caepio. He carefully did not look at his client, who was on the verge of apoplexy.

'Wow,' muttered Scaevola, 'They must really, really want their own judge.' He looked at the Praetor like a puppy waiting for a bone. Under his breath he urged Glaucia, 'Dismiss or commit, don't postpone.'

Suddenly he leapt to his feet. Glaucia looked at him, and with raised eyebrows signalled Scaevola to speak. Mustering maximum indignation, Scaevola said, 'The charges have been laid in public. Panderius has been denounced in the street. His own manager has called him a poisoner. These are serious accusations that cut right to the heart of my client's reputation and public standing. The prosecution can't make such allegations and then just walk away from them. They must either stand by what they have said, or admit the allegations are false, and allow my client to leave right now without a stain on his character.'

'Which is why if the prosecution had withdrawn earlier, I would have dismissed the charges with the stipulation that they be considered false and therefore cannot be brought again later,' retorted the Praetor, drawing a strangled yelp from Fadius.

Looking at him, the Praetor explained. 'My job here is not just to assign a court and a judge. I also have to give my *praescriptio*, and the whole point of a *praescriptio* is to prevent the prosecution from laying multiple charges related to the same case. So you've laid your charges, and now you get one shot at proving them. In fact, the charges can't be withdrawn any more. The case is now a criminal one and already assigned to go before the standing court.' He turned to Caepio. 'If you don't want it, I'm sure someone else will step up.'

Scaevola was still standing. 'The judge of the poisoning court is Lutatius Catulus, Praetor. I took the liberty of checking with him this morning. He's got some administrative procedures to clear up, but he's happy to hear preliminary arguments this afternoon.'

'Give me ten days at least,' pleaded Caepio.

'You've got two,' Glaucia informed him. He looked at me and Scaevola. 'Are you two content with that?'

'Content,' agreed Scaevola. And that was that for the day.

Liber VI

There was a throng of people wanting to ask questions of us as we left the basilica, and even more wanting to shout opinions.

'It's a set-up! Caepio wants Panderius dead or exiled!'

'You killed her, admit it!'

'Is this how we treat our heroes? It's a frame-up!'

'How can I help you, Lucius Panderius?'

Scaevola smiled, waved and made encouraging gestures to those shouting favourable comments.

I tried to look suitably modest and pleased by the support but still outraged that the accusation had been made at all. Then someone at the back of the throng tried to start a chant of 'Panderius, murderer! Murderer!' He abruptly vanished to reveal a sour-faced Tancinus standing behind, looking downward with little sympathy in his expression.

We pushed through the crowd, I holding my toga tightly lest the encouraging pats and slaps send it sliding off my back. Without looking at me, Scaevola muttered, 'A good turn-out.'

'And some of them are doing it for free,' I agreed in a low murmur. 'Not all of them are the people we hired last night.'

Scaevola heartily shook the hand of a well-wisher and then we were through into the more general crowd of the Forum.

'Caepio didn't have much of a claque out there,' I remarked.

Scaevola nodded. 'We took him by surprise. He put all his effort into making sure that he'd have the judge sewn up in a regular trial, so now he's running to catch up. You can bet he'll have people doing the rounds of Lutatius Catulus' poison court jurors today. Fortunately we got to most of the bribeable ones last night. I'm glad you have a large war-chest for this, because Caepio is going to work hard to outbid you.'

'I have friends in high places – as you well know.'

'You are accumulating debts in high places too. Check with

me before you accept favours from people. You might as well accept them from me instead, and I'm beginning to understand what Sulla meant when he said you might be ... useful.'

There in a nutshell is how Rome works. In this town, no-one does things out of the goodness of his heart. It may be that in a few months' time Scaevola would ask me to quietly check the background of a particular individual that he was considering lending money to, or recommending for a state job. Or Scaevola might not want the favour for himself, but for a friend, thus leveraging the payment of a favour owed by me into the more worthwhile debt of a favour owed by someone higher up the food chain.

My patron Cornelius Sulla occasionally asked me for even more extensive 'favours' such as the months spent spying on the Vidacilius household. He had sent word this morning that he was working at repaying that particular debt in the manner suggested last night, though it was tacitly understood that this meant that I now owed Sulla all over again for getting me cleared in the Tolosa enquiry. On the other hand, I was doing the Tribune Norbanus a massive favour by testifying against the elder Caepio, since Norbanus would gain huge political credibility and clout if he managed to bring Caepio down. Now I could point out to Sulla that Norbanus would soon be prepared to do him a favour as a favour to me. Therefore my patron now had social credit with (yet another) Tribune. By passing the favour Norbanus to owed me on to Sulla I could pretty much cancel out the favour I owed to Sulla already.

Aristocrats such as Scaevola kept track of this sort of thing as easily as breathing. Personally, instead of keeping a mental set of accounts of who owes what to whom, I prefer the simpler transactions of the brothel. They are ever so much more honest and straightforward. Talking of honesty and directness, it would soon be time for a rather unpleasant chat with Tancinus. Employer-employee relations would take a dive during that conversation, but it had to be done.

Scaevola arranged for us to meet tomorrow for a strategy session, and we both turned to our respective homes, vowing to catch up on much-needed sleep. Sure enough though, as soon as we were alone on the street Tancinus fell into step beside me, the metal tip of his staff click-clicking on the flagstones of the pavement.

'So how did it go, boss? Looking in from the outside, so to speak, it seems like they can make you look pretty guilty. That bitch Helga turning on you like that, if you'll excuse my language.'

'Yes, Helga was a setback, no doubt about it,' I agreed casually.

'So why take the poison court? I mean, if they can convince a jury ... I'm not saying they've convinced me, because I know you, but looking at it from outside ... if they convict, you get your neck wrung like a chicken.'

'It's a risk, certainly.'

'So why do it?' Tancinus persisted. 'You must have a trick in reserve that the other side aren't expecting. It's suicide other-wise.' A street urchin ran up and tugged at my sleeve. He must have reckoned that a man formally dressed in a toga might part with a good bit of small change. Instead Tancinus whacked him with unnecessary but understandable force, and the kid hared off down the street bawling loudly.

Tancinus had been moody and out of sorts all day, and it was time to sort that out. I had chosen this route home because there was a small tavern along the way, a converted house, really. It was filled with nooks and quiet alcoves where two people could have a tense conversation undisturbed.

'Oh, I've several tricks in hand. I'll play them when the time is right. In here ... .' I steered Tancinus into the tavern with a neat nudge, and strode to a table at the back. Sulla's man was sitting a few yards away. He was using an unnecessarily large knife to tackle an early lunch of artichokes and beans. He ignored us, and I hoped that we would soon leave the building without Tancinus being aware that the man even existed.

'So what tricks?' asked Tancinus eagerly. He leaned forward with his elbows on the table and watched me impatiently as I signalled the slave girl to bring drinks.

'Well, for a start,' I said, 'I know where they're holding your daughter and grand-child.'

Tancinus went very still. For ten long heartbeats he did not even breathe, but kept his eyes steady on my face. Then he said, 'Ah.'

We were silent as the serving girl plonked two clay mugs of wine in front of us. One advantage of having set up the confrontation beforehand was that I had been able to ensure that my wine was a sweet heavy Volconian selected from my own cellars. Tancinus was getting the house brew - a cheap blend from the Vatican hill. They mix in honey to take the edge off that stuff, and I had seriously considered having them add opium as a sedative as well. My bodyguard was in for a stressful chat.

'So what's the arrangement?' I asked conversationally, 'You get the grandchild back after you've reported our defence strategy, and your daughter safe home if you kill me once the trial is over? Otherwise, both suffer horrible torture, etcetera?'

Tancinus looked at me. His hands still rested on the table, knobbly knuckles bobbing as he clenched and unclenched his fists. 'How did you know?' he demanded hoarsely.

'It's what I'd have ... er,' I mentally reconfigured the sentence to make myself less villainous. 'It's what I'd have expected Sabaco to do. I've had dealings with him before.'

'Ah. Try this. It's Lucarnian sausage. Mixed herbs, fish sauce and bay berries rubbed into well-tenderized beef and smoked. It's got a strong enough flavour to cancel out the taste of your wine, which I imagine is like having a saw dragged over your tongue.'

The gastronomic advice was unheeded, as was the sausage itself; which was unfortunate as it really was rather good.

'Where's my babes?' Tancinus wanted to know.

'In a house by the Aventine docks. There's seven guards that we know of, and Sabaco himself. Taking out the guards isn't the problem. The trouble is that the captives become hostages if we don't play it right. Sit down. Do you think I don't want to rush over there? It's almost certain that they've got Ava in the same place, because my man heard someone screaming. Muffled by the walls, but screaming. The thing is, if we go in hard, all we get is three corpses. So shut up, eat your sausage and smile, because someone is probably watching.'

'Your man heard screaming?' asked Tancinus with sudden suspicion. 'I thought I was 'your man'. So that's how you know where they took the girls?'

While keeping my face impassive, I allowed myself an inward wince. This was going to be the tough bit. Again I regretted the lack of opium in Tancinus' wine, though on the other hand, he had not yet touched a drop.

'Drink,' I urged him. 'Remember this meeting has to look like you busily at work spying for Sabaco. You are successfully pumping me for information. So look pleased with what you are hearing.'

Obediently Tancinus took a swig from his tankard. 'Well,' I told him, 'at least now no-one can tell if your sour face comes from the conversation or the wine.'

'To answer your question, I've had someone watching your house. As soon as it came out that Sabaco was behind this court case, it was reasonable to also suppose he was also the one behind the attempts to kill me.'

'Knowing how he works, there was an obvious risk that he

would try to get to me through my bodyguard. He's done that sort of thing before. I have no family to be used as leverage, but you have, and Sabaco has no scruples in that department. Note also, he would certainly deliver on his threats to harm them. His promises to release the pair safe and sound afterwards though - that's another story. Sabaco doesn't leave witnesses.'

'His men came for your children last night, just as it was getting dark. Four men with a cart. Straight in, straight out with the pair of them. Some burly individual with a beard got in their way, so one of the kidnappers hauled a club out from under his cloak and took him down.'

'Aye,' growled Tancinus. 'That was Scarvius. A good man. He has concussion, but he'll recover.'

'My man alone could not do much, so he just followed them down to that the house by the docks and then reported to me. Then we watched your meeting with Sabaco early this morning. You have commendable self-restraint. I had my doubts, because you looked positively homicidal while he told you what you have to do to keep your family safe. After that I went down to the house by the Aventine docks and had a look at the place for myself. Which is,' I added with some feeling, 'why I've not had any sleep for the past thirty-six hours.'

It is a real shame that Tancinus has a devious mind. You don't need one for hitting people on the head, which was the reason why I had hired him. Well, one reason. The other reason, well, that was where matters were about to get tricky.

'You knew about my family before you hired me,' Tancinus said slowly. 'I remember you made a joke about it. And you haven't had time to hire watchers for my house, not while I've been bodyguarding you. There's been the trial, your other investigations, the Ava kidnapping. ... You must have set the watchers up before all that. As soon as you hired me. You didn't need a bodyguard. You needed ... bait.'

'Not at all,' I said urgently. 'I needed, I still need, protection.'

'Not half as much as you needed to know who was behind it all. You bastard. Oh, you total bastard. You hired me because you thought that someone - not Sabaco maybe - but someone, might try to use my daughter and grandchild as a way to get at you through me. So you were waiting already, just waiting to see who would do it. That was it, wasn't it?'

'Calm,' I urged. 'If you don't cool down, we won't ever get the chance to stage a rescue. Look like we are discussing my legal defence strategy.'

'Your defence strategy? Your sodding defence strategy was to hire poor bloody Tancinus so you could get a good look at whoever attacked the sucker's family. Are you proud, right now? Saving your noble skin by putting a child and an innocent woman in danger?'

'Now hold it right there. Lectures on morality don't come well from you. Remember, you're the man who, just a few minutes ago, was going to betray and then murder your employer - the man who pays you to protect him. I didn't put your children at risk. You did. As soon as you agreed to take the job. You're the bodyguard - it's your responsibility to take the proper precautions, yet it was me who ended up guarding them. I didn't kidnap your girls and it is not my job to protect them. If I do deserve some blame, I should also get some credit. You now know where your children are and who's got them - thanks to me. Now we are going to set about rescuing them. Not bad service from the person you are meant to be protecting.'

'Protecting? You? You need protecting about as much as a viper does.'

'Hah! If I'm a viper, I'm a viper in a scorpion pit. Highly endangered, believe me. So, are we going to sit here swapping recriminations, or do you want to hear how we go about getting your children back?'

I sliced some sausage onto the rough brown bread, and raised my eyebrows enquiringly at Tancinus as I chewed. It was evident that Lucius Panderius was far from Tancinus' favourite person at the moment. After several seconds, Tancinus put his hand to his knife. Behind him, Sulla's man casually wiped his mouth with a napkin. You needed to look carefully to see the outline of the dagger under the napkin, as Sulla's agent was holding the hilt backwards, a trick which kept the blade flat against his inner forearm. Dabbing away the residue of the beans from around the man's mouth took a few moments, and the action only ceased when Tancinus carefully sliced some sausage, laid down his knife and forced a smile. It looked like a death's head rictus.

'If I actually have to eat any of this, I'll throw up,' he informed me through rigid lips.

'Just push it around your plate. No-one's expecting you to be truly relaxed.' I gave an encouraging smile, and noted the slight but visible easing of the tension in my 'other' bodyguard's shoulders.

Of course, Tancinus was completely right. My shadowy opponents knew that I would need a bodyguard, because they had made it too dangerous for me to survive without one. Therefore I had given them a bodyguard to find; Tancinus, just the sort of the bodyguard they were expecting. He was unobtrusive, skilled and dangerous; exactly the man for the job.

Because Tancinus met their expectations, I had hoped that potential killers would stop looking for who was really protecting me and instead concentrate their energies on undermining the man they had found. Tancinus was indeed a bodyguard, and a good one. He was also a diversion from my true protectors, and as he had rather brutally described himself, bait.

Just as I had researched Tancinus before I hired him, my enemies had researched the man afterwards. We had both found the same weak spot, and they had exploited it, exactly as expected. My plan had been to identify whoever it was that put pressure on Tancinus, but as it turned out, we had known that it was Sabaco by the time he struck. Until last night, though, I hadn't known where Sabaco was based, or where Ava was imprisoned. As of this morning I knew both. In the matter of bringing my enemies into the light there was definitely progress, albeit not progress made in a manner of which I was at all proud.

'Here's what you'll do,' I told Tancinus. 'After lunch I'm going home to sleep, and I mean it this time. This wine was stronger than anticipated, and the days I could push an all-nighter without feeling it are long gone. '

'You on the other hand, are going to wait for Sabaco's man to approach you. Even if there's no-one watching right now - and there probably is - they'll be desperate to know why Scaevola is confident enough to put my life at risk in the poison court. Tell the man that you have information so important you want to renegotiate with Sabaco. You want both family members freed, now, in exchange for what you have learned. Got that?'

Tancinus responded with a terse nod.

'Arrange to meet at sundown by the fountain of the Marcian aqueduct. The one near the Temple of Fortune on the Quirinal Hill. It's a well-known lover's rendezvous, and on the other side of Rome from the Aventine.'

'Sabaco never moves without his bravos. He'll take at least three with him, so that should leave between four and six at the house. There are people watching the place for us, and they should have a clearer picture of who's inside by the time we get there. So as soon as you've arranged your meeting with Sabaco, come back to the Temple, wake me up and we'll move out.'

'What if I'm followed?'

We had been talking in tones well below the buzz of lunchtime chatter and the clatter of earthenware crockery at the food counter. Nevertheless, a careful eavesdropper at the table behind Tancinus could have followed our conversation if he had been listening attentively. Now that man's head dipped slightly, once. Tancinus would indeed be followed. If anyone else also decided to follow my bodyguard back to the Temple, the stalker would get as far as the first dark alleyway - and never come out.

'Don't worry about anyone following you. Just come straight to the Temple afterwards. And, well, it's embarrassing, but I have to point this out – don't try to make any independent deal when you talk to Sabaco's man. As we've discovered from the start, betrayal doesn't suit you. Play to your strengths. You are honest, decent and have an unexpected talent for violence. But everyone else in this game is more duplicitous than you, so please don't try duplicity. You'll lose, and there's a lot at stake.'

Tancinus gave me a sullen glare in reply.

'Look, Sabaco killed my father. Murdered him, actually. Do you think I'd not rather go to wait at the Marcian aqueduct and see if I can't cut off more than his ear this time? But the safety of Ava, your daughter and granddaughter takes priority. So I'll do the right thing and put the rescue first, because I'm one of the good guys. Well, at least I'm one of the less bad guys.'

'On the other hand, if you really were to turn up at that meeting with Sabaco and give him everything he needs, you'd probably not walk away from the conversation alive. Once you've served your purpose, you're a loose end and you're dead - along with your family. You did not realize that? Instead of taking orders from Sabaco, your best move would have been to tell me everything as soon as we met this morning. You didn't, which proves again that double-crossing and espionage isn't your thing.'

'I'm not saying you should trust me. I don't deserve that. But trust your instincts and decide – are you going to get through this alone, ally with me, or ally with Sabaco? You might not like any of those choices, but you have to make one, and only one choice is going to end well for you and your children.' My little homily delivered, I rather breathlessly turned my attention back to lunch.

Tancinus thought about things for as long as it took me to finish off my sausage and wash it down with a final swallow of wine. Then he pushed back his stool.

'I'll set up the meeting,' he announced abruptly. Then he walked out, manoeuvring his staff with care between the increasingly-crowded tables of the tavern. From the corner of my eye I saw another diner rise casually from his seat by the door, pushing aside a half-eaten plateful of beets, corn and mutton. Sulla's man had already left, and would undoubtedly pick up the pair when they hit the street.

Alone, drowsy and unprotected, I would have to make my own way home to grab a few hours of sleep.

'That's them?' Tancinus considered the rescue party through the gathering gloom of dusk. There seemed to be one more person that I had been expecting. My bodyguard sniffed disparagingly. (Or should that be my former bodyguard? Once we'd got Ava and his children out of Sabaco's clutches, Tancinus and I needed to have a long talk about our future relationship.) Apparently unaware of any irony, the skinny man leaning on his staff remarked, 'Seriously? They don't look so very dangerous to me.'

Indeed, four of the men we were walking toward looked like clerks who had stopped for a modest snack on the way home from the baths. On seeing our arrival, the group arose from their benches at the pavement eatery and came to meet us. One looked like a somewhat corpulent and benevolent uncle, with white tufts of hair protruding from behind his ears. Another was a slim twenty-something whose face was scarred with teenage acne. The other two were so remarkably ordinary that Tancinus failed to recognize either of them, despite having seen each man a dozen times over the past two days. In fact, one had been sitting just behind him at lunchtime.

'Don't confuse scary with dangerous,' I responded. 'If you think about it, scary people are insecure - being scary is a way of telling the world to keep away. Now ask yourself why a viper wants to look like a scatter of dry leaves, or why a wolf wants you to see just a patch of shadow in the forest. Real predators don't do scary. They try hard to look as harmless as possible. That's also true of the human variety.'

This is why I was rather puzzled by the only dangerous-looking gent in the group. He was a well-muscled individual with a scarred face and a nose that had at some point been badly broken and poorly re-set. This beauty was hunched over, cradling one hand with the other, which was wrapped in a napkin. He didn't look up as we approached. 'Who's he?' I asked the avuncular character by way of greeting.

Uncle smiled, crinkling up the edges of his eyes. 'This is Alvidus. He's a legionary. You might remember meeting him at the Samnite's Helmet.'

'Not one of the pair who confronted me inside. He must have been one of those waiting in the mist, I think. Hmmm ... so you are a legionary, Alvidus? Do you know, when we first met I mistook you for a builder?' Stepping forward I grasped the man in a friendly and familiar manner by the elbow, and then dug my thumb viciously into the ulnar nerve at the joint. 'Have you recently dropped bricks on anyone interesting, you son of a swine?'

Alvidus made the high keening noise of a man who would scream except that it would hurt too much. His already grey face went ashen. Acne-face stepped over quickly to help the man before he keeled over on to the pavement. 'Careful, Lucius,' he warned me. 'Alvidus has already had a long chat with us. He can't take much more.'

I nodded at the hand in the napkin. 'He's from the house?'

Uncle nodded. 'Came in here a little while back to get a take-away supper for eight. Talk about walking into the lion's den. We've got a while yet. Cook's still preparing the order, and Alvidus is keen to chat with us some more. Isn't that right, Alvidus?'

The legionary nodded immediately. Whatever had been done to his hand had completely taken the fight out of him. Over uncle's shoulder Tancinus looked on with horrified fascination.

'Did he describe the interior of the house?' I asked.

'In loving detail. My friend here,' Uncle nodded at acne-face, 'will give you the run-down. The room you want faces into a side alley. The alley's a dead-end with a guard on the street side. Two men in the vestibule, which is the only entrance, and one in the room with the prisoners.'

I counted mentally. 'Four? How many did Sabaco take with him?'

'Just two. He obviously doesn't rate your man highly.' Uncle's eyes flickered over Tancinus' stony countenance, and then gave the quarterstaff a long, thoughtful stare. 'A mistake, maybe. Sabaco had more men than we thought. All legionaries and all from the same contubernium. The man you killed in your bed-room that night was the decanus.'

Legionaries are grouped in squads of eight. Each group shares a tent and a mule which carries the tent, a cooking pot and whatever gear the men don't lug around for themselves. By and large legionaries choose as tent-mates people of a like-minded disposition, and elect their leader, the decanus, from among themselves. The decanus is either the longest serving soldier, or the one who has seen the most combat. Quite often the men of a contubernium became as close as brothers, bonding together in an alliance against centurions, the enemy and the world in general. It is not unusual to find an off-duty squad painting the town red together, or all taking leave at once to go see the sights of Rome. It was less usual for a contubernium to do a little freelance kidnapping and assassination while in town, but Alvidus was clearly dying to tell us how that had been arranged. And 'dying to tell us' was no more than the grim, literal truth. Like Sabaco, Sulla's men were not keen on witnesses.

'I don't believe it.'

'As I live and breathe.'

'It's Lucius Panderius. Come here for us to kill him and save us the bother.'

'Very funny, gentlemen.' I looked at the two thugs in the vestibule and the guard from the alley-mouth who had followed me in. 'But the game has changed. Sulla has done a deal with Caepio. I've been sent round to call Sabaco off. Where is he?'

'Caepio can go shove his head in a latrine as far as we're concerned, right boys? We answer to Marius, and we didn't hear otherwise from him. You're going to make a beautiful corpse.'

'Ooh. I'm terrified. If Caepio wasn't talking to Marius through Sabaco, do you think I'd be here? How do you think I even found the place? Sabaco doesn't tell you everything that's going on, does he? So get off your lard-filled backsides and go get your boss. Time's too short to spend it gossiping with the hired help. Tell him to bring the women and I'll get out of here.'

'The women? Why should Caepio or Sulla give a tinker's fart about them?'

'They don't. I do. One is my cook ... among other things.'

One of the men sniggered. He was a pleasant-looking young man with curly brown hair. 'Ava? Don't plan on using her oven soon, if you get what I mean.'

'You are the torturer?'

The man looked from side to side at his comrades and then answered with bravado, 'Yeah. Want to make something of it?'

97

'Oh, I do. And I shall. But first I've got to talk to your boss. Unless you want this to become unpleasant, let me see Sabaco right now.'

'You've missed him. He'll be back in an hour or two. What do you mean by 'unpleasant', eh?'

'Caepio knows I'm here. So does Sulla. What do you think they'll do if half a squad of ragged-ass legionaries screw up their plans? To those ragged-ass legionaries, I mean?'

'Marius wouldn't stand for it.'

'Sure, he'll back you up. Come on. The Consul will publicly admit that he's sponsoring kidnappers and assassins? Assassins of me - a war hero?' I spread my arms. 'Sure he will. Or perhaps you'll all disappear into the nearest midden and everyone will pretend you never existed. Because you see, Sulla and Caepio are right here in Rome, and Marius isn't here for you to run to his skirts. But, hey, all Sulla will be doing is helping Sabaco with his dirty work anyway. You were never coming back off leave, lads. You know too much.'

'What does that mean?'

'Figure it out, soldier boy. Figure it out as an investment in your health. Meanwhile I'm off to that tavern on the corner to wait for Sabaco. You lot can get back to romancing each other, or whatever you do to pass the time.'

The older of the legionaries looked at me, narrow-eyed. 'I think not. Terentius, get back to the alley. If you leave your post without permission again, I'll skin you alive. You,' he jerked his head at me, 'get inside.'

'Why?'

'Because I'm not telling Sabaco we had you, and then let you go. So you can stay here as our guest, and have your little chat with the boss when he gets back. After that, if the Gods have any decency, we'll be allowed to kill you. Slowly. Like you did our friend.'

'The decanus?'

'Yeah. Him. Did you come alone?' The legionary was turning his head back and forth, peering into the twilit street.

'I might have. Or not.'

The senior legionary glanced at the younger man whom I now thought of as the Torturer. 'You. Get to the tavern and call Alvidus back. Forget dinner. We're too stretched right now. Food can wait. I don't like this at all.' He looked at the wall of the vestibule where five scabbarded swords were stacked, then made up his mind and strode over, strapping on one sword and picking up another. Then he nodded at me. 'Let's go.'

'Where?'

'You wanted the women. Well you can pass some time with them until we're ready for you. Then you can tell Sabaco whatever Caepio has worked out with your boss. And if it isn't good enough ... .' The legionary grinned nastily. 'Let's hope it isn't good enough.'

'Orco?' The legionary knocked on the door of the prisoner's room and got a muffled query in reply. 'Another one for you. It's Panderius. Watch him closely. Don't kill him. But if he gives any trouble you might want to break a leg or two. I'm bringing you a sword, just in case.'

The man lifted the heavy wooden bracket that was used to bar the door, and opened it carefully, sword in hand. I noted that the door was made of heavy oak, and that it swung outward from a wall three hands thick. Beyond was some sort of storeroom. In the shadows were sacks, and some planks stacked against a wall. There was a smell of must and mould.

Hardly had I caught a glimpse of the room when I was rudely shoved into it. I staggered to keep my balance, because after patting me down for hidden weapons, the legionary had taken the precaution of firmly and expertly tying my hands behind my

back - an unexpected and annoying development. Behind me
came the sound of the thick wooden bracket being replaced on
the door. A figure in a grimy white tunic turned, strapping on the
sword he had just been passed. Orco, I assumed. Near the wall a
female figure in brown robes moved her child aside as she rose
silently. The child was dressed in a chiton, sucking her thumb
and regarding me solemnly.

Then my attention was fully taken up by Orco as the man
advanced purposefully. He had unshaven jowls and small blue
eyes, and from the leonine stink that came with him, it appeared
he'd not had time to bathe recently. A snarl showed the yellowed
pegs of teeth in his top jaw. I recognized him. This was one of the
legionaries who had confronted me in the pub, and he was
clearly intent on picking up where he had left off at that point.
He pushed his face at mine.

'I'm going to ... .' Whatever (or wherever, I suppose) Orco
was 'going to' would never be known. I had reared my head back,
in a natural enough reaction to the reddened, sweaty face being
pushed into mine. Then I slammed my forehead hard into the
bridge on the man's nose, feeling a satisfying crunch as something broke. Stepping forward, I slammed my knee forward into
his groin, but like a hardened street-fighter, Orco still had the wit
to turn the blow with his thigh. He threw a quick punch at my
head which I dodged, and then leapt back. Blood streamed black
from the legionary's nose and his eyes gleamed in the gloom. He
said nothing more, but I heard a rattle and a hiss as his sword
came unsheathed.

Then there was a strange, loud 'thwock!' and the sword
dropped from Orco's hand as his eyes slowly crossed. He
dropped first to his knees and then pitched forward, hitting my
sandals with his face.

Behind him, the woman dropped the plank which she was
holding and stooped for the fallen sword. With an economical

twirl of the finger she signalled me to turn around, and there was a release of tension on my wrists as the cloth bindings were sliced through. So far the woman had not uttered a sound, and her face was hooded by a mass of auburn hair. But there was only one person she could be.

'Tancina? I'm Lucius Panderius. Pleased to meet you.'

'If this is a rescue, it's a damned poor job.' The voice was a pleasant contralto, and for all her circumstances, Tancina seemed mildly amused.

'Oh, it's just getting started,' I assured her, taking the sword from her unresisting fingers. After briefly ensuring that Orco would never bother anyone again, I started to strip the tunic off the corpse.

'Was that really necessary?' Tancina seemed genuinely curious rather than indignant. She was certainly her father's daughter.

'Necessary, no. Advisable, definitely. Were you two planning on becoming friends if he had woken up? Pass me that plank ... no, even better, that pickaxe handle, over there. Oh, perfect.'

'Is Ava behind that?' As I headed for the door I jerked my head toward the far corner of the room where a cloth had been hung to make a crude partition.

'The slave girl? Yes. She's been drugged for a while now, ever since she agreed to say what they wanted. The official questioner is coming tomorrow, and I guess they need her fresh, well sort of fresh, to answer his questions. They'll torture her again for that, I suppose. What are you doing?'

On our side, the door was set into the wall with a simple curved handle with which to push it open on those occasions when it was not secured by a two-inch plank on the other side.

'I'm locking the door.' As I spoke I lifted the tunic which had belonged to the late Orco. I fed one end of this through the gap between handle and door. When the tunic was halfway through, I slit the skirt side, and pushed one end of the cut cloth through the sleeve hole at the top of the tunic and the other end through the neck. Then I knotted the ends together so that a crude but thick loop of cloth dangled from the door handle. Tancina regarded it dubiously.

Taking the pickaxe handle I shoved it into the cloth loop and started twisting. Seven turns later and the cloth was a thick, twisted rope pulling the pickaxe handle toward the door. Two more turns, and the pickaxe handle was clamped against the wall by the twisted cloth, each end resting against the wall on either side of the door.

'Lucky the wall is so thick,' observed Tancina.

'It's a structural support wall,' I said vaguely, 'I knew it would be thick before I came in - I asked. Now let's grab Ava and get out of here.'

Tancina looked around the darkened room. There was one window in the outside wall. It was less than a foot wide and barred in any case. There was the door, now secured on both sides. In terms of exits that was about it.

'Get out?' she asked. 'Hmm ... Well, the mortar on that far wall is really crumbly. We can carry on working on that. I think the wall is one brick thick - look at the window. I was digging out one of the bricks when they caught me at it. They put him,' she jerked her chin at the late Orco, '... in with us so I wouldn't try doing that again. I won't tell you how he passed the time while he was here. He said he'd hurt the child if I didn't play along. Come to think of it, I'm rather glad you killed him. He stank.'

The brick in question had indeed a deep groove in the mortar along two sides. After a brief study I announced, 'Good, but it lacks ambition. There's a faster way out.'

'The roof? I could stand on your shoulders. Actually since there's not much to you, you could stand on mine and work some tiles loose.'

Tancina was indeed my own height, and the set of her

shoulders reminded me that she was a laundry-woman. Lifting and stirring water-soaked clothes in a tub day after day builds up a healthy set of muscles. The roof was supported by heavy beams running crossways over our heads, and these would certainly support our weight if we tunnelled our way up through the tiles. Mind you, there would then be the unconscious Ava and the child to manhandle through the gap.

'We'll take the simpler way. We're going through the wall.'

'It's a wall. You don't go through them. That's why they are called walls.' Tancina's was only a token protest while she watched me curiously. She was already catching on.

'Damn that Plato and his theory of forms. Give something a name and you define and limit it. You see a wall, and of course, as you say, one can't walk through a wall.'

Behind us someone knocked on the door, then knocked again, more urgently. A muffled voice shouted something.

'On the other hand. Let's say that what we have here is a rickety pile of bricks eight feet high and one brick wide, held together with lousy mortar. It's a curtain wall, put together quickly and with hardly any foundations. It's already starting to lean outward – look at the corner. It would probably fall over by itself in a few years time. That's why the roof beams go crossways to the more solid side walls instead of resting on it. The builder was a cheapskate. Want to bet the two of us can't push that pile over?'

The bracket had been removed from the door, and vehement cursing greeted the discovery that it was held shut on our side. Tancina brushed the hair from her face, showing a broad, pale forehead. White teeth gleamed in a grin.

'Why don't we bet our lives?'

We positioned ourselves at the middle of the wall, an arm's length apart. There was shouting and hammering at the door. Much more of that commotion and I reckoned it would be hard to keep Tancinus out, no matter what he had been instructed.

'Not you sweetie,' Tancina informed her daughter, who had positioned herself between us, imitating our pose by leaning against the wall with outstretched arms.

'Ready?' Tancina asked. 'Then push ... and push ... it's moving ... keep the rhythm.'

On the fourth push, the wall swayed so violently that for a moment I thought it was going to fall inward, but one more mighty shove from the pair of us sent it toppling in the other direction. A U-shaped chunk of brickwork from the height of our knees to the roof fell entire into the alley, breaking in two as it landed. I grabbed the sword and stepped out over the low barrier that remained, looking up the alley for the guard. First I saw the guard's feet. My gaze travelled up from there to the rest of the shadowy, recumbent form. Even in the gloom there was something dreadfully wrong with the shape of his head. Then Tancina was pushing past me, child in tow, and her father came hurrying to meet her. Three shadows, silhouetted across the mouth of the alley, slipped by like wolves tracking a deer. Sulla's men were heading into the house to dispose of the remaining occupants.

Tancinus and his family were locked in a hug that a crowbar couldn't break. I left them to it, and turned back to the broken wall to retrieve Ava.

Liber VII

If a man has to go to trial, he may as well make a performance of it. So, clean-shaven and in a spanking new toga - of purest lambs-wool from Apulia, no less - I set off to see what the fates had in store. We had all agreed to meet about an hour before the case was due to start, and then make an impressive progress through the Forum to the basilica. By 'we' I mean my friends, patrons and other supporters.

Who turns up to support a man in a court case is almost as important as who sits in the jury. In court, one need not necessarily bribe the jurors to influence their verdict. The fact that Sulla, Metellus, the elder Scaevola and a number of minor senators were expected to turn up for my parade to the court was a powerful public statement that these men believed in my innocence. It was also a clear indication of the powerful men whom the jurors would upset if they came up with a guilty verdict. This matters.

A while back Metellus senior was accused of extortion against the provincials while he was in charge of the African war. No-one likes to upset the Metelli, and when Metellus' accounts were passed to the jurors, the jurors looked instead at the massed ranks of the accused's brothers, sons and cousins, many wearing their insignia of office. There were also powerful friends in their senatorial togas, and influential Metellan clients packing the benches and stonily regarding the jurors. Not a man in the jury so much as looked at the account books, just in case this was construed as doubting the integrity of the accused. Metellus got off, naturally. In Rome it never hurts to show that you have influence.

Given the circumstances, I had decided the procession to the law court should start from the Oppian Leucadia. This is now a posh apartment block, but a century ago the building was the oldest and best-known bawdy house in Rome. As the name suggested, the enterprise had been owned by the Oppian family, a clan so ancient that the family's first Vestal Virgin is recorded on temple scrolls four hundred years old. Indeed, the Oppians had been in Rome for so long that the spur of rock where the house was located was generally known as 'the Oppian hill'. My point was that if the venerable and painfully respectable Oppians could own a brothel, then Caepio should think twice about reproaching me with the same fact.

There was mulled wine laid on at the rendezvous, and some honeyed sweet-cakes. The morning chill in the air was enough to make us glad of our togas, though the peacock-blue sky showing over the looming roofs of the narrow street suggested that the day would warm up nicely. There was the usual bustle of people meeting old acquaintances and catching up with gossip, and I and Scaevola moved together through the throng, greeting friends with real enthusiasm and thanking well-wishers. Overall, the crowd consisted mainly of my friends, my patrons, their clients and customers from the business, but a considerable number had come along just to see how young Scaevola did in his first case. One or two of those anxiously wishing my counsel well evidently did not recognize the accused who was standing right beside him.

The procession started slowly because we had to make our way over the ridge of the Velia into the Forum proper, and the Velia is crowded with the stalls of butchers, bakers and merchants with huge piles of cloth, Cappadocian sandals and other goods which retailers buy in bulk here and then sell off in their own stalls around the city. From the top of the Velia, jostled by the crowd, I looked across the Forum to the blocky cube of the Senate House, and at the Capitoline Hill soaring beyond. There was the golden roof of the temple of Jupiter, and there, bathed in morning sunlight were the Gemonian steps leading down from the Capitoline to the speaker's Rostra. Those steps were where my strangled corpse would be displayed if the jury brought in a guilty verdict.

As we swept past the temple of Castor I looked back toward the banker's benches which are located so that the money-changers can sit with their backs securely against the temple's high granite pediment. As expected, more than a few of my retinue peeled off here to lay bets with the bankers on the trial's outcome. I had already put my money down at good odds for an acquittal, and I had bet quite a lot - since after all, what did I have to lose? If I was found guilty I would not be poor for long.

Once past the financial area, the Forum narrows slightly. In the past I have often taken visitors to Rome down this very road, and noted their disappointment that the slightly shabby brick buildings lining the pavement are the very heart of the city and its empire. It's a sad fact that there are small Greek municipalities which no-one has never heard of that have better public spaces than our higgledy-piggeldy Forum, with the day-labourers waiting for hires spilling out from the Etrurian street and a whiff of sewage floating across from the air vents of the Cloaca Maxima - Rome's principal sewer, and appropriately enough, the pride of our city's civic engineering.

This middle area of the Forum is the most disreputable - here the layabouts swap lies with the gossips and both haggle for the services of the worn-out harlots who peddle their services in the back streets. Here there used to be what was known grandly as 'the canal' - though in truth it was a glorified drainage ditch and mosquito hatchery. Though now paved over, the line of flag-stones still acts as a de-facto border. On the one side are the fish-mongers and merchants selling takeaway lunches to labourers or those going to the chariot races. On the other side, no-one with a reputation to lose would dream of appearing without a toga, for this is the 'proper' side of the Forum.

Here, instead of gossips and layabouts, gentlemen of leisure exchange the news of the day, and senators' sons hang around the doors of the curia listening to their parents running Rome's empire. Instead of cheap harlots, you can rent a witness at the Puteal Libonis scroll depository who will happily perjure himself by providing the best testimony that money can buy. The Puteal Libonis is also where records of witness testimonies are stored, and a sign that we were reaching the business end of our walk. The basilicas beyond are where the court cases are held, and a crowd gathering at one end showed that the *Inquisitio de Veneficariis*, the poison court, was preparing for the day's session with Lutatius Catulus presiding.

You would think that marching up at the head of a huge crowd of friends and allies would have been a huge morale booster, but instead the walk through the Forum had left me unaccountably depressed, and almost a bit lonely. Few in the bustling mass of humanity knew who I was or where I was going. Crowds heading for the courts were an everyday experience at this time of the year, and it mattered nothing to the people we passed whether I would be alive or dead in a few months. They would still celebrate the Saturnalia, and Rome would go on without me. In a few years time someone would look down the via Patricus and ask, 'Wasn't there a house with German girls here once? What became of it?' Between Sulla and Metellus I could be sure of a decent funeral, even if most of the mourners would be paid for turning up and showing the appropriate emotions. This was appropriate enough. My employees did much the same thing in their current jobs, after all.

As we approached the basilica, different emotions came to the fore. There was an eagerness to get started, to test the plans laid beforehand against the skill of the enemy and the vagaries of chance; to begin the struggle of life and death knowing that at the end lay a survivor's euphoria or the bleak emptiness of defeat.

This was my first court appearance as the accused, but the feeling was very familiar. It was just like going into combat.

'Gentlemen of the jury - there before you is the Palatine hill, where Hercules once trod. Indeed he might also have walked here, on the ground of this very forum. Mighty Hercules brought order to Italy, slew monsters and brought peace to much of the world. And yet ... when Hercules in his divine madness slew Iphitus, he had to face judgement. Yes, even that hero's great deeds did not excuse murder and Hercules was punished for his wrongdoing.'

'Expect, gentlemen of the jury, that the defence will lean heavily on the acts of Panderius in war, as if spilling foreign blood in combat excuses senseless killing at home. Doubtless this man's homicidal fury has served his country well. His bestial nature revels in slaughter - be it of Rome's enemies, or of Romans themselves. It is common knowledge that once, maddened by panic and blood-lust, he even tried to kill my own father - his commanding officer - when he tried to reason with Panderius on the battlefield. There are soldiers here on the witness bench who will testify that as an officer Panderius is a morose, savage creature, given over in turn to wild overconfidence and craven terror. His punishments are brutal, as reflects his nature, and on occasion he has so forgotten his humanity that, carried away by the infliction of pain, he actually killed a man under the pretence of enforcing discipline.'

'Did you?' enquired Mucius Scaevola of me out of the corner of his mouth.

'Yep,' I replied. The man in question had raped the ten-year-old daughter of the headman in a strategic Numidian village, and he had done so in flagrant disobedience of stringent orders to keep the locals friendly. The place had stayed loyal because I'd had the offender flogged to death in the town square. No doubt

Caepio knew the full story, but in a Roman court misrepresentation, slander and distortion of the truth are as standard as outright lies. We would get our chance to twist the facts later.

Caepio's opening was a small classic in its own way. Not only was he discrediting the 'war hero' defence before we had a chance to play it, but Caepio was also taking the chance to cast doubt on the credibility of the testimony I would be giving against his father at the later enquiry. It looked as though Caepio had rounded up every soldier that had ever been punished or fined while under my command. If they all testified we'd still be here in autumn, but that was the point – they were meant to make Caepio's case by their very number. Meanwhile Caepio's oration was moving past its preliminary.

'A wolfhound may serve well in the rough woods and meadows by chasing down prey at the command of its master. Just so in the past, the bestial nature of Panderius has worked in the service of Rome. Yet if a wolfhound took advantage of his master's indulgence and came into the house, and if, while in the house that savage beast slew one of the master's tender babes with his blood-slavened jaws, how quickly would the master take his sword and put an end to the murderous beast? So it is with Panderius. Without the trumpets of war as an excuse, he lured into his chambers the tender maiden Fadia, and there mercilessly murdered her.'

Caepio stopped, and threw me a dirty look. I had inadvertently and loudly spluttered at the description of Fadia as a 'tender maiden'. From across the court the sibling Fadius glared at me murderously. I smiled beatifically at both prosecutor and plaintiff and leaned back in my warm woollen toga. The toga itself was a sign of disrespect, both to the prosecution and the court. Traditionally, the accused wears a dark toga and presents himself before the jury looking haggard and unshaven, showing by his appearance how the stress of the unjust accusation is wearing him down. The grandfather of the Caepio currently prosecuting had done all of that a few decades back when (rightly) accused of murdering a tribe of innocent Spaniards for their loot. Caepio Maior had carried his infant babies in his arms and tearfully beseeched the Roman people to care for them if he was found guilty. Such histrionics were the conventional way for the accused to behave.

So my appearance, clean-shaven and immaculate in a snow-white toga, told the court that the charges were insignificant and that I snapped my fingers with contempt at the prosecution. Even Catulus on his judge's curule stool had raised a curious eyebrow at my outfit. It had been a strategic choice. Scaevola and I wanted our confidence to worry the prosecution.

Behind me Sulla noted my reaction to the 'tender maiden' reference and muttered an aside to Metellus Numidicus who guffawed loudly. Naturally the audience picked up on this. There was quite a crowd in the basilica to watch the trial, and - this being a matter of considerable interest and debate beforehand - to see who had shown up for each side.

The prosecution had naturally mustered its own heavy-weights. Among the luminaries in his support, Caepio had of course his father, Caepio senior, an Appius Claudius, Cassius Longinus and old Aemilius Scaurus himself. While these men were leaders of the Senate and the driving force of the Optimate faction, they were also rather good for our cause. As Scaevola (senior) had loudly remarked as we took our seats, on the one hand we had the progressive, popular element and on the other the corrupt remnants of the Optimate regime. Public opinion was passionately opposed to the Optimates, both for their mismana-gement of the African war and Caepio senior's incompetence in losing an army of Roman soldiers at Arausio. Consequently the crowd was firmly pro-Panderius on the basis that the average citizen supported anyone that the Optimates did not. I was interested to see that no Marians had stepped up to declare support for the prosecution. Whatever Marius had against me, he was not yet prepared to make it public.

Thus the audience responded to my and my patrons' reaction with boos and catcalls at Caepio, even though none of them had ever known the Lady Fadia or her reputation. Fadius, the plaintiff, was seated beside the elder Caepio in an obvious attempt to make the pair into a sort of 'victims-of-Panderius-club'. Whatever good this might be doing Caepio senior, it was certainly not helping the cause of young Fadius. His face was flushed scarlet and his fists clenched and unclenched as he listened. Annoyingly, the young man did indeed look like the innocent victim of crime. His inability to hide his feelings gave the impression that he was honest, open and guileless, and Fadius alone on the prosecution bench received some sympathy from the watching crowd - sympathy that might yet prove fatal for my health if it was sustained.

Caepio sensed this advantage. 'For shame!' he bellowed at me. 'It is not enough that you have taken the life of an innocent woman? Must you also take her good name?' Ignoring the jury, Caepio planted himself before the watching crowd with his arms akimbo. With the unbreakable self-assurance of a born Roman aristocrat he glared at the spectators until an uneasy silence fell.

'Let me tell you about the Lady Fadia,' Caepio growled. 'Let me tell you of her as I heard it from her nursemaid,' he gestured at an elderly woman among the witnesses. The nursemaid sat bolt upright amid the gathering of reprobate soldiery, glancing about nervously and evidently wondering when their infamous licentiousness was going to break out.

'The nursemaid raised Fadia from the time she was a babe. She will testify that her charge was open, honest and trusting. As a girl Fadia would patrol the grounds of the family estate to look for baby sparrows that had fallen from their nests. It was her pleasure to make pets of these and feed and care for them until they were grown, such was her gentle nature. She had friends, mainly female, who can testify that as a young woman Fadia was sweet, modest and chaste. Her education was that of a young lady - some reading of the classics, and tuition in the womanly virtues. Even when her parents had passed away, she would spend several hours a day weaving at the loom, a proper pastime which befits a young lady.'

'I challenge the defence to produce a witness, a single witness, who can attest that the young Lady Fadia took any interest in witchcraft, or poisonings, or that she ever associated with any persons of infamy. They will not do so.'

Caepio paused in his pacing and stood before us, waiting. Scaevola and I stared back blandly. The sun was getting stronger, for the day was warming nicely. Prickles of sweat already adorned Caepio's forehead, testimony to the energy with which he was working crowd and jury alike with eloquent gesture and carefully modulated turn of phrase.

'So she came to Rome – naive, excited, wanting to see the big city at least once before settling down to life as a married *materfamilias*. Can't we all understand why she would want that? To see the Capitoline hill and the temple of Jupiter, the shrine of Vesta and the hut of our father and founder Romulus? She was a Roman and she wanted to see the city of the seven hills for herself. Who can blame her?'

'So what academy of darkness did she throw herself into, that within two months she learned all the arts of poisoning and seduction? How could this gentle, friendly and overly trusting young woman so suddenly transform herself into the man-eating poisoner that this villain' - Caepio flung out an arm to indicate me - 'pretends her to be?'

'Yet she did indeed meet a master of poisons, a man whose dark savagery hides beneath a genial nature. We know this from her own words, spoken from beyond the tomb.' Caepio gestured and a young woman rose from behind the prosecutor's bench. She held a small roll of papyrus and from this she read in a well-rehearsed voice.

'Brother,

Know that I am well and expect to return to you by the Kalends of May. I have no complaint of my new lodgings which are cleaner than those of the inn where I first stayed. My friend Lucinda is a constant companion and the innkeeper knows her well - he positively jumps to fulfil her wishes if she so much as glances at him!

We went to the Circus Maximus this month, and the chariot races were as exciting as they say. Our dear father was always so strong a supporter of the Blues, and it pleases me to relate that on my visit the Blue chariots won most of the races. The crowds! There were more people there to watch than are in all our little town, and the town beside it too. It was packed in the stands, and I was forced to remonstrate with the man behind me, who kept pushing his knees into my back. Eventually the man beside me intervened on my behalf. He is a called Lucius, and he is a businessman and a soldier. We talked together between the races, and I hope to see him again. He seems to know everyone in Rome and everything about the city.

But do not worry, dear brother, for I can so well imagine your eyebrows rising as you read this! I shall ensure that I am properly chaperoned at all times and that nothing will happen between us which is not befitting of our family and our name.
I remain your loving sister,
Fadia.'

With some disquiet I noted that Caepio seemed to be gaining ground. Both jury and spectators were now following attentively. The young woman rolled up her scroll and stepped back into the shadows of the basilica, leaving centre stage once more to Caepio.

'Let us now look at this 'Lucius.' He cannot deny that 'Lucius' is he, Lucius the procurer, the whore-monger, the brothel-master. Many of you believe that you know him - yet you see only the smiling mask that he turns to the world. I have spoken to those who have seen him in private, where like some savage beast in his dark lair, he prowls and plots while beating and abusing those at his mercy. He pretends to be a gourmet, yet we have discovered that his interest in cookery is merely to disguise his real interest, which is exotic and lethal poisons. His cook was made his accomplice in the brewing of these deadly potions, and his housekeeper daily had to dispose of the corpses of the dogs on which he tested his concoctions.'

'The cook has attested that she saw him preparing the apple seeds that were used to poison the Lady Fadia. She saw the poison, she helped him test it on a rabbit and watched the creature's death throes. Then she saw him stir the deadly mixture into the wine ... what?'

Scaevola was on his feet, trying to attract the attention of the judge. Catulus was displeased. 'The agreement, you will recall,' Catulus chided my counsel, 'was that the speeches for each side should be given without interruption, and that you could question the witnesses afterwards. I understand that you are new to this, but you need to have a very good reason for flouting these terms.'

'I do have good reason,' Scaevola replied mildly. 'My friend Caepio is telling us what the cook did and saw, yet I do not see the cook on the witness bench. How are we to confirm the veracity of his words if the cook herself is not there to attest to them? What we are hearing now could be - and is - wholesale invention.'

'He has a point,' admitted Catulus. 'Do you intend to produce this cook, Caepio?'

'Awareness of his own guilt has led Lucius the Procurer to obscure the evidence.' Caepio confessed. 'Knowing that the cook had seen too much, he arranged for her to be sold into slavery. His housekeeper was present when he arranged the infamous deal with the poor girl's father, and the housekeeper is here to so testify to that.' Helga sat among the witnesses, her face stony. She looked neither right nor left, and had not done so since the proceedings had begun.

'We traced the cook to the place where she had been sold, and the new owner interrogated her. That is when we discovered everything. That owner too is here to verify what the cook told him.' This would be one of the 'businessmen' who had purchased Ava from her father. He was a middle-aged individual, balding and running slightly to fat. Scaevola was definitely looking forward to questioning him.

'But the cook herself?' Catulus wanted to know.

'She is missing,' Caepio admitted. 'We believe that she realized that Panderius would not permit her to testify, and she fled for her life. It was the same with the housekeeper. She discovered that Panderius was coming to silence her and she fled to my protection. He is sinister, determined and ruthless, and he has military companions who are every bit as bloodthirsty as he. Nowhere in Rome is safe, and we believe the cook knew that. Even with the penalties facing an escaped slave, she must have believed flight to be her only option.'

I wondered how much Caepio knew of the house on the Aventine, which we had left neat and corpse-free as though abandoned without fuss. Sabaco would have come back to an empty house with no indication of what had happened other than a collapsed wall. What Sabaco had told his masters, and what they had told Caepio, I could only conjecture. For the moment I relaxed and let the prosecution give hostages to fortune.

Catulus considered. 'I'll allow the testimony,' he conceded. 'But the jury should be aware that Caepio is repeating what one person heard from someone else. Consider it hearsay, and one level above gossip.'

Caepio recovered swiftly. 'Then perhaps we should once again hear from the victim herself, in her own words.' The young woman stepped forward once more, with another scroll in hand.

'My Brother;

You are ever dear to me, and your concern for my well-being is my shelter and refuge in these times. I fear you were right about Lucius. He is not the man I thought him when we first met. Recently he has become demanding and possessive. Even this letter I am dictating in secret, for he tries to keep me from communication with my former friends and family. However, he has not been able to prevent my visit to this morning salon. Still, I must prepare this letter in haste.

Tonight I shall tell Lucius that I no longer wish for his company. I shall collect the things he insisted I store at his house of infamy 'for convenience', and then I shall arrange to return home. Rome has little appeal for me now. I am sure that there is no need for this, but you should not fear for my safety. My friend has arranged for a bodyguard to accompany me, a soldier on leave. He is a relative of one of the house servants. He looks very stern and martial, and will certainly intimidate Lucius.

I cannot wait to be home again, and by the time you get this I shall already be on the road. Prepare please, to be reunited with
Your foolish sister,

Fadia.'

'Well,' resumed Caepio, 'we know how that story ends. Lucius Panderius confided to his housekeeper that his original intention was to romance the woman, and perhaps get a substantial inheritance in her will. Fadia was young, but Rome is an unhealthy city, especially when one associates with a poisoner. The cook's testimony proves that the plan was originally to slip the victim a slow poison such as arsenic while Panderius was a devoted attendant at her bedside.'

'However, Fadia became aware that the man courting her was not who he pretended to be. She wished to leave and return home. So Panderius, in fury and spite at the loss of money he already considered his own, prepared the fatal potion. The cook watched him prepare it, and mix it into the wine. The housekeeper saw him carry it into the room. We know not how Panderius inveigled the girl into his personal quarters, but even now perhaps, Fadia was too willing, open and trusting. Once there, we know from her pitiful nakedness that Panderius attempted to force himself on the girl, but she got loose, and somehow lifted the bracket barring the door.'

'Outside the bodyguard, already worried, had been pacing restlessly. As soon as the door opened, he rushed in at once, and at once he was foully murdered. Like Fadia he recognized too late that human life means nothing to a man accustomed to death on the battlefield, a man whose experience of war has released savage passions that cannot be controlled in peacetime. Roused by the pitiful screams of the girl, the housekeeper rushes to the rooms. In truth she could have come sooner, but screams of fear and pain are not unusual when Panderius takes his pleasure. It was only when she realizes that these are the desperate cries of the hapless Fadia that the housekeeper hurries to the scene.'

'The horror of the sight that confronts her! There in the lamplight, the darkened sheets soaked and heavy, reeking with blood! The gallant soldier dying, his final spasms unnoticed. For there is Panderius, his face contorted with fury and hate, as he wraps his arms around the tender neck of the woman he would violate. She sees as he grasps the fatal vessel, forces open with a savage hand the clenched jaws of his victim and pours the deadly wine down her choking throat. It ... .'

Seized with emotion, Caepio seemed for a moment to be unable to go on. The court listened with fascination. Even I was spellbound, and I had been there the first time around. The prosecutor shook his head, visibly pulling himself together. 'It is a crime that cries to the heavens for justice. An innocent lamb, lured into the blood-stained den of this human wolf. And then, by the Gods! That very wolf pretends he, yes, that he is the lamb and his poor dead victim was the ravening lion come to slay him.'

'Why the pretence? Indeed, why not dispose quietly of the bodies as doubtless Panderius has done before? Because of the only witness he can call to testify in his defence.' Caepio gave a stiff nod to Sulla. 'This man, the patron of Panderius, was at his establishment that night. He came too late to witness the killing but he was in time to see the bodies. While perhaps too ready to believe the best of his clients, Cornelius Sulla is a man of integrity and honour. Once he had seen the massacre which Panderius had wrought, Sulla's honesty would insist that the vigiles be called. Thus it was known where Fadia had spent her final night.'

'Then, alarmed by her last letter, and that she had not returned as promised, her brother came to Rome to find her. This is when the tissue of lies Panderius had wrapped around his killings began to dissolve. Those who knew Fadia in life knew how foully Panderius had besmirched her reputation in death. Threats of violence seemed so real to the housekeeper that instead of remaining silent as he intended, she fled for her life to the authorities, and the plan to get rid of the cook by selling her into slavery rebounded to Panderius' detriment.'

'Now the web of lies has unravelled. His treacheries and lies have been brought into the daylight. And there Lucius Panderius sits before you, smirking and defiant, still hoping that he can bluff his way out of it by sheer effrontery. Gentlemen of the jury, by the evidence, by the irrefutable testimony of witnesses, by the vengeance of Nemesis, Lucius Panderius is guilty. He is not fit to remain in the light of day. He is a monster to be cast into the shadows of the underworld, there to face true judgement and the spirits of those he has sent before him. It is your task, your duty, to send him there. Justice demands no less!'

This last was delivered at a shout, with Caepio pointing a trembling finger at me from an arm's length away. There was complete silence as he dropped his arm and walked away to collapse, panting, on the prosecutor's stool.

Catulus sat back. 'This may be a good moment to break for lunch,' he said.

Liber VIII

'Well,' conceded Scaevola judiciously, 'that was a pretty good speech. Who knew that young Caepio had it in him? If I were a juror eating lunch right now, I'd be convinced you won't be able to talk your way out of it this afternoon. The whole story hangs together too beautifully - character, motivation, the lot. It's a really credible narrative, isn't it? If you had an evil twin, he would have done exactly as Caepio described.' Scaevola selected a bread roll. 'You don't actually have an evil twin, do you? No? Pity. Mmmm. Nice cheese this. Metellus does pretty well for himself if this is what his clients can afford.'

We were in the Palatine home of one of Metellus' richer clients. It was five minutes' walk from the courtroom, and a world away from the dingy shop-fronts of the mid-Forum. We reclined on couches in the atrium, where the gentle splashing of a fountain and the song of caged thrushes filled the courtyard and muted the sound of Roman life roaring along in the streets outside. A serving slave waited in the shadows across the court-yard, discreetly just out of earshot. Scaevola examined one of the stone columns holding up the roof around the little sanctuary. 'Pink granite, polished to a mirror finish. Do you know how much it costs to get this stuff imported from Egypt?'

'Not that much. This fellow is a pottery exporter - he's got factories churning lamps out by the thousand in Aricia. Probably sent a load to Egypt and brought the columns back as ballast on the return journey.'

'Pshaw!' with a genial wave of his bread roll Scaevola dismissed my sour objection. 'Grain! Egypt is drowning in the stuff. If I sent oil lamps to Egypt, I would have brought back a shipload of grain and sold it to the Ostia merchants. Or shipped it up the coast to Syria - the harvests are bad there this year. No, importing the marble was pure extravagance. Hold on... .'

Scaevola slipped off his couch (helping himself to another bread roll as he did so), and examined the nearest column closely. He seemed to sniff at it, wolfhound style. For a moment I wondered if he was going to raise a leg and pee on the thing. Instead, he gave a little yip of triumph. 'Thought so! It's just facing. Look, you can see the join here, hidden by marble dust and resin. The marble is a quarter inch thick - I bet the actual column is brick.'

'Wow,' I said unenthusiastically. 'Now shall we discuss the provenance of the flowers by the atrium pool, or perhaps the colours of the butterflies fluttering around them? I know! Maybe something of passing interest ... like the trial? I'm fighting for my life here, remember?'

Scaevola dropped back onto the couch beside mine, and helped himself to a handful of honeyed dates. 'Actually, those granite columns are rather like Caepio's case. Impressive and convincing at first sight, but on closer examination, a façade.'

'The disgruntled soldiery make up most of the witnesses, and they are fluff, just there for show. We might ask Caepio how many soldiers his father has punished. I recall an entire *ala* of 500 cavalry for a start. The witnesses that count are Ava and Helga. Just those two.'

'What about the nursemaid?'

'What about her? Forget nursemaids; is there a mother in Rome who really knows what her teenage daughters get up to when her back is turned? You can have slave chaperones, have the girls followed, but it's all part of the game. You may recall from recent scandals that even some of our Vestal Virgins ... weren't. Little Marcia is allegedly on a tour of Greece, though I happen to know she won't be moving from Baiae until the baby is born. Last year's Tribune of the Plebs thought that his daughter spent the winter weaving and spinning. If he can be fooled, well, want to bet that young Fadia picked up more than baby sparrows on the grounds of her estate?'

'Do you think Caepio knows we have Ava?' I picked at the dates, but my stomach was so clenched I could not even pretend to have an appetite. The insouciant manner with which my advocate had polished off his lunch was proving more aggravating than reassuring. Now Scaevola was examining the grapes and pears in the fruit basket with predatory interest.

'Hmm?' You really ought to try these pears. The darn things on my Alban farm manage to go from unripe to rotten without ever becoming ripe. Have one. A good pear should be treasured, because the bad ones are so bad.'

My eyelid twitched involuntarily. I was almost the only person in Rome who knew for sure that I had not murdered the Lady Fadia. Since everyone else seemed certain of my guilt, I reckoned I might not have much to lose by also strangling Scaevola. There were times when doing that would be, oh, so very satisfying.

'Caepio actually doesn't care if you have Ava, or if reality flatly contradicts everything his witness has said.' Jupiter be praised, Scaevola's attention had wandered back to the case. 'You can't produce her, because she's an escaped slave - and Caepio will happily take a hit to his poisoning case if he can be certain of nailing you for abetting the escape of a slave. Either way you're marked by *infamia* and your testimony as a witness is practically invalid. And um, I understand that persons went unaccountably missing at the time Ava disappeared. So producing Ava in court actually exposes you to further charges of murder and robbery while not actually getting you off the poisoning charge. Ava would just go back to her owners, and you'd be up before the standing court on robbery right after the poisoning court had done with you.'

'Or that's what Caepio thinks.'

Scaevola's grin was suddenly savage. 'Yes, I can't wait to see that little prick's expression when he finds out just how wrong he was.'

'So it all depends on Helga, then.'

'Oh good. It's not as if Helga has ever let you down before.'

Some of the audience had obviously enjoyed wine with their lunch, for semi-inebriated cheers arose from the spectators as Scaevola stood in the afternoon sunshine to deliver his maiden speech for the defence.

Turning to the plaintiff Fadius, Scaevola began politely, 'Lucius Panderius and I would like to offer you our condolences for the death of your sister.' Then, oration concluded, he sat down again to a stunned silence. This lasted for some time until the judge finally broke it.

'That's it?' Catulus wanted to know. 'That was the whole opening speech of the defence?'

Scaevola rolled his eyeballs up as he mentally reprised his words. 'I left something out?'

'Does this mean that you are throwing yourself on the mercy of the court?' Catulus asked incredulously. 'Because ...'.

'Indeed not,' Scaevola rolled smoothly over the judge's expostulation. 'We've had pretty words all morning, so expertly delivered by our Caepio here. I'm not going to waste more of the jury's time with speechifying. It is time that everyone heard the facts, and discovered that this case has been a sham from start to finish. We'll be wanting the prosecution witness Ofella first.' The businessman who owned Ava shifted uncomfortably, but Scaevola pressed on, 'Immediately after we've heard from King Burones of the Suebi.' To a general murmur of surprise and speculation, the German exile stepped forward to be questioned.

'King' Burones was a short, chubby man with a black, spade-shaped beard. His lively, intelligent gaze darted around the court as he stood to take Scaevola's questions.

'You are chieftain of the Runcini?' The Suebi are one of the largest confederations of people who occupy the endless forests of Germania. The individual sub-tribes - such as the Runcini - are constantly feuding and falling out with each other, and this produces a regular flow of exiles such as Burones to Rome.

'I am the rightful chieftain, yes,' Burones said carefully. 'Currently seeking the help of the Roman people to place me back on the throne from which I was treacherously deposed. My brother allied with the Chattii against Rome, persuaded my foolish people to go along, and ... .'

'No doubt you will tell the Senate all about it,' interrupted Scaevola soothingly. 'The next senatorial session dedicated to foreign affairs will be fascinating. But I need to know something else. Who among your people came with you to Rome when your brother expelled you?'

'My sworn bodyguard, of course. A few headmen and their families, and my daughter Ava.'

'*Your* daughter, Ava? Yours?'

'Yes.'

Without turning his head, Scaevola gave orders to the court officials. 'Do not let the witness Ofella leave the bench.'

The balding businessman had shown no signs of leaving, but Scaevola's comment drew everybody's attention to him. Under the sudden scrutiny the man looked startled and not a little agitated. Scaevola waited several seconds for the implications of Burones' testimony to sink in. Then he pretended to consult his notes.

'Ava is your daughter? It was my understanding that this girl was the daughter of, let's see ... one Pracardus, of your retinue?'

'No, no. Ava is my natural child. A relationship I had with her mother before either of us was married. I couldn't marry the girl myself, of course. My father had already pledged me to the daughter of the chief of the Sacidi because of ... well, politics, to be brief. But after she had given birth to Ava, I arranged for the girl to marry one of my retainers. That retainer was Pracardus. He brought up Ava after her mother died, but she is my acknowledged daughter. One of several. Sadly, my line produces more daughters than sons.'

'Legally speaking, what is the relationship between Pracardus and your daughter Ava?'

The chief looked worried. 'Is there one? My knowledge of how the law works in Rome is rather limited. There is no blood relationship, and he never formally adopted her or became her guardian. She just lived with him. She had to live somewhere. My family would be as uncomfortable living with her as she with them, so my household was out of the question. Dynastically, Ava is a by-blow of no significance. So when I heard she had made a life for herself in Rome as ... ,' Burones coughed, 'as a cook, I saw no need to get involved.'

'Did you arrange to sell her,' Scaevola looked at his notes again, 'for an amphora of wine?' I nudged my counsel's leg, and he corrected himself, 'An amphora of cheap Etruscan wine?'

'I did not,' said Burones indignantly. 'And Pracardus had no right to do it either. The scoundrel appears to have fled Rome, or he would be in the courts right now. My daughter, a slave? Never! She might be my natural child, but she is a child of Burones, and Burones does not sell his children.' The dark beard jutted forward proudly.

'Ofella,' Scaevola's voice was almost caressing as he addressed his next witness. He prowled toward the businessman who stood before him, sweating gently.

'Ofella, can you describe Pracardus for us?'

The question seemed so innocent that Ofella, expecting much worse, answered eagerly. 'Of course. He's well-built, tall, even for a German. He has shoulder-length hair, blond ... um ... high cheek bones, and I think his eyes were blue. He .... '

'Can you describe Ava, the girl you purchased?'

Ofella paused. He was starting to get it.

'I can get other witnesses to help jog your memory. But the jury might wonder at your reticence. Go on.'

'She's not very tall, sort of plump.'

'And her hair?'

'Dark and curly. Look, girls don't always resemble their fathers.'

Scaevola turned to study Burones, and after a while everyone else in the court did too. 'Ava does, though,' Scaevola remarked mildly. 'She looks just like her father.'

'I didn't know. Pracardus said he was her father. They said there wouldn't be any trouble.'

Scaevola pounced. 'They? Who are 'they'? Do please tell.'

'Um, I meant the German. Pracardus. He offered, we purchased.'

'Your associate is back in Arpinum, is he not?'

'Yes. I should be too. I only agreed to stay in Rome to testify because the girl went missing.'

'Even though not a Roman, you do understand Roman law? As a businessman you should.'

Instead of answering, Ofella closed his eyes. He knew what was coming. Scaevola spelled it out anyway for the benefit of the jury and the spectators.

'Nowhere in Roman law more than slavery does the rule 'caveat emptor' more rigidly apply. Let the buyer beware. The purchaser of a slave must ensure that his slave is legitimately owned, and owned by the person doing the selling. To him falls the task of due diligence. Otherwise we would have anarchy.'

Scaevola turned to face me. 'Lucius Panderius. Do you claim to own this slave, Ofella?'

Solemnly I replied, 'I do.'

'Will you sell him to me for, oh, say five denarii?'

'I would not. It would be cheating you of his value. He's yours for a bent copper *as*.'

To laughter from the crowd, Scaevola turned and explained to Ofella what everyone already knew. 'See? You can't have people buying and selling random Romans to each other. There must be proof of ownership, properly claimed, proven - and checked. We discovered Ava's true father within a morning. If not blinded by greed, you could have done so as well. You are liable and guilty.'

Approaching the witness, Scaevola handed him a scroll of vellum. 'It's an indictment. You are charged with the kidnapping, false imprisonment, rape and torture of a free woman. Since neither you nor the girl are Roman citizens, you'll go before the Praetor Peregrinus. It's an open and shut case, so we'll see you next at the Saturnalia. My money says you get thrown to the beasts at the games.'

'It was a mistake,' Ofella pleaded. 'I didn't know. They said ... I mean, I thought we just had to sign the contract, hand over the amphora and go. I didn't even want to be there when they questioned her. It made me sick.'

Scaevola looked thoughtful. 'There may be a way for you to redeem yourself. Perhaps. Think carefully about your testimony. By 'your' testimony I mean the testimony which Caepio here says you told to him. Think hard about it. All that detail about Panderius preparing the poisons. Is that testimony completely accurate? Is that really what the girl said? Now that you have heard the prosecution case, and weighed it against all the relevant facts? Perhaps you might reconsider?'

'I ... I see. Yes, yes, after consideration, I may have exaggerated, slightly ... .'

'A lot.'

'Yes, that's it. A lot. I exaggerated a lot. Also, Caepio exaggerated my exaggerations. Come to think of it, the whole thing is rubbish. Exaggerated out of all proportion.' Ofella looked at Scaevola desperately. 'Almost the opposite of the truth?' he suggested hopefully.

Caepio could take it no more. He leapt to his feet and appealed to Catulus. 'This is farcical. Everyone can see that Scaevola is blatantly coercing the witness.'

Scaevola turned to him and held up a hand as though stopping traffic. Then whirling back to the witness he demanded loudly. 'How was the girl Ava questioned when you saw her?'

Ofella gulped, but answered straightforwardly. 'She was hanging naked from a roof beam by her wrists. Her ankles were tied back to her thighs, and a man was beating the soles of her upturned feet with a split cane. By the look of things, he had been doing this for some time.'

'Now that,' Scaevola informed Caepio gently, 'is coercion.' He suddenly raised his voice to a shout. 'They kidnap and torture a girl to testify against her employer, and you accuse *me* of coercion? Where do you stand, Caepio? Does a witness lie when coerced? Because if this pathetic Ofella is lying now, when I have not laid a finger on him, what would Ava not say after a few hours of being whipped? What? What! Ava tells the truth because you torture her, but your man lies after ten minutes of gentle questions? How dreadfully convenient for you.'

Scaevola paused to collect himself. He was genuinely angry. 'We take your point, Mucius,' Catulus told him. 'The testimony of the cook is worthless, and the jury will be instructed to completely ignore it.'

Scaevola nodded at the judge. 'Perhaps not, Sir. It would be better if the cook herself testified that the prosecution evidence given in her name is a pack of lies. We said at the start that the case against my client is a sham, and we intend proving it.'

'You have the cook?' asked Catulus, astonished.

'She was brought in a litter just last night. Those who brought her told me that they had been lied to. They had been informed that she was a slave. However, the girl convinced the men that they had been torturing a free woman. Smitten by conscience, they decided to hand her to my custody and leave Rome. It seemed from their bearing that they were legionaries. It makes me proud that our army has such men of integrity and honour.'

Caepio was on his feet again. 'If you had the cook, why did you not produce her earlier, as your witness, instead of ...?'

'Instead of letting you make a fool of yourself? Because the girl was so hard used that we could not be sure until the lunch recess that she would be able to testify. Because we did not want Ofella to seize her before we had heard from her real father, and because she is still under the care of our doctor - there.'

Like the heads of the audience at a ball-catching game, those of jury and spectators swivelled to the corner of the basilica indicated by Scaevola's outflung arm. A covered litter had been set unobtrusively on the ground. Whoever was within had a clear view of the proceedings through the litter's thin curtains of gauzy Amorges cloth. No-one had paid the litter much attention, because bored aristocratic ladies occasionally like to drop in anonymously and watch some of the more sordid trials of the day. These ladies have sturdy and antisocial litter-bearers right on hand to discourage unwanted curiosity, so spectators tend to ignore such intrusions out of a learned sense of self-preservation.

Now, at a signal from Scaevola, the curtains were lifted back to reveal a pale but evidently alert Ava sitting up straight on the cushions. The crowd murmured with interest and several looked back and forth between Burones and Ava, drawing their own conclusions. Ofella looked as though he was going to be sick.

Catulus signalled to the litter-bearers. 'Bring her here.'

When the litter had been set down before him, Catulus studied Ava, who looked solemnly back with her round, brown eyes.

'Is this your daughter?' Catulus asked Burones.

'Yes,' the chieftain replied. He had hardly looked at the girl.

'Listen,' Catulus told Ava carefully. 'You are now a free woman. You can go to your father, or if you wish, after your testimony you can be sent to my household where I will make sure that you will be taken care of. 'Neither that man,' a finger jabbed at Caepio, 'nor they' - Scaevola and I were indicated by a similar gesture - 'can harm you. Do you understand that?'

'I want to go back to my job,' Ava told him, 'back at the Temple, The Temple of Freya. I work there. I'm the cook.' She looked over at me, agitated. 'I'm not well, but I'm getting better. I can work.'

'Are you ready to answer some questions?' Catulus enquired.

At this, Ava flinched violently and shrank back into the cushions with a frightened whimper. Her already pale face went as white as a sheet. With unusual sensitivity for a Roman aristocrat, Catulus immediately understood the response.

'No, no, not like that. No-one is going to hurt you. You don't have to answer, and you won't be harmed, no matter what you say. You are safe here. You can say whatever you want.'

Ava studied him with a child-like gaze. 'They hurt my feet,' she informed him. 'I can't walk.'

Scaevola stood up. 'She was drugged after her torture, we think with some poppy mixture. The doctor says she is still recovering. Also, there are the after-effects of what was done to her ... .'

'When I want your opinion, I'll ask for it,' Catulus snapped. 'If you interrupt me again, I'll have you ejected from my court. Is that clear?'

An abashed Scaevola sat down promptly, red-faced.

Catulus turned back to Ava. 'All we want is for you to talk about some things. Things that really happened. Not things that you might have been told to say.'

Ava was crying. Not sobbing, but tears streamed silently down her face. 'They hurt my feet,' she insisted. 'He kept hitting them.'

'That man has gone Ava. He won't be back. Do you know that person over there?' Catulus indicated me, and Ava twisted to look at my face.

'Yes,' she agreed carefully.

'Does he make you scared?'

'Yes,' said Ava firmly. There was a sigh from the crowd.

'Why does he scare you?'

'Because I want to work. But I can't walk. I can cook, but he might not let me.'

'Did he ever make any poison in your kitchen, or ask you to make any poison?'

For the first time Ava's face showed colour. Her cheeks flushed. 'I told you, and told you and told you. There was no poison. We didn't make any. Lucius didn't make any. I didn't see any poison and I didn't see Lucius make any. So you can hit me, and I'll tell you, no poison, no poison. There was no poison. Don't hit me, please. Please!'

Ava wailed and collapsed back, trying to burrow herself into the cushions. From her panic it was clear that it would be a while before she could say anything more. The doctor hurried up, and Ava clung to him while he spoke quickly and soothingly.

Catulus signalled the litter bearers. 'Take her back.' He looked over at Scaevola. 'I can see why you were not sure she could testify at all.' Then, to Caepio, 'You heard what we heard. If you have any questions for the girl you will put them to her through me. Later.'

Even with the curtains of the litter back up, Ava's sobs were still audible. Caepio stood up. 'I will seek only to make clear that neither my client nor I had any part in this deplorable affair. This was some misguided friend of the Lady Fadia, or an enemy of Panderius trying to blacken his name even further. We had nothing to do with it. We accept that the cook denies handling poison, and that she denies Panderius ever did so. However, you have seen that she is desperate to return to her place of employment. Obviously she would be reluctant to implicate her employer. Just because she insists that something did not happen does not mean that thing did not happen.'

'But you accept her testimony?'

'She has said what she has said. We are content for that testimony to stand, though we dispute its accuracy. We also withdraw that part of my speech which contradicts what the witness has now said. But we still insist as strongly as ever that Panderius is guilty, and that he did kill Fadia, with or without his cook's knowledge or help.'

'So do you want to quest- ... will you require me to talk to her again?'

'Only to make clear that we had no part in her unfortunate treatment,' Caepio stated.

Scaevola arose. 'We are prepared to accept the claim of Caepio and his client that they knew nothing about the treatment of this witness. We ask that the court does the same. We accept that they had no part in attempting to force the witness to perjure herself. We also ask that this gentleman here ...', a contemptuous gesture indicated Ofella, '... be kept for questioning so that we can establish who did.'

Catulus said briskly, 'So noted. Now, the afternoon is getting on, and I'd like to get this wrapped up by nightfall. 'Are you ready to continue?'

Scaevola nodded happily. 'The prosecution's case is falling apart at the seams. One more tug should unravel it completely. Everything alleged by the plaintiff now depends on the false and lying testimony of one person and one person only. The witness Helga.'

'There's also the letters,' Catulus reminded him.

Scaevola looked politely incredulous. 'The letters? I really did not think anyone would take that second letter at all seriously. But very well, we can deal with that issue right now. Is the person who read them aloud still here?'

After a slight delay, the woman was duly produced.

'Is that the second letter?' Scaevola asked. 'Good. Now, can you tell me if the name at the bottom was written by the same hand which wrote the rest of it?'

It was agreed that the letter had been written by someone else, and then signed by the Lady Fadia. 'In fact,' remarked Scaevola, 'we know this in any case. In the text, we are told that the letter is being 'dictated in haste'. So the only reason we have for believing that this letter comes from the Lady Fadia is her signature at the bottom. A signature which is printed in block letters. Easy to forge.'

Scaevola turned to the nursemaid and courteously enquired 'Is it correct to assume, ma'am, that the Lady Fadia was not of a scholarly disposition? She was a weaver, and had potential as a *materfamilias*, but did she show signs of being a scholar?'

The nursemaid was intimidated by the size of her audience and the intensity of the attention suddenly turned upon her. Scaevola's savage filleting of the previous witness had doubtless served to terrorize her further. She answered the question by shaking her head violently, and slumped back in relief when Scaevola turned his attention elsewhere.

'In short, we have no evidence that this second letter, so convenient for the prosecution's case, was ever written by Fadia. After just one look at that shaky signature I could probably manage a reasonable facsimile, but there would be no need for that. Just outside this court here,' Scaevola gestured for emphasis, '... are men who can produce entire screeds in the handwriting of anyone you wish. And all for a few denarii. How many cases of forged wills have been heard in this very basilica in just this past month? To save you from checking, the answer is five - and the month is not over yet.'

'We know, from the treatment of the cook, Ava, that there are those who are prepared to go to great lengths to ruin and discredit my client. As to the motive, well, that is not hard to guess. We all know that Lucius Panderius will be testifying at another hearing later in the year. Who might like to ensure that Panderius gives the useless testimony of a condemned murderer is not for us to speculate about here. We need only note that someone has spent significant resources to ensure a guilty verdict in this case. After Fadia had died, for such a person to forge a letter that made Panderius look guilty was child's play. The writer already knew from the perjured Helga exactly what had happened that fateful night, so all he had to do was twist the circumstances around. Then he sent the letter on its way, and waited for Fadius to receive it and thereafter arrive in Rome, worried and in haste.'

Scaevola chewed his lip like a puppy worrying a slipper. 'I'm going to take a chance here, because I believe that you, Fadius, are an honest man. So I will ask a question to which I do not know the answer. Was that second letter from your sister delayed? Compared to her other letters was it significantly late in arriving?'

Inwardly I grinned. For all the ingenuous manner with which he had asked the question, Scaevola was lying through his teeth. He knew the truth. It had cost a small fortune to suborn one of the servants in the *domus Fadii*, but Scaevola and I both knew that the letter which should have been a few days on the road had taken well over a week to arrive. The servant was prepared to so testify if need be, in exchange for relocation to Rome and a job in the Scaevola household.

With his question, therefore, Scaevola would win whichever way it went. Fadius could either tell the truth, and confirm that the letter could well have been written after the Lady Fadia's body was stone cold, or he could be caught in a blatant lie by the servant's testimony.

Fadius stood. He frowned at Caepio and then glared at jury and spectators from under lowered brows, looking like a bull at bay in the arena. 'Yes, the letter was late. What of it? Correspondence is often delayed. The surprise is when a letter comes in good time. My sister did not use a dedicated messenger but relied on the goodwill of travellers from Rome. The letter could have sat in a roadside inn for days before someone saw my name and decided to take it to me.'

In fact most letters moved around Italy in this manner. One wrote a letter, went to the gates and enquired for someone going to, or close to, the letter's destination. Then you handed over the letter - and maybe a small payment - and left delivery in the lap of the Gods. That as many letters reached their addressees as actually did was one of the few things that kept alive my faith in human nature. So a late letter proved nothing. But as Scaevola pointed out -

'You do accept that the letter could have been forged after the attempt of Panderius' life, carefully tailored after Fadia's death to make him look as guilty as possible, and then sent to you by dedicated delivery so that it arrived late but not unusually late?'

Fadius did not reply. He merely grunted and sat down.

'I'd like to see that letter,' said Catulus. 'And pass it to the jury too.'

We sat patiently while the incriminating letter was examined, passed around, and discussed between earnest jurors with their heads together over the papyrus. Finally the tiny scroll was passed back to the prosecution bench, and we were ready to resume.

'Only one pillar stands in the crumbling edifice of the prosecution case,' Scaevola declared. 'It is now time to pull that pillar down; and pull down with it this whole sad and scandalous prosecution. Let the witness Helga rise and be questioned.'

Liber IX

Helga arose and faced jury and crowd fearlessly. With her blonde hair swept back and chiselled jaw set firm, she looked the very model of a Germanic warrior woman. Helga being Helga, I had no doubt that she had gone through every line of her testimony with meticulous thoroughness. She would have prepared herself for every rhetorical trick and attempt by Scaevola to prise open a chink in her story. Our only hope was to blind-side her from a direction she had not anticipated. Helga was organized, thorough and hard to shake. However, she was not good at unexpected developments, and was slow to adapt. We were going to work with that.

'Ma'am, could you please step over here, and stand facing the jury?' asked Scaevola politely.

Helga looked around her. 'Here is good. I can answer your questions from here.' She wasn't giving an inch.

Scaevola sighed. 'It was not a request, actually.'

Helga looked at Catulus. She asked the judge, 'Why do I have to move? All the other witnesses stand, answer questions and sit down. Why does he want to move me around the courtroom like a child's doll?'

Catulus looked at Scaevola. 'Why indeed?'

The real answer was that we wanted get Helga out of her comfort zone, to have her answering our questions in a place different from where she had imagined she would be answering them. We needed to take away her illusion that she was in control and get her slightly off-balance.

Of course, Scaevola could not actually give this reply, so instead he informed the judge, 'The witness will be lying. As she is a clever and accomplished liar, there will be only the slightest pause, the merest flicker of uncertainty on her face when she invents an untruth. I don't want the jury - or the spectators - to miss it.'

Catulus grunted. 'This smacks of theatricality. However, I see no harm in indulging it.' He looked over at Helga. 'Move to where he asks, and let us get on with this.'

Mulishly, Helga seemed for a moment to consider standing her ground. Then ostentatiously letting everyone know that she was being unfairly put-upon, she walked to the spot which Scaevola courteously indicated and stood glaring at him.

'You are the *vica puellarum*, the manager of Panderius' brothel?'

'Yes, but he manages it himself.' This was true, but a low blow. There was no shame in owning a brothel - several senators owned one, and it was a point of pride with me that they frequented my premises nevertheless. However, actually managing the bawdy house one owned was a disreputable job unbecoming of a member of decent society. It was the difference between owning gladiators and actually training them. The gladiator owner was respected, even admired, while the *lanista*, the trainer, was a person like my prostitutes, someone permanently marked in the census lists with *infamia*. The main reason I had Helga on the payroll was to officially distance myself from the day-to-day running of the establishment, though in reality, as Helga had bitterly pointed out, running the place day-to-day was exactly what I did anyway.

Scaevola had to allow Helga to get her in dig about my working habits so that he could get in a shot of his own. 'Tell me why the word of a brothel manager such as yourself should be taken above that of Lucius Panderius, a respected soldier and citizen?'

Helga did not blink. This was one she had prepared earlier. 'Because Panderius is a murderer and I am not.'

My counsel followed up smoothly. 'Is that a lie?'

'Eh? What? No. No, it is the truth.'

Scaevola turned to the jury. 'You see? When she has to lie suddenly, her expression changes somewhat – watch for it as the questioning goes on.'

The jurymen looked doubtfully at one another, and I was sure that, like me, they had seen no tell-tale flash of guilt. However, Helga would not be at all sure of what her expression had betrayed, and would school herself to give nothing away next time she lied. Once she began to doubt herself, the effort of trying to look innocent would begin to show. Since Scaevola knew the true story from me, he needed no subtle indications from his witness's expression to know when she had told a lie. And every time that she lied, Scaevola would helpfully point it out to the jury, and Helga's uncertainty would grow. She would try harder to look natural every time she told an untruth, and she was not that good an actor.

After a few more preliminary skirmishes, Scaevola asked a series of innocuous questions one after the other. Helga began answering with monosyllables, while the jury shifted restlessly.

'Did you get a replacement cook for Panderius?'

'Yes.'

'Was this because the cook Ava had disappeared?'

'Yes'

'Were you at the brothel on the night Fadia died?'

'Yes.'

'Did you hear a disturbance at Panderius' rooms?'

'Yes.'

'Did you see the Lady Fadia poison herself?'

'Y ... No! No, I saw Panderius do it.'

Scaevola smirked at Helga who glared back furiously. The questions had been all of the same length and asked with the same rhythm. All of them required Helga to honestly answer 'yes'. Caught by the pattern, Helga had only at the last moment remembered to deviate from truthfully saying what she had done and seen, and change her automatic 'yes' to a 'no'. So she had hesitated before the lie, just as Scaevola had predicted she would. By his smirk, Scaevola was letting Helga know that he knew, which made Helga even more angry and uncertain.

It was all good fun, and helped to show future clients that Mucius Scaevola was a counsel who knew how to interrogate a witness. Also, it attacked Helga on a front she had expected to be attacked. Because it was a very good attack, fending it off took all of Helga's mental energy. I was restless, and tried hard to conceal this behind a bland expression. The time was coming for Scaevola to launch our ambush. It had to work, because discreet enquiries by Scaevola's agents had confirmed that Caepio had bribed enough of the jury to ensure that that nothing but overwhelming proof of my innocence would now save me.

My gaze wandered over the spectators. There were a goodly number of women among them. Some were taking a break from tending market stalls, and others were wives who had accompanied their husbands to watch the entertainment of a legal knockabout. A few women were alone, one of these a veiled woman in black who stood by the jury box, right against the ropes which held spectators back from the court. Another group consisted of noisy spinsters still reeling slightly from the effects of lunchtime wine. These received angry and scandalized looks from many in the crowd. A 'proper' lady did not drink at all, and for a woman so show the effects of wine while in public was outrageous. Not that the women seemed to care - every reproof was answered with a torrent of abuse that would make a legionary blush.

The spectators too were getting restless. Up to now, Scaevola had mostly gone over ground covered by Caepio's speech, but with Helga slightly off-balance my counsel launched into the offensive.

'Let me tell you what actually happened. It goes like this. Your entire tale is correct right up to the moment you arrived at Panderius' rooms. There you saw the dying assassin whom Fadia had let into the room, and there you saw Fadia herself trapped in a corner. You saw her curse Panderius for foiling the planned murder, and you saw her drink the wine with which she had earlier tried to kill Panderius. Isn't that the case?'

'No. I saw him kill her. He forced her jaws open and .... '

'He killed her?'

'Yes.'

'Are you sure she died? Did you personally check the body?'

'No but .... '

'Do you know the penalty for perjury?'

'I am not lying,'

'In this court you swore by Castor and Pollux to tell the truth, and not only will the authorities in Rome punish you for lying, but even in the afterlife you will be hunted down and punished by the Furies for your crime. You understand that?'

'I am not lying,' insisted Helga stubbornly.

'What if there is one here who can throw your lies back in your teeth, someone who can testify personally that what you have told this court is a malicious deception designed to ruin my client.'

'There is no such person.'

My breath would not come. This was the moment. Scaevola made the most of it, pausing, and then almost snarling out his revelation.

'What if ... what if that person was the Lady Fadia?'

To the accompaniment of shouts and gasps from the crowd, Scaevola flung out an arm dramatically toward the spectators, and toward the veiled woman by the ropes - the woman in front of whom Helga had been carefully positioned.

This woman swept back her veil and the hood of her cloak,

and faced Helga, silent and proud. Her face was expressionless and her complexion yellowish and waxen, but it was beyond doubt Fadia as Helga had last seen her, lying on the floor of my bedroom.

All the blood drained from Helga's face, and she put a hand to her throat. Her eyes were wide with shock and for several seconds she struggled to speak.

'I ... it. It ... can't be. You ... dead. Saw. No.'

The crowd waited tensely, and I even more so. Come on .... My hands clenched into fists as Helga made a massive effort to regain her composure.

'No ... it can't be. You died. You fell to the floor of the room, you were not acting. You were so still afterwards. Not breathing, not blinking. You're dead.'

Helga stopped for a moment, and thought.

'Of course! When Sulla had left, Panderius stayed by the bodies.' Helga looked at me, sure of herself now.

'You told me to get wax, and oil. I watched from the dark outside. You put oil on the faces, and then used melted wax to make death masks of the corpses. You wanted to ... .'

I had wanted to identify the one assassin, and identify where the other had been and whom she had been working with, but Helga could not say that without supporting my side of the story, so she temporized.

'I do not know what you wanted to do by this, but you did it. Look! You can see this is not the Lady Fadia, it is an actor wearing a wax mask. Panderius has painted it with cosmetics to look lifelike. He took that mask from her face. This actor looks like the dead woman, but it is not her. It is just a stupid trick!'

The blood was back in Helga's face now and she looked at me scornfully. Her flush was pure relief, and under the cloth of her stola I saw her ribs heave as she whooshed out a sigh. I too sighed deeply. Thank you, Helga. Got you. Now, ... my gaze shifted to Fadius. His part was less essential, but it would be good to know that we had read him correctly.

Fadius was on his feet. He shook off Caepio's restraining hand, ignored Catulus' weak protest and marched across the court to stand just a few feet from the fake Fadia in her wax mask.

'What in Hades is this nonsense?' Fadius shouted, his voice almost breaking. He whirled on Scaevola, jabbing a forefinger so close to my counsel's jaw that he risked getting it bitten. 'What is this stupid game?' Unconsciously imitating Scaevola's earlier gesture, he threw out his arm to indicate the woman by the ropes. 'Who is this woman? Why do you say she is Fadia? That mask is not of Fadia. That's not my sister. I've never seen her before in my life!'

'That's not Fadia?' asked Scaevola with feigned surprise.

'Of course it isn't! Her nose is longer and straighter, the mouth isn't as wide, her … her face is more narrow … gah! It looks nothing like her.'

'It's not a likeness of your sister?' Scaevola wanted to get that fact unambiguously on the record.

'Are you stupid, man? That's what I keep telling you. That mask is not of my sister. It's not Fadia. It is some stranger. I don't know who it is.'

Scaevola turned to Helga, his eyebrows raised high. 'Yet you identified this woman as the Lady Fadia, did you not? Clearly and unmistakeably. You almost fainted when you saw her.'

Wisely, Helga said nothing. She knew she had been tricked somehow, but had not yet worked it out. However, the look she gave Scaevola was so downright murderous that for a moment I genuinely feared for his safety.

'Wait,' Catulus was imposing his presence on the proceedings. He looked at Fadius. 'So you say this mask is not a likeness of your sister?'

'I do not just say it. It simply is not. Her face says it. I can bring a dozen people who can testify that they knew Fadia, and that woman is not her. She looks nothing like her.'

Scaevola interjected smoothly, 'On the other hand, I can bring Cornelius Sulla who saw the body, and the captain of the vigiles who took it away later, and both will corroborate the testimony of the brothel manager that this is the true likeness of the woman who died in Panderius' rooms that night.'

Catulus asked in bewilderment, 'Well, if she's not Fadia, who is she?'

'She's a murdering bitch!'

This last contribution came from a woman in widow's clothing who was near, but not with the group of tipsy spinsters. Like everyone in the crowd the spinsters had been craning their necks to see the woman in the wax mask, and she had obligingly half turned to give the spectators a better look.

Suddenly aware that she had everyone's attention, the accuser hesitated. Being in widow's garb she had her head covered, and all that was visible was a shadowed face and a mass of dark, tangled hair. But raised arm and pointing finger clearly indicated their target.

'She killed my husband! Oh, I know they said it was his heart that gave out, but just two weeks after she seduces him from me and they run away together, he drops dead. Coincidence? I think not. She poisoned him, and ran off with my money. Yes, my money! If he's left me to run off after her like a dog chasing a bitch on heat then I get to have my dowry back. Right? Right?'

'Yet after the funeral, when he's hardly gone cold, she's sold off everything he had, taken my dowry and vanished. She killed my man! She took my money! May Mercury and Hecate take her stinking spirit to the underworld and there let the fates punish her with whips and scourges! She killed him. Killed him!'

At this the speaker could take no more, and she collapsed into sobs, her body bent over and hands covering her face while the dark hair hung tangled around it. The bevy of spinsters surrounded her, clucking sympathetically as they led her away. There was a small swirl in the crowd as people turned to watch their departure.

Catulus on the bench had been as riveted as any of the spectators. Now he stirred himself. 'Guards! Detain that woman! *What* now?'

This question was asked in a dangerous growl, for Scaevola had held up a hand to the guards in an unmistakeable signal for them to stop. Scaevola turned to the judge with grovelling politeness that barely hid his inner delight. 'May I ask why you want to detain that woman, Sir?' You could have greased axles with his voice, it was that oily.

'Because she is a material witness in this case, blast it!'

'Erm, what case is that? Because if it's the case against my client Lucius Panderius, I'd say that case is holed below the waterline and sunk beyond retrieval. If I may recap the Praetor's formula ... .' Scaevola fished out of his sleeve a little papyrus he just happened to have handy. Loudly enough for everyone to hear he proclaimed, 'Here's what the Praetor instructed "As plaintiff, Quintus Fadius through his agents and counsel must prove to the judge - and any jury that judge might appoint - beyond doubt, that on the night in question Lucius Turpillius Panderius did with malice and intention kill with poison the sister of Quintus Fadius, namely the Lady Fadia." Well, it's completely evident now that whatever happened that evening, my client did not kill the Lady Fadia since we have the word of her brother that the deceased is not that person. There's no longer a case to answer.'

There was silence for a moment, and then murmurs in the crowd as they worked it out. Tucking the little scroll away, Scaevola beamed at Catulus. 'The case is pretty much a dead letter wouldn't you say? Quintus Fadius can't even prove that my client even met his sister, the real Fadia, let alone killed her. And if he did it at all — which we vigorously deny - my client certainly did not do it on the night in question, because he was too busy trying not to be killed by the fake Lady Fadia and her accomplice.'

'So, by each and every count on the Praetor's formula, the charge against my client fails. Whoever died in my client's rooms that night, the real Fadia did not. So my client did not kill her, with poison or otherwise, and certainly not with malice and intention as per the formula. The formula is clear, so the plaintiff must admit *nolle prosequi* - that he is unable to proceed. There is simply nothing left to prosecute. The case has fallen apart. I submit Sir, that all that remains is for you to so rule. The shipwreck is complete.'

'Wait!' Caepio was on his feet. 'Even if that is not Fadia, some-one died in Panderius' room that night, and we still have witness testimony that Panderius killed her. Murdered her.'

'Ye-ees,' remarked Catulus thoughtfully. 'But under Roman law, the state does not prosecute crimes without an accuser. It's the family of the alleged victim who have to bring the prose-cution. If relatives of this unknown dead woman wish to bring suit, I will happily hear that case in this court as a separate charge. What is clear that Panderius did not kill the plaintiff's sister, and that's the case which we are, hmm, were trying today.'

Catulus reiterated, to make himself clear, 'It may be that a new case might be brought against Panderius for poisoning whoever that woman was. I would like to see someone make that case. Perhaps that someone can also explain why the deceased was using a false identity, and what happened to the husband and the money of that widow who spoke up just now. Did you get her by the way?'

The guards shook their heads helplessly.

'But ... what happened to my sister?' Fadius was near tears.

'Did you see the body?' enquired Scaevola. This was another

question to which he already knew the answer.

'No, no, she was cremated before I arrived. They said the poison accelerated the corruption of the corpse. Actually, that was odd.' Fadius turned and gave Caepio a long, suspicious look.

Scaevola and I had worked it out much earlier. It was a common enough scam. Con-men meet a visitor from the country who is on an extended visit to Rome. They befriend that visitor, and learn everything they can about his or, in this case her, personal life. Then the scammers get a sample of the victim's handwriting.

Thereafter, the victim can be disposed of while the fraudsters write 'home' with a simulated emergency that can only be solved by an immediate transfusion of cash. They keep up the scam up until their mark runs out of money or becomes suspicious. Then the thieves drop their assumed identity and fade into back into the shadows to wait until another wide-eyed victim comes wandering into the big city. Rinse and repeat.

Scaevola explained a part of this to Fadius. 'We believe from our enquiries that the woman pretending to be your sister was the 'Lucinda' described in the first letter. That part about Lucinda getting her transferred to a new inn, that was probably genuine. That move put your sister completely in Lucinda's power - but the bit about meeting 'Lucius' was added later.' Fadius merely looked bewildered.

'But why?'

'Because Lucinda - which was almost certainly not her real name either - had already stolen the identity of your sister when those wishing Panderius ill needed to place someone close to him. Originally she was just there to point out his movements to the assassins.' (It had belatedly occurred to me that it takes time to set up ambushes such as those with the builders in the alley or at the Samnite's Head. Those attacks could not have been set up in advance without someone who knew my schedule passing this information on.)

'It was only after these murder attempts failed that Lucinda was told to take a more direct role in the killing of Panderius. Had there been need, we could have produced the market trader who sold her the sack of apples just a fortnight ago.' A man on the witness bench timidly raised a hand.

'He identified Lucinda by the very mask held by that woman.' The mask now dangled from the hand of Brangita, the girl from the Temple whose build was closest to that of the late Lucinda. 'With those apples, Lucinda brewed the poison which eventually killed her.'

'Your sister's identity was a convenience. A disguise donned by a murderer to catch her victim off guard.'

'But what happened to Fadia? My Fadia?' asked Fadius, almost in a sob.

'I can only repeat the sincere condolences with which we started the defence. Naturally, we have been scouring the city for her, but so far not a clue has turned up.'

'You think she is dead?'

Scaevola nodded solemnly, but I was not so sure. In my profession you come to know the price of a healthy young woman. The fact that Ava had been sold so cheaply should have immediately roused my suspicions about the sale, and I doubted Lucinda would have made the same error. My best guess was that Fadia had been shipped to North Africa and sold off for extra profit on the side. Quite possibly Fadius' sister was right now toiling as a slave in the olive grove of an unscrupulous land-owner, and bitterly regretting the trust she had placed in her new 'friend' in Rome.

'This is interesting, but outside the purview of my court,' declared Catulus. 'It has certainly been one of the most remarkable cases I have heard while seated here. However, I am ready to rule.'

'Firstly, Quintus Fadius, do you still allege that Lucius Turpillius Panderius did kill your sister with poison, in the manner described on the night in question?'

Fadius looked to Caepio for help, but the prosecutor sat glumly on his bench and refused to meet the young man's eye. 'Um, no, no, I can't say I do. It seems he killed this woman here,' a gesture indicated the mask in Brangita's hand. 'And a blessing on him for doing so.'

'If it were only this man's friends who identified the corpse, I might have hoped they were lying. But that woman - the manager - she was the chief witness, our chief witness, and she identified it too. It was this Lucinda who died that night.' Fadius put his face into his hands. In a muffled voice he continued, 'My sister was probably dead already.'

'So you withdraw your charges?'

'Yes,' the reply was hoarse and strained. Scaevola put a comforting arm around Fadius, and led him back to our bench. Even now my counsel was playing to the gallery, for the symbolism of his action was unmistakeable.

Catulus gave a little grunt. He looked over at the jury. 'I thank you for your time, gentlemen but it seems there is no need for your verdict. The plaintiff has withdrawn, and even had he not withdrawn, I would anyway have ruled *actori incumbit probatio* - that the plaintiff has failed to present a valid case. The defendant is accordingly acquitted of all charges. The trial is over. I thank you for your service, jurymen. You may now depart.'

Dropping his voice so that only the nearer jurors could hear him, Catulus scornfully added, 'I hope those of you who were bribed were at least intelligent enough to insist on non-refundable deposits.' Then more loudly, 'Good day, gentlemen. We're done.'

With that the judge left the court, to where his retainers were waiting at the side of the basilica. I noted with envy that one servant carried a drink cooled with snow, probably from the last falls on the Apennines. These snowfalls were hauled to Rome by cart at horrendous expense for the delectation of the very wealthy. There were a few cheers from the crowd at Catulus' decision, but the evident grief of Fadius had put a damper on the festive mood. We were a somewhat subdued group as we left for the Temple, where dinner and celebratory drinks were waiting.

When I glanced back, the crowd at the basilica had dispersed, leaving Helga alone and forlorn where we had left her, still standing by the jurors' empty benches.

Liber X

Tancina selected a peach and bit into it. This was a spectacle worth watching, so I lay back against a hay bale with a peach of my own and enjoyed the sight. My bodyguard's daughter had a physique that would get any sculptor worth his salt instantly grabbing for a chisel. A naturally full frame had been rounded out with shapely muscle from hours at the laundry tub, giving Tancina the appearance of an Amazon queen. That, combined with her huge blue eyes and tumbling mass of auburn hair, would have made her a beauty for the ages – if not for a dramatically huge set of buck teeth. Tancina was the only person I have ever met who could eat a peach without actually opening her mouth.

Since she had never considered herself beautiful in the first place, Tancina was totally unselfconscious about her dental bounty, or indeed about her appearance in general. Her lustrous curls were currently tied back with a rawhide leather band, and since she intended mucking out the pigs later, she was wearing a set of leather breeches taken from one of the German field hands. Snugly packed into these leggings, she had preceded me up the ladder to the loft of the hay-barn, and the sight had brought a small prickle of sweat to my forehead.

We were at the Alban farm, to where we had evacuated Tancina and her daughter until the Sabaco threat in Rome was eliminated. Tancina had taken to country life with gusto. Never one to sit idle, she had first watched, then joined in, and then - when the foreman had been called away to cope with a flooded ditch - organized the remainder of the peach harvest. This harvest was now stashed in the hay-barn, neatly boxed and awaiting transport to Rome. On my arrival Tancina had taken me there to show off what were literally the fruits of her labour.

Consultation was needed because handling peaches was an art which all Italians were still learning. This farm had been among the first in Italy to start growing peaches, mainly to cater to Roman aristocrats who had developed a taste for them in Greece, where the fruit had been introduced by Alexander the Great two centuries previously. In Italy peaches remain an expensive - and therefore very profitable - novelty.

I had taken to coming over to the farm when ever I had some spare time, a habit of which Tancina's father heartily disapproved.

'Daddy doesn't want you keeping me company,' Tancina informed me, and dabbed at some peach juice running down her chin. She wrinkled her nose and continued judiciously, 'He's right, of course. It's not just that you are dangerous and a degenerate, or even that you are dangerously degenerate, though actually you are both. Or is that three?'

'Thanks. I try to please.'

'No, the main thing is no-one can trust anything about you. You are as twisted as a Celtic locket and slippery as an eel. You can't believe a damn word he says. I'd not believe him that it was winter if he told me so while standing in a snowstorm. I'm quoting from memory here.'

'That's a bit harsh.'

'No, it's true. Nothing about you is what it seems. You look so boyish and enthusiastic and naïve. But you have to admit you are manipulative (daddy's word), and totally cynical. I've already seen you kill two people, and you do tell an awful lot of lies.'

'Two people? I thought it was just the one.'

'After you saw your slave girl ... I suppose I should not call her that any more. When you saw your German princess, back in that room. That was the other one. You pulled the open the curtain, and looked at her. Then you went to the door and stabbed the man who was unblocking it on the other side. I was watching over daddy's shoulder. Afterwards you picked the girl up and came over as if nothing had happened.'

'Can we forget that? Please? It was a world away. Relax and

enjoy the afternoon.'

I waved an arm languidly at the farm which we could see through the open front of the barn. The light was golden, and the late afternoon had raised a glowing mist from ground damp from a morning shower. The mist lay in cloudy piles about the orchard, and puddled below the slope of the pasture, so the cattle became smudgy shadows and glimpses of horn. Beyond lay the Alban hills, russet, green and gold in their early summer finery, with a sky of delicate robin's egg blue stretching beyond. To our left, a field of barley lay green and still behind a row of towering pines. It seemed the sort of rural paradise that city folk dream about, never understanding the hours of back-breaking work, risk and pain from which such idyllic scenes are made.

'Yes, this farm for example. It's another lie.'

'Er, what?'

'Come on. The manager jumps when you talk to him, and when you arrived this afternoon the pair of you spent an hour in the offices together. The farm workers know that the senator Albus comes around every now and then with his family, and often with guests, but he's not the one they call 'dominus' - the boss. They seem to think that's you.'

'A misunderstanding. I like to help Albus out, that's all.'

'Ooh, another lie. Well, not quite, because you are helping Albus out. You are letting him pretend the farm is his, so he can impress his friends and clients with his elegant little rural hideaway. Meanwhile, someone - let's say someone with more money than he likes people to know he's got - has a nice little investment in land, and somewhere to hide away his bodyguard's family when things get too dangerous in Rome. Thanks again for doing that, by the way.'

'My pleasure.' I meant that. Tancina was remarkably good company. My somewhat hectic life had included any number of women; workers, lovers, clients and priestesses among others, but until now, it had suddenly dawned on me, never one that I could call a friend. It was a novel and definitely enjoyable experience, even if Tancina shared her father's ability for unwonted and disconcerting insights. Tancina meanwhile, had switched her thoughts to another track.

'That trial was another example. Total lies. Your defence was a lie from start to finish. If you let a word of truth slip in, it was by accident.'

'If you mean that widow who denounced Lucinda as the fake Fadia – well, you should know.'

'Indeed I should, since it was me in that wig shrieking like a harpy about her killing my husband. Poor Marcus died on the battlefield, and I had never seen either of those 'Fadias' before in my life. And those awful people who rushed me away afterwards. Where ever did you find them?'

'I have friends in low places.'

'The theatre, I would guess. They got that wig off me and stripped off the widow's dress awful fast, so I'm guessing they are quick-change artists. By the time the guards reached us, I was just another woman wearing a stola. And red-headed of course.' She tossed her pony-tail carelessly.

'Well, it was a little lie to help a larger truth come out. Fadia was a fake, after all. I mean the assassin was a fake Fadia. There was a real Fadia too, the poor girl '

'But you knew all along that Lucinda had been pretending to be Fadia. Well, by the start of the trial anyway, when your man came back from the Fadius estate after showing Lucinda's death-mask to the servants. The whole thing with that Helga person, and her identifying the wrong woman was just a charade.' Tancina licked peach juice from her fingers. 'Exciting though.'

'Not a charade. If Helga had been thinking clearly, she could have denied ever having seen the person in the wax mask before. She could have insisted that the person she saw die that night was someone completely different, namely the real Lady Fadia. It was absolutely essential that she identified the corpse she saw in my bedroom as 'Fadia'. If Helga did not make that identification, clearly and unmistakeably, I might have been sunk. Her testimony was vital.'

'What about the other people – Fadius and the nursemaid?'

'Oh, they knew that the person in the mask was not Fadia, but so what? I could have still killed the real Fadia that night and later produced the mask of any random person. Sulla and the captain of the vigiles knew that we had the death-mask of the person who was with me that night, but the captain could have been bribed, and Sulla, well Sulla can lie like a bedspread. On the other hand, Helga had no reason to help me - exactly the contrary. When she identified the person in the mask as the person who died that night, the prosecution was sunk. The problem was setting Helga up to make that identification. You just confirmed it afterwards. As a real widow, you had your own robes, too.'

'Which I've had to get rid of, since your actors re-tailored it for a quick strip.'

'Sorry.'

'Let's look at how it went. Helga was uncertain, because you had destroyed the supposed evidence from Ava so comprehensively. She didn't know what you had planned for her. Just when she thought she had seen through your trick, that was the exact moment when she was actually being tricked. Not at all sneaky and twisted, was it?'

'We had to keep her off-balance. Caepio was absolutely correct in one part of his case. Once we knew Fadius was the plaintiff, we checked. The real Fadia was exactly the person Caepio so convincingly explained she was - a pleasant, old-fashioned country girl. As Caepio said, there was no way she could arrive in Rome and within a few weeks become an expert seductress with the contacts to obtain exotic poisons. I really doubt she would even have known how to procure the wine that the poison came in.'

I went on, 'Caepio was right. It didn't add up. The Fadia I knew was so different from the person that her brother knew that they had to have been different people. As in fact, they were. Fortunately I had taken Fadia's - well Lucinda's - death mask because I wanted to find who she had been dealing with and who her associates were. I had already used the mask to track down the merchant who sold her the apples that she extracted the poison from. Then suddenly the mask became immensely more useful than I'd thought it would be. A life-saver, in fact.'

Tancina was like a puppy with a slipper. She just wouldn't let go. 'Then there was the fact that Ava looked like that king, Burones. A lucky coincidence - and another huge lie.'

'Coincidence? He might really be her father for all we know. It's a small tribe, and family life is probably as complicated in the German forests as in the back-streets of Rome. Even if Burones hadn't looked like Ava, well, as the merchant said, girls don't always resemble their fathers. Ava didn't resemble Pracatus either, and that's all that mattered.'

'What happened to Pracatus? Did you ...?'

'No! I don't go around killing people as a first resort. He was planning to leave Rome anyway. That's why he sold Ava for whatever he could get. We just helped him on his way with a fast horse and a letter of commendation to a Galatian prince I know in Asia Minor.'

'Now, with Sulla and Metellus backing him, Burones gets to make his appeal to the Senate. Ava told me he had been trying for months. He'd spent almost all the gold he had left and no-one would listen to him. Then, suddenly, all he had to do was discover that he had a new daughter, and his Senate hearing is assured. Ah, the beneficence of the Gods!'

'Uh-oh! Daddy alert!'

Hastily I swallowed a mouthful of peach and sat up. The golden sunlight was bright outside, and I was sure that we were invisible in the shadows of the loft. Nevertheless, Tancinus was squinting suspiciously upwards as he made his way along the path towards us.

'We'd better get down.' Tancina wriggled and started to rise. Seizing a leather-clad thigh I pushed her back into a seated position.

'Be still. He'll see movement. Anyway, what's the problem? All we've done is come up here and eat peaches. Hardly the ultimate in debauchery.'

'Do you think Daddy will believe that? Anyway, just the sight of these leggings will give him apoplexy. He's got his staff.'

Knowing what that quarterstaff could do, I gave the thing a worried look. 'Well, he's my bodyguard and your father. He's got reason for finding us both. Slip a work dress over those leggings before you see him and we'll be fine. Once he has gone to the stables we'll leave here and go to the villa.'

'He's just come from the stables - look! He's coming here now. He's not above spanking my backside, you know, for all I'm a widow and a mother. We have to move!'

'Relax. He'll get as far as that byre there, and then sidestep into the shadows. Wait for it ... there he goes. Now, crane your neck towards the cowsheds. See him running along the back there?'

'What's he doing?'

'He thinks we might have been in the stables and made a run for it when he came into sight. Now he's checked the stables, so if we wanted to hide we'd come back to them thinking it's safe. So he's doubling back to catch us. Let's go.'

'Daddy's totally right. You do have a twisted mind. How did you know so well what he would do?'

'I've studied him. He's my bodyguard. My life might depend

on knowing exactly what he will do next. Coming?'

Six hours later, with the evening drawing late, I was back in Rome, in the basement of the Temple. This was going to be Cyrenicus' bedroom, but since I had established that the new cook was no threat we'd moved him upstairs, where he now shared a room with some of the cleaning lads. The bed we had taken downstairs was still in the basement room. Stretched out on it, one hand and both ankles tied to opposite ends of the bed-frame, was the legionary I still thought of as the Torturer. The young man's swagger was long gone, his braggadocio replaced by an earnest desire to please me.

That's the advantage of dealing with a professional. He knew that with plenty of time and the right techniques there is nothing that a truly determined questioner can't discover. Apart from all else, after a while the mind breaks down and whatever remains within the broken shell will tell practically anything to stop the pain. The cocky ones go first, because once you have broken the image they have of themselves, they have nothing to fall back on. Withstanding torture is mainly about self-respect, which is why a good interrogator will make sure that the subject has none left. That's why the Torturer had stripped Ava naked, and why I had left the man for over a day in the dark. I had wanted to let his imagination conjure up nightmares of the future.

The Torturer knew what I had done and why I had done it. This let let him know that he was in expert hands - hardly a reassuring discovery in the circumstances. The man knew himself as well. When I'd come in over an hour ago, bearing nothing more terrifying than a lamp and two beakers of Sabine wine on a tray, his first question had been, 'What do you want to know?'

We had a long talk after that, and I was preparing to wrap things up. Then the door swung open with a loud creak. It had taken close to an hour with a toolkit and a pitcher of boiling water to make the creak that loud, but I had wanted everyone to hear if Cyrenicus decided to leave his bedroom in the dead of night.

'Hello, Ava?'

Those shuffling footsteps as Ava hobbled down the corridor had been a dead give-away even before the door was pushed open, so I didn't turn my head when she came in. I had freed one of the Torturer's hands so he could drink his wine, and had no intention of taking my eyes off him until he was fully secure once more. Consequently my first clue came when the Torturer's eyes opened wide in panic. He screamed once, then Ava pushed past me, and the breath the Torturer had drawn for a second scream came out instead as a horrid gurgle mixed with blood.

'You had finished with him, yes?' Ava asked me tightly. Her hands were shaking violently and her unbound hair hung over her cheeks. There was a gleam in her eye that was downright disturbing. I looked past her to the handle of the large kitchen knife buried to the hilt in the former Torturer's chest. I groaned.

'Nooo, Ava, what have you done?'

'I killed him. If he was still alive, I would kill him again. The things he did, I hate him. It was my right to kill him, and I did it!'

'With that meat knife? Seriously, did you have to use that one? It was Anatolian steel, perfectly balanced and it keeps an edge like nothing else in the kitchen. Do you know how much a blade like that costs? Now I'll never eat another lamb cutlet without knowing where it's been. You've ruined it.'

'You could have stopped me.'

'If I'd known you were going to use that knife I would have. Otherwise, well ... .'

The fact is I had not been sure what to do with the Torturer once he had told me everything. It is hard to kill someone in cold blood once you have shared a beaker of wine with him. Yet at the same time, there was no question of releasing the man so that he could return to Sabaco and make another attempt on my life. Nor could I keep him in the basement indefinitely. I had been considering shipping the Torturer off to Africa, reflecting that it would be a nice irony if he finished his days working as a slave in the olive groves alongside the kidnapped Fadia. Then, unexpectedly, Ava had come in and taken the matter out of my hands.

Now she was matter-of-factly turning the corpse's head so that blood would not flow from the gaping mouth to soak into the mattress. When the head flopped back, she backhanded it with vicious fury. Then suddenly she was hitting the corpse with her fists, pounding and slapping it with a furious intensity while a low animal growl came from her throat. Eventually she grabbed a wine beaker and hammered and hammered until the man's face was a shapeless pulp.

After what seemed a very long while she stopped, and fell against me, sobbing violently. As gently as possible, I took the dented cup from her hand and hugged her close.

'You've got to think of him like that,' I told her. 'In the dead of night, when the horrors come. That is how you have to think of him. Not as the laughing man who could do whatever he liked to your body, not as the man you wanted to please so much because then the pain would stop - he has gone. You killed him. Here's how you must remember him. Remember him as someone who was terrified by just the sight of you, a man who cowered back on the bed when you walked in. An abject young man who at the last screamed in fear for his mother. Remember him like that.'

'You have had your revenge. Before, you felt powerless, humiliated and worthless because that is how he needed you to feel. If that is how you still let yourself feel, then he has won, even now. Don't do it. Tell yourself you are a German warrior woman. You have wiped out with blood the memory of what he did. With your knife he paid for every insult, every deed. Tell yourself that, each night. Because it is true, and you will sleep better.'

PHILIP MATYSZAK

'What did you do with the body?' Sulla asked.

It was the next morning. I don't usually do the daily grovel customary in Rome, whereby a client goes to salute his patron in the morning and reminds him of the services he has to offer in return for the patron's favour and protection. Nor does Sulla insist on it. We both have better things to do. Nevertheless, every now and then it is no bad thing to don a toga and head out for a bit of hierarchically-stratified social networking - especially when you find your patron breakfasting on devilled eggs, cheese and honeyed ham on fresh-baked bread, and he has just invited you to pull up a chair and tuck in.

'Great ham,' I enthused in a muffled voice. 'There's a bit of a tang there, hmmm.' With my cheeks bulging like a dormouse's I studied the bread in my hand.

'Pear and saffron chutney,' said Sulla dismissively. 'My cook will send yours the recipe. For personal use only, mind you. I don't want my darkest culinary secrets wasted on those ne'er-do-wells that frequent your brothel.'

'Er, aren't you one of those 'ne'er do-wells'? I've seen you around.'

'I am. What's your point?'

'Nothing, nothing at all.' Politeness prevented me from immediately grabbing more ham, but I looked at it like a puppy denied a treat. Sulla sighed and pushed the plate across the table.

'You were asked to be the last client today because Metellus junior will be coming over when he's finished the morning session with his lot. You've nothing against him hearing what you've told me?'

I shook my head.

'Then be a good fellow and get that ham down your throat so you can fill in the details as needed. I'm assuming the body won't embarrass anyone?'

'We left it on a rubbish dump on the Esquiline hill just after

162

midnight. A couple of prostitutes carrying what looked like a passed-out client in a cloak raises no eyebrows in those parts. When Ava had finished with him there was not much face to recognize, and by now I'd imagine the locals have stripped the corpse of its clothing and the dogs have pretty much mangled the rest. Just another random corpse adding colour to big-city life; nothing that will come back to us.'

Sulla grunted. 'That's okay then.'

'Sabaco has had over half his men go missing without trace. That's a start.' I paused as I remembered something.

'Oh, and to go off on a tangent somewhat - guess who was waiting to see me when I got back from the farm yesterday? None other than the back-stabbing Helga herself.'

'Is that so? What did she want?'

'In a word, help. She was left high and dry when the case collapsed. Caepio, being a Caepio, naturally blames everyone but himself for the failure. Helga was the obvious scapegoat. She didn't get the money or the reward she was promised. Actually, once the case collapsed there was no way she could get the reward she wanted.'

'Which was?'

'The Temple. Helga said it was never really about the money. It was the Temple. As far as she could see, what should be an excellent, tightly-run business was being run into the ground by my playboy ways. I've tried repeatedly to explain to her that you can't run a place like that without a bit of personal freedom and creativity. If the girls aren't having fun, then no-one's having fun. But she was having none of it. Odd that. One does not think of Germans as being organized, meticulous types, but our Helga has the military mind of a Praefectus Castrorum - the sort of mentality that thinks of people as things that perform set actions to a fixed routine, and everything else has its proper place, properly filed and maintained. She would have run the Temple just as a Camp

Prefect would – and be wondering why it was empty within a year.'

'So in the end it came down to a clash of management styles?'

'Another unexpected danger in the brothel business. The job is full of them.'

'And Helga?'

'Well, she looked a wreck. No money, no friends and no prospects. She'd spent the previous night on the streets, sleeping rough and trying to fend off amorous and drunken beggars. Given the competition from younger street girls, those beggars might be her only customers if she tries to make a living as a prostitute in Rome. She's a competent manager, but has no connections that would get her a management job. So Helga is really desperate. She was eager to tell everything about her involvement with Caepio and Sabaco in exchange for just a glimmer of hope.'

'She didn't have a lot to add, as it turns out. Not much there, but it rounds off the picture we have already from various sources and confirms a few speculations.'

Sulla nodded. 'After that you sent her on her way with a few whip stripes across her back for good measure?'

'Um, no. Actually, I'm thinking that Helga has potential. Let's use it. She has nowhere else to turn, so why not send her to Ofella? The man is still terrified that we're going to prosecute him for taking Ava. No-one knows her in Aricia, so we'll give Helga a new identity as a freedwoman. She is a good book-keeper, which is why I kept her around. After she's worked for Ofella for a while, and everyone in Ofella's circle has become used to her, we get Ofella to move her on. He can vouch for her management skills and place her in a job with one of his shady Italian connections. I'm thinking of something like a clerk or warehouse manager for a rebel sympathizer.'

Sulla understood instantly. 'Nice. A two-for-one deal. If he does as we say, Ofella becomes our agent, since we could ruin him at any time by letting on that he's planted a spy among the Italians. We also get an actual spy in the ranks of our would-be Italian rebels. Hmm ... I'll bet that your Helga will be a good spy too. She has the character for it.'

'A good idea, Lucius!' My patron grinned hugely. 'I let my eagerness for revenge on your behalf blind me for a moment there. You are absolutely right. When you come across someone with a talent for treachery like your Helga, it's criminal to waste it. The bitch should take to her new life of double-dealing like a duck to water. Leave her in my hands.'

From there, we chatted idly, with Sulla recounting some of the deeds of Cornelia, his daughter from a previous marriage and a girl of whom he was indulgently fond. The conversation had moved on to the prospects of the latest charioteer for the Greens, and how long this latest darling of the crowds would survive the dangerous races at the Circus Maximus, when a stir in the vestibule let us know that Metellus had arrived.

'Ah, Lucius Sulla and Lucius Panderius!' exclaimed Metellus cheerfully as he strode in. 'Oh, sit, sit!' He plonked himself at the table to join us and grinned across enthusiastically. The younger Metellus and I were more or less of an age, though he far outranked me. As a Turpillius, my children unborn would need several generations of consulships before a Quintus Caecilius Metellus counted them as equals. Sulla, of course, was of the ancient Cornelian family and already Metellus' social equal and elder. Yet he too had risen to greet Metellus, both out of politeness and because though he was not socially obliged to rise when Metellus came in, I was, and Sulla did not want that fact to be obvious. That's the sort of thing Sulla does so well, and why people love him for his social skills and overlook the occasional touch of blackmail, extortion and murder.

Metellus beamed at me. 'Congratulations on your success at

trial, Lucius Panderius. Didn't Scaevola do a great job? It was a delight to see how the truth came out like, like ... like the sun emerging from behind a cloud of lies. It was good of Burones to acknowledge that girl as his natural child, and just amazing how after that the prosecution case just fell apart the way it did. So your would-be assassin was not that Fadia woman after all! Who could have seen that coming? It was a stroke of luck that your counsel tried to frighten that manager of yours with that woman in the mask, eh?'

'They do say that Jupiter protects the innocent, and I swear by his name that we certainly saw him do that during your trial! A white ox, that's what you owe Jupiter. There's a few on my estate - I'll order one brought up, so that you can do the honours. We'll make a big ceremony of it. A sacrifice of thanksgiving on the Capitoline hill. It won't hurt anyone to know whose side the Gods are on.'

Sulla and I took care not to look at one another. The younger Metellus was that rarest of creatures in Roman politics, a genuinely nice guy. He was also direct, honest and believed the best of people. (Fortunately, he made an exception for Marius.) In deference to Metellus' honesty, during the trial my patron and I had carefully not involved our ally in the more underhand aspects of my defence. Metellus had seen and believed exactly what the general public were meant to see and believe, and we could only pray that things remained that way. If Metellus found out, for example, that we had stolen back a girl legitimately sold by her father and then bribed a third party to lie under oath about that girl's paternity, he would probably turn us in to the authorities himself. At times I felt decades older than Metellus, and wished I didn't. It would be wonderful to live in the city of Rome that Metellus thought he lived in.

Sulla sometimes mused aloud whether Metellus' trusting openness was a drawback or an advantage, politically speaking.

Certainly with Metellus what you saw was what you got. Nevertheless, honest politician though he may be, Metellus was still a politician and more than ready to make hay with the temporary discomfort of Caepio and his faction.

He leaned forward, elbows on the table, and looked expectantly from Sulla to me. 'So, what have you got?'

Liber XI

My gaze flickered from Metellus to Sulla.

'I'm not sure how much my personal problems would interest you,' I said frankly. 'The trouble is that private issues and state affairs seem to be rather intertwined at the moment.'

Metellus grinned. 'Until you've repaid the money my father lent you, all your problems are my problems,' he said heartily. 'Tell us the lot and we'll sort it out afterwards.'

More of that honeyed ham would have gone down well right then. Chewing a mouthful would have given me time to get my thoughts in order. Unfortunately Sulla's servants had unobtrusively cleared the table while my attention was on Metellus. I would have to snag a morsel later.

'Okay - the issue is in two parts. First, Caepio wants my silence, and second, our Consul Marius wants me dead. The pair of them combined their plans and decided that the silence of the grave works best with me.'

'Caepio, I can understand,' Metellus said, frowning slightly. 'You're going to give testimony and tell the world how he mismanaged the battle at Arausio. That will certainly get him fined and most probably exiled. During the battle you did chuck a javelin at him with murderous intent, so it's understandable that he would take that personally. Now that we've seen the younger Caepio fronting the recent failed lawsuit, there is no doubt that the Caepio faction were behind the prosecution. So I understand that the Caepiones are out to get you, and they have good reason.'

'Marius, though? That baffles me. Why would he be behind the assassination attempt that caused the trial in the first place? All of us here have history with that man, and not the one of us but doubts that he is a world-class scumbag, but why is he so eager to kill you?'

'He has a lot else on his plate right now, with Roman politics and the Cimbri returning to attack Italy. Apart from that, he stands to lose a hard-won reputation if any of this becomes public. With all due respect, my dear Lucius, why is killing you worth the risk - or the effort, since you are not proving to be that easy to kill?'

Sulla grunted. 'Oh, Marius can afford the risk. He will keep command of the legions for the coming campaign no matter what. He's got the popular support and he has insulated himself from any direct involvement with the dirty deeds themselves - just as he always does. He's got Sabaco working for him again, so in killing of our Lucius, the effort and the risk fall on his henchman.'

Metellus' eyebrows rose. 'Sabaco? That nasty piece of work? I'm surprised that he has popped up once more. The man's a wanted criminal. There have been forgery and murder charges outstanding ever since the Turpillius affair.' Metellus shot me an embarrassed glance.

'The men I'm holding responsible for my father's death are Sabaco and Marius,' I assured Metellus. 'Your father was their unwitting instrument.'

'My family are no-one's *instruments*,' growled Metellus. 'That Marius used us is another reason why your fight is my fight. Trust me, if it hurts Marius and gets Sabaco killed, you can rely on the Metelli for whatever you need. But you still have not told me why Marius wants you dead. Why now?'

'You'll need a bit of background later, but basically Marius has got his hands on a prophetic priestess.'

'Momina?' Sulla interjected. 'Didn't that remarkable young woman go back to Greece?'

'Who is Momina?' Metellus asked.

'An enslaved priestess that Panderius stole off the state. They confiscated her along with the rest of his property when he didn't pay his fine over that aqueduct business. As you know, after not paying his fine, Lucius fell in with a bunch of Gallic thugs who were on the run after they had assaulted the City Praetor. That's the reason that he ended up in Narbo Martius and at the battle at Arausio after that.'

'When Lucius got back from the wars two months ago, he formally purchased the priestess from the state with some of the money he borrowed from your father. There was not much choice but for him to do that, as by then he'd already pre-emptively freed the girl and sent her off to Greece - or at least that's what I thought. It appears that she has now turned up in northern Italy instead.'

'You do lead an interesting life,' Metellus remarked to me. 'I suppose that's how you meet so many interesting people. '

I took up the tale. 'The how and why of Momina ending up with Marius is a bit vague at present, but you can be sure that if our prophetess is with Marius, it is because that is where she wants to be. She is called Martha now, by the way. Apparently Marius decided that an oracle would be more exotic and have more credibility if she was Jewish.'

'They're a strange lot, the Jews,' agreed Metellus.

'Well, Momina/Martha is getting luxury treatment from our leader. He has her accompany his retinue in a litter with silk curtains, and when she tells him it's time to sacrifice, he leaps up and gets the proceedings organized personally, no matter what else he was doing beforehand. Then she turns up for the sacrifice itself wearing a double purple robe, and holding a spear. It definitely impresses the troops, which is great for morale, and that's certainly one reason for the whole rigmarole. That - and the fact that Momina's prophecies are invariably right, which also helps.'

'The problem for me is that Marius believes her completely.'

'Why so?'

'Well, I got this story third-hand from a would-be assassin and torturer who got it from Sabaco who got it from a guard who was there at the time. But it is credible, because you know how annoying Marius can be.'

'Oh, I do, I do,' Metellus and Sulla intoned together like a dramatic chorus.

'Well, Marius even managed to get under the skin of our Momina. One evening he was in her quarters - it was all very respectable with witnesses present. Marius was after information, not hanky-panky. After a few standard questions, he started pressing her for details of his future. The number of consulships he would hold, what honours he would receive, well, you know the sort of things that insecure egomaniac would love to hear. Marius wanted the replies as unambiguous as possible. When it got to his posthumous honours - how large his tomb would be, whether it would be within the city walls, that sort of thing, Momina became very evasive. At one point Marius caught her wrist, and would not let go, though it caused her pain. So she laid it on him straight.'

In my best oracular tones I repeated the words that the Torturer had told to me during our basement interview.

'You will be honoured by the river Aniene into which your disgraced ashes will be thrown. You, who have laid hands on a priestess of Aphrodite, will die at the hands of a servant of Aphrodite. A servant of Aphrodite shall overthrow your works and your memory. You will be honoured in life as the saviour of your country, but after your death men will know you as Marius the monster - and your legacy will be blood and ruin.'

Marius was stunned. He just gaped at her in peasant awe while everything he had heard sank into his thick head. Then he slapped her, hard. That caused Momina to produce this little addendum.

'Before your ashes are cast into the Aniene, Aphrodite's servant will mix them with meat and feed them to a street dog. Only when your remains have passed through the bowels of a

171

diseased cur will they be tossed into the river. Do you wish to know more, Marius? Perhaps I should tell of how you will flee Rome and the events of your exile? Shall I give details of the death and beheading of your son? Ask me!' Marius got to his feet and ran from the tent as though the Furies were pursuing him. Momina shouted after him 'Come back! I can tell you everything. Ask the oracle!'

'Since then Marius has given Momina all honour, but he is never long in her presence. It seems she scares the wits out of him. But he has built 'Martha' up so much with the army that he can't abandon her now. It would hurt morale. And when she prophesies about the Cimbri, where they are going, what their leaders will decide, she is always remarkably accurate. So Marius is stuck with his seer.'

I grinned, knowing I did so rather smugly. 'Here's something Marius doesn't know. Apart from me, the other survivor from the Arausio is Quintus Sertorius. Like me, Sertorius swam the Rhone, but unlike me he chose to join the enemy and spy on them. Well, the go-between who takes messages from Sertorius to the Romans is a Gaul called Madric. He was one of that gang of Gallic ruffians whom Momina and I joined up with when we left Rome in a hurry last year. Madric has been a friend of Momina's ever since. He also 'deserted' to the Cimbri, but had the good sense to do his deserting before the risks of the battle. I'll lay gold to copper that Madric passes on his information to Momina in full before he gives an edited version to the Romans. There's nothing like hard intelligence to make prophesy easy.'

'So Marius dreads his oracle, but thinks he can't do without her. Nice to know he is in an uncomfortable situation, but why does that mean he has got it in for you?' Sulla wanted to know.

'This is just a theory, but if you were Marius, would you not be giving some thought as to whom this so-called 'Servant of Aphrodite' might be? Would you perhaps decide it was someone who owns a brothel dedicated to Freya, since Freya is Aphrodite in her Germanic aspect?'

'Then remember that man quite justifiably holds Marius responsible for the death of his father. If that man is already seeking to kill one of his henchmen - I've never stopped looking for Sabaco – might not such a man next move up to killing Marius himself? We Romans take revenge very seriously, and I have a lot to avenge when it comes to Marius. My disdain for the man is no secret. In short, it seems that our Consul has decided that the Servant of Aphrodite, the man he must fear, is none other than myself. Evidently, he has decided to get his retaliation in first.'

'The soldiers in Sabaco's kidnap and assassination squad were legionaries from the army in the north - picked men who have done this sort of dirty work before. Someone had to release them from military duty, and it's a fair bet that the orders came straight from the top. As our legalistic friend Scaevola might say, Momina has given Marius motive, the legionaries have provided the means and problems with Caepio presented the opportunity. Put the motive, means and opportunity together, and the finger of guilt points at Marius.'

'Hmm,' remarked Metellus. 'It all sounds credible. The next question is, what can we do about it? Taking down Marius right now is beyond us. Going after Caepio is one thing. He's unpopular, and vulnerable. But Marius? We all might hate the thought, but the man is untouchable right now. If there was a way to get to him, half the Senate would stand in line for half a chance to do just that.'

'He is untouchable in the short term, I agree,' said Sulla. 'But I like the sound of what's in store for Marius in the long term.'

'You don't really believe that, do you?' asked Metellus with incredulity. 'That was nonsense. Simply the spite of a girl angered because Marius was hurting her. You can't take it seriously.'

'Well, it does have a certain dark kind of style.' Sulla looked at me teasingly. 'The sort of thing our Lucius here might be capable of.'

'Not that you would ever consider doing anything of the sort,' I shot back. 'Especially as you now have oracular authority for the deed.'

Metellus was distressed. 'Please gentlemen, please. I understand soldierly raillery and all that. But really, this is overstepping the line. Whatever we might think of Marius, he is a Consul of Rome. The rank deserves our respect, even if the person holding it does not. To do ... that ... to a person who has held the highest office of state and has sacrificed to Jupiter as triumphator after a victorious war, well, it is unthinkable. It would be an eternal stain on the reputation of our city!'

Sulla appeared chastened. 'You are absolutely right.' He gave me a reproving stare. 'Lucius, whatever were you thinking?'

'My apologies, sir. I got caught up in the moment.'

'Okay troops. Here's the situation.' Rubbing my hands together, I surveyed the motley band that had gathered in the courtyard of the Temple. The girls, several wearing diaphanous robes entirely unsuited for the outdoors, lounged about in the golden evening sunshine and watched the rest of the group with interest. This interest was mostly directed at four pug-ugly gladiators who stood in a truculent group, warily watching Sulla's men and Tancinus. Like the girls, but for entirely different reasons, Sulla's men were studying the gladiators in a measuring, thoughtful manner that the gladiators found distinctly off-putting.

'Pay attention now. My enemies have so far failed to kill me directly, and failed to persuade the judiciary to kill me instead. We can expect them to step up their efforts in the coming weeks. We can also expect that there will be attempts to put the Temple out of business by persons whom Rome's libel laws prevent me from naming; that is, Caius Marius, Servilius Caepio, Aemilius Scaurus, Licinius Crassus and their friends and allies. So -'

'Girls, after you have finished with a client, conduct him - or her - to the door of your room and make sure that the gladiator in the courtyard sees you alive and well on that person's departure. The easiest way to ruin the business is to get rid of the staff. Please let us know of anyone who tries to threaten you. Help yourself to any bribes that are offered, but let us know about them. I'll be checking. House calls to clients are off the menu for a while, because we can't guarantee your safety away from the Temple. If you do have to go out of the Temple for any reason, please ask one of these gentlemen to accompany you.'

I indicated the 'gentlemen' with a wave of the hand, gloomily aware that the female staff were at that moment inventing excuses to leave the premises. What is it with women and gladiators? While girls and gladiators exchanged looks of mutual appreciation, I gave a more cynical look to Sulla's men that said clearly, 'If any girl does decide to go out unescorted, make sure that you report back where she went and whom she talked to.'

The gladiators - supplied by Metellus - were not present at the later chat I had with Sulla's men. This focussed on the less obvious aspects of security. We met in the basement, in a room both large enough for the entire group and secure from spying ears. It was also close enough to an urn of vintage wine for me to offer high-value refreshments to the group - an offer that fell flat, as it turned out that Sulla's men were basically teetotallers.

'Takes a fraction off reaction time,' the group's avuncular leader informed me. 'Not so you'd notice because ordinarily it's too little to make a difference, and in extraordinary times you don't notice being slower on account of being dead. So thanks, but no thanks.'

Tancinus ungraciously helped himself to a flagon. Being more accustomed to the fiery wines they serve on the Aventine, he pronounced the smooth vintage to be 'soppy stuff'. Since his daughter had come into the picture, there was very little that I could do right in Tancinus' eyes.

Ignoring my recalcitrant bodyguard I began the briefing. 'Listen up. First, Sabaco is hiding out somewhere in Rome. That's probably in a house, warehouse or other property owned by friends of Marius. We've got clerks investigating the property records in the *tabularium* [the Roman record office on the Capitoline Hill - ed] and tomorrow you'll each get a list of places to discreetly check out.'

'Second, Sabaco likes to keep a gang of retainers about him. He's lost half of them, and the best half at that. He'll be recruiting, so keep your ears to the ground. If you can get recruited, that's great. In any case, we know the kind of people Sabaco is looking for, so if any of them change their habits or seem suddenly flush with cash, investigate. Sabaco tried to put pressure on us through Tancinus here ... .' Tancinus scowled over the rim of his flagon, daring anyone to make a further comment. No-one did.

'So let's see if we can return the favour and subvert someone in Sabaco's gang. An inside line on the group would be a great help. Finally, I'm expecting to be followed. Handle this with care, because Sabaco will know I'm expecting him to put a tail on me. So he'll be looking to take out whoever follows his followers. Those are the guys I want you to focus on - the ones who follow the people following whoever follows me.'

'Just as well we didn't take any of that wine,' commented someone in the audience. 'I'm having trouble keeping up as it is. What if Sabaco has foreseen this and has someone following the follower of the ... Hades, I've lost track already.'

I grinned. 'Just remember the first part - handle with care. Everyone in Rome knows by now that Caepio has it in for me. If I get killed, it will be blamed on him, not Marius. That allows

Sabaco to be pretty blatant in his assassination attempts from here on in, because Caepio and Marius are not natural allies, and Marius doesn't care at all if Caepio's reputation suffers by my death. From his perspective, the time for discretion passed away with the Lady Fadia, or Lucinda or whoever in Hades she was. Now there's a large target on my back, and another on my front.'

'I want a pay rise.' This from Tancinus, to general laughter.

'Done,' I said promptly. 'The funds are available gentlemen, and this is no time to scrimp. Don't throw money around like water, but if you need a few gold pieces to ease the flow of information, ask and you shall receive. This is war, and I understand that wars cost money.'

I did not add that the one good thing about this sort of underground war was that no-one would ask me to explain where the money was coming from. If some of the gold pieces were the proceeds from Gallic treasure discreetly disposed of, I could not think of a better use for my ill-gotten gains. Both Sabaco and I had played this game before in the cities of Numidia, and in my case more recently amid the flames of doomed Tolosa in Gaul. In Numidia, much as we had courteously disliked one another, Sabaco and I had been nominally on the same side. After my father's death I had searched for Sabaco in vain. Had Momina known that? Was the priestess putting Sabaco in my path as her way of returning the favours I had done her? Or was I over-estimating her powers? That was the thing about Momina. You never knew.

Once security had been set up in the temple, everyone dispersed to their various tasks for the evening. Ava had resumed command of the kitchen. Being still unsteady on her feet, she did much of her cooking by proxy, giving orders to the hapless Cyrenicus who did not take this quietly. At present the pair were hotly bickering about how much basil to put into thrush soup, and hardly noticed when I popped in to pick up a loaf of rosemary bread for the road.

'Going somewhere?' asked Tancinus, materializing at my elbow as I emerged from the kitchen.

'I thought we might slip out of town and spend the night in the Alban hills. There's nothing happening at the Temple that needs me here tonight, and the rest of the week looks busy. You won't get another chance to visit Tancina or your grandchild until next market day has been and gone, so let's do it while we can. Anyway, I sleep more soundly these days when I'm out of Rome.'

'As long as you sleep alone,' Tancinus informed me. 'Tancina is a sweet girl, but too naïve to be allowed around the likes of you. Remember our agreement and stay away from her.'

Despite his grumbling, Tancinus followed me readily into the vestibule where we pulled on our road cloaks. He too enjoyed his evenings on the farm, where he played with his grand-child in the yard and drank home-brewed cider with the farm-workers after the girl had gone to bed.

We stepped out on to the pavement, each automatically turning to look in a different direction - my gaze going east towards the shadowy bulk of the Circus Maximus at the end of the street, Tancinus taking the left, squinting into the shadows cast by the setting sun. The street looked clear. That is, it was packed with pedestrians, street traders and all the bustle of a late Roman afternoon, but there were no anomalies in the swirl of people on the road. No-one was trying too hard to look inconspicuous, and no-one had quickened or slowed their pace as we stepped into view.

I remarked, 'Looks okay,' and had taken half a step forward when Tancinus' staff scythed the legs out from under me. The cobbles of the road hit my shoulder with bruising force as I went into a roll, directing my momentum toward the apartment building over the street. I too had seen the flicker of movement as the archer in an upstairs window released his arrow. As my feet came under me I bounded upright and threw myself at the sturdy iron-bound door blocking our way.

'Locked,' Tancinus grunted as he tugged on the metal ring of the door handle.

'It should be.' Muscles in my shoulder twanged as I rubbed it. 'The building is condemned. Structurally unsound. Even the rats have abandoned the place. It's centuries old, and was built on the cheap even back then.'

Tancinus was looking up at the wealth of balconies and gutters overhead. 'Bastard is well away by now. If we cut over to the back alley we might catch him coming out.'

'Only if he's stupid enough not to have left his bow behind. Otherwise he might be any citizen taking a short cut, or stopping in the alley for a piss. I'll ask Sulla to have a word with the Aediles. We've got to have those windows boarded up or I'll be in a shooting gallery every time we step out of the front door.'

We both turned to look over the street. The sun cast a thin black shadow at an angle across the stucco of the Temple wall. That shadow was cast by an arrow embedded in the plaster, and already a small knot of curious pedestrians was forming to examine it.

'Low,' said Tancinus. 'He was either a bad shot or aiming for the gut.'

'It's harder shooting downward than most people imagine,' I agreed. That's why when you storm a city wall it's safer in the front rank. Archers on the walls either shoot over your head or over-compensate and hit the ground in front of you.'

'But I imagine our boy knew exactly what he was doing. This is a thick cloak I'm wearing, and shooting at the chest runs the risk of the arrow hitting a rib and tracking around. Aim for the centre of mass, and a gut shot is more likely to go home because there's no ribs to protect it. Doesn't even have to be immediately lethal since a bowel infection is almost inevitable.'

Tancinus raised an eyebrow, and I realised I was babbling somewhat. My hands were shaking too, so I put them under my cloak where they couldn't be seen. Some of the pedestrians noticed us across the street, and came over, curious to discover what had happened and asking if we were all right.

My bodyguard hefted his staff. 'So that wine takes your timing off a fraction, does it? Can't say I noticed.'

Liber XII

'Watch out!' yelled the dealer.

I had already whipped by foot off the railing and was studying a neat notch in the tip of my sandal, a hair's breadth away from my toe.

'Are you some kind of idiot?' the dealer demanded furiously. 'Didn't you see the straw?'

There was a generous twist of straw tied around the top bar of the pen. In the Forum Boarium, Rome's premier livestock market, straw tied to an animal or its cage indicates that the animal within is dangerous. Going by the condition of my sandal, the dealer had not used enough straw.

'He's fast,' I commented.

'If you were half a heartbeat slower you'd be walking with half a foot,' agreed the dealer. 'He'd eat the rest as well.'

'What's the weight?'

The dealer pushed out his lower lip as he made an assessment. 'We haven't been able to weigh him recently, for obvious reasons. Last time they put him on a scale he came in at just under ten *talents*. [320kg or 710lbs – ed.] He's a big boy and no mistake.'

As we talked, I kept a wary eye on the pen. The occupant still regarded me with bloodshot yellow eyes as he backed up to the far side of his cage. There was not a lot of room there, but at the end of his short charge, the beast still managed to hit the bars with an almighty crash. For a moment, his head was level with my shoulder, and wicked tusks snapped together as the boar made a fierce effort to get at my upper arm. The thick timbers sprang back as the pig rebounded.

'Gods,' I said, shaken.

'He jumped a barrier high as my waist not a fortnight ago,' the dealer told me. 'Killed the bull in the neighbouring pen and started eating it. That's when the farmer decided to get rid of him. I mean that's a lot prime pork on the hoof. He wanted to breed from that, but the risks were not worth it. His name is Bocchus, by the way.'

Almost as if he recognized his name, the beast gave a strangled 'Mmmgaarph!' sound, and slurped at the saliva running generously from his slavering jaws. Every muscle in his body trembled with fury and hatred, and his intelligent eyes searched his prison for a means of escape. Bocchus was covered in a bristly layer of brownish-black hair, and was nothing like his namesake, the king of Mauretania. When I'd known him, that Bocchus was soft, plump and weak-willed. If the king had possessed a fraction of the fire of the porcine hellion before me, I would never have left the country alive.

'Why Bocchus?' I wanted to know.

The dealer shrugged. 'You'd have to ask the farmer. He just liked the name, I guess. So do you want to buy the boar or not? There's enough pork there to feed a cohort, and not an ounce of fat. Cutlets, hams, bacon. It's all there, magistrate. Just that one beast would feed a family for the winter. Tell you what. We close the deal now, and I'll get the market butcher to kill the thing for you, and arrange a litter to take the meat around to wherever you want it dressed. You don't want this animal to leave his cage alive.'

The dealer patted the pen by way of emphasis, then realized what he was doing and yanked his hand away as though the bar was red-hot. Bocchus studied him intently, and the dealer looked back uncomfortably.

'I'd sooner the creature was dead, to be honest,' he told me frankly. 'I know people like to buy their livestock on the hoof, but the sooner that thing is pork chops and ham, the happier I'll be. If he got loose, I got a feeling that he would track me through the streets of Rome just to do me in. Look at him.'

We looked, and I came to a decision.

'Well, I'm in the market for a boar, and Bocchus here ... far exceeds my expectations. If the price is as we discussed earlier, I'll take him.'

'Great,' said the dealer with relief. 'I'll get a sword put through his neck immediately.'

'Not necessary. I want him alive. We'll get him boxed up and taken out of here. I've a cart ready. But you're going to have to give me a bit of time. We will need a stronger crate.'

Even on a gloomy morning with a sullen drizzle sweeping out of low-hanging clouds, there is something cheering about the atmosphere of the Forum Boarium. I don't mean the atmosphere itself, which on market days is generally polluted by the bowel movements of several hundred confused and justifiably worried animals, but the general ambience of the market-place. The site itself is a pleasant one, sloping gently down to the smooth, mud-brown waters of the Tiber, and at the top of the slope, the little circular temple of Hercules Victor looks down over the scene.

'It's the oldest marble building in Rome,' I told Cyrenicus. We stood in a nook between two pens, aside from the jostling crowd, and had a good view of the temple. My slave cook studied the building curiously.

'Why is it round?' he asked. 'Most Roman temples are sort of rectangular stone boxes with a porch in front.'

'As if your Greek temples are any more imaginative. That temple is round because it is incredibly ancient. It was here before Rome was. The original was of wood, and those marble pillars were tree trunks. They were put up to impress the big H, Hercules himself, when he was here in person and had just killed a cattle rustler named Cacus.'

Cyrenicus studied the vista of stock pens and damp, steaming livestock. 'Plenty of potential for rustling here,' he commented.

'I like it. This market works. It's not like the Forum Romanum where they sell you Persian slippers and other fripperies you don't really need ... .'

'Wouldn't mind some Persian slippers,' Cyrenicus interjected.

'Oh shut up. What I mean is that this is the real Rome. People with proper jobs, here to do business. There's a city of thousands and thousands needing to be fed every day, and the people here are the ones who make it happen. There's deals being done all around us, and as a result people will be going to bed with full stomachs tonight. It's busy, purposeful and peaceful. What's not to like?'

'Being ankle-deep in cow pats?'

'That's better than being ankle-deep in shepherd guts, which was the usual method of taking possession of livestock before the Pax Romana got a grip on Italy. Now we get the cattle - or the pig in my case - and in return the farmer gets a profit instead of his house burned down. I've seen how it's done in less civilized parts, and by comparison, this,' I grandly swept out a hand, and nearly knocked the leather hat off a nearby peasant, 'this is pretty. What?'

This last was addressed to a workman in a grubby tunic. The man had slipped one arm out of his sleeve and knotted the tunic behind his neck to take up the slack. I have done the same myself at times because it's more comfortable if you're doing physical labour, as this fellow evidently had been doing. The workman was looking startled and slightly offended, because as he pushed up to me, the staff of Tancinus had slammed across his path and blocked his progress. Until that moment the workman had not even noticed my bodyguard. Now, looking at Tancinus' mightily frowning face, the workman decided to ignore the staff pressed against his chest and addressed me over it.

'Your crate's ready. What we did, we took a crate just a bit larger, and fitted your original crate into that, so now it's got a double layer. Oh, Gods. Are you putting *him* in there?'

The workman had just got his first sight of Bocchus. 'Um, I'll just go back and tell the boys to put some extra planks into the spaces, maybe nail some rails around the sides ... not very friendly is he? Rope reinforcement too, are you okay paying for all that, magistrate?'

I made a gesture indicating assent, and the workman backed off into the throng after giving Bocchus a last, assessing look.

'Lots of bacon on that thing,' he assured me.

'How's Ava?' I asked, necessarily having to make conversation with Cyrenicus as Tancinus was busily ignoring me. My body-guard hated being in places where strangers could get very close to me, and he had vigorously opposed coming to the market at all.

'A *sicarius*,' he had said, palming a vicious little knife from his belt. 'Sharp as a razor and not even as long as your hand. You fit it sideways behind a wide Samnite-style belt, or reach for it through a slit in your tunic. Then I go past you like this, stab back with the blade like this. It goes in here, just below your hip. Then a twist to make sure the artery is wide open, and I'm walking away while you're still wondering why you're dead. No-one else in the crowd notices a damn thing. There's eastern assassins who make a profession of it. I can go down to the Transtiburine district by the tanning vats and hire half a dozen of them by tonight. Want to make a bet that your friend Sabaco hasn't already hired the others?'

Nevertheless, I had insisted on plunging into the crowds of the Forum Boarium, and after his initial hissy fit, my bodyguard had maintained a stony silence. I did want one of those little belt knives though.

'Ava?' sighed Cyrenicus, bringing me back to the present. 'She's simply impossible. Impossible. Oh, she can cook, but her technique! Look, if you're going to put cumin in a dish, you measure it out, so you know the right amount for next time. But no, she just pours in a dollop and stops when it 'feels right'. What kind of cooking is that? And she's obsessive. You brought back some honeyed ham the other day, and she won't let off. She's experimented with the recipe a dozen ways already, even with garlic. Seriously. Garlic and honey. Now she's marinating the ham with herbs. I mean yes, it's a promising approach, but who had to do the breakfast for everyone while she was at it, eh?'

'The slave?' enquired Tancinus, breaking his silence with a snarl. That was something else Tancinus had on the ever-growing list of things he held against me. I was far too familiar with the servile classes. 'Treating them like people,' he called it with contempt, though he, like everyone else was benefiting mightily from the creative tension in the kitchen. In fact he was developing what looked suspiciously like a paunch, something else for which the corrupting Panderius influence was doubtless to blame.

'That reminds me,' I commented as a hurt silence descended on our little group. 'Can anyone make a guess at the time? I'm due to meet my patron at the second hour and attend him at the Senate. Yet with these accursed clouds it's hard to tell the second hour from the fifth.'

Tancinus studied the sky for a moment and then said, 'We've got about three-quarters of an hour to get home, change you into something that doesn't reek of pig dung, and present you at the Four Temples for the meeting.'

My bodyguard had some sort of internal timer and was rarely wrong in his estimates of the hour, though as they say in Rome, 'Sooner two philosophers agree than two clocks'. I gave my pair of retainers a bright smile and said, 'Okay, I'm off. Not you Tancinus - I'll have to look after myself for a while. You and Cyrenicus need to stay here and get our Bocchus ready for shipping to the farm. You all play nice together, okay? I'll meet you back at the Temple after the Senate session has finished. Bye!'

Timing my adieu carefully, I slipped past a knot of merchants and was into the crowd before the outraged Tancinus could stop me.

'Take this cushion,' Sulla told me, indicating a reddish affair of lambs' wool held by one of his retainers. 'And these wax tablets, and this flask of mustum.' He gestured at the appropriate objects.

'How many hands am I supposed to have?' I complained. Another thought struck me. 'Mustum? You can't even have proper wine? Why the unfermented stuff?'

'This is the Roman Senate,' Sulla reminded me primly. 'A generation back, you could have nothing at all to drink during a sitting, and you did all the sitting with your bony bum on a marble bench. Thank heaven we live in more decadent times. Now we're allowed a servant to take care of our basic needs.'

'As long as the servant is one of the hekatonkheires,' I muttered as I struggled to get a grip on all the equipment Sulla's retainers were loading onto me. The hekatonkheires were hundred-handed monsters in Greek mythology. If Sulla heard that, he loftily ignored me.

Acting as a servant for Sulla would in normal circumstances be considered a major demotion in status for me. However, the key word was 'acting'. I was not a senator and was highly unlikely ever to become one. Nevertheless, a number of powerful people wanted my attendance at the meeting and since the only way to get me there was as a servant to an attending senator, a servant I had become.

One advantage of being a servant rather than a senator was that my attendance was not compulsory throughout the entire meeting. This convocation of the Senate had actually begun at dawn, with the taking of the auguries (to see if the Gods approved of this particular meeting), followed by various rituals to satisfy this God or that, or - this being the Roman Senate - because something last relevant four centuries ago meant that the same pointless rigmarole had to be solemnly performed today. These rituals reminded me of the 'Salian hymns' which the priests sing in March; songs that might actually be dirty ditties about the butcher's daughter, because the verses are so old that no-one understands the words any more.

The good thing about these ceremonies is that the timing is precise to the last minute - unless someone screws up, in which case it all has to be done again from the start - so it was not hard to time my arrival for just as the officials were wrapping up the final sacrifice. This sacrifice was of a bullock, an animal probably procured from that same livestock market I had been frequenting while the Senate was busy sucking up to the Gods.

The 'Senate House' where the meeting was taking place on this occasion was one of a group of four temples tightly packed into an area just north of the Forum. The Senate is a body of men rather than an institution, and it can meet in any Roman temple. Usually it meets in the building in the top right-hand corner of the Forum – in fact so usually that this building is generally called the 'Senate House', though a shrine to Victory within makes this also a temple, technically speaking. (When it comes to the Senate, reality and 'technical' often diverge.) At the Senate House the only place for spectators is in the crowd by the door. The temple we were currently loitering outside had a somewhat more open-plan layout. As convenor of the session, the Tribune Cassius got to select the venue, and he had selected this one so that as many voters as possible could see and hear him in action.

As I arrived and located Sulla there was a general stirring among the toga-clad mass of Rome's great and good, a drift towards the temple doors, and the general buzz of a crowd looking forward to a good political punch-up. Sulla had just enough time to load me up like a donkey and give me last-minute instructions.

'The objective of this meeting,' remarked my patron jovially, 'is basically to stick it once again to the miserable Servilius Caepio, and through him, to stick it to his faction in the Senate. You're here to observe, so once you have seated me, take your place with the others by the back wall and keep out of the way. Take copious notes of events, and afterwards we'll compare our impressions.'

'You mean who's backing this senatorial lynch mob, who's agin it, and who's perched on the fence?'

'In your case, it's a matter of keeping an eye on the Marians. Now that the murder case against you has failed, the question is whether the Marius-Caepio alliance is intact.'

I nodded. 'I'm not going to be called on to testify, am I?'

'No, not today. This is a procedural motion. Technically it's got nothing to do with Caepio at all, other than that he'll be affected by it. Unofficially, it's another turn of the screw that ratchets things up to the big trial by Norbanus in early January. It also puts Marius in a bit of a bind, which is not the objective of the exercise, but it's a useful bonus.'

'The first step in the political destruction of Caepio was taken while you were away skirmishing with the departing Cimbri in your hit-and-run cavalry actions. While you were being a hero, Caepio slunk back into Rome with his tail between his legs. You missed the outrage - Hades, the fury - when people suddenly discovered how many of them Caepio had made fatherless and husbandless.'

'For a while it looked as though a lynch mob would storm the Senate House. In the end Caepio's own faction persuaded the Senate to strip him of his command. The hope was that this unprecedented humiliation of a serving Roman Proconsul would calm the crowd. That worked, but only as a stop-gap.' Sulla sighed. 'Painful to say, but people have reason to be angry with

... ,' he quickly glanced about to check that no-one was paying attention, '... the incompetence, arrogance and corruption of Rome's top men. Now that anger and yes, hatred has found physical focus in Caepio. Even months after the battle, the hatred simmering in the streets is still palpable.'

'I know all this. But I don't see how it hurts Marius.'

'Because Caepio was not the only general who screwed things up at Arausio. Mallius Maximus helped - and even though Caepio disobeyed his orders, Mallius was technically in charge. So this legislation today can be used against Mallius as well as against Caepio. Now Mallius is a fervent supporter of Marius, and he will desperately want Marius to block the passage of the law. Marius has to decide whether to leave one of his most loyal supporters in the wind, or outrage the crowd baying for Caepio's blood by blocking the measure that would affect both.'

Beyond the ropes that separated the senators (and their humble servants) from the general populace there was a large and growing crowd. Some of the members of that crowd were already getting somewhat vociferous.

'It looks as though the baying for blood has started,' I remarked. 'And this is just the Senate Consultation. The actual passage of the law should be quick but lively.'

Technically, the Senate was meeting today to 'advise' on legislation proposed by one of Rome's twelve Tribunes of the Plebs, a certain Cassius Longinus. This proposed legislation was to the effect that anyone who had been stripped of his command by the Senate of Rome could no longer be a Roman senator. When the Senate is called upon to give advice on a proposed law, the Senate's decision on the matter is called a *Senatus Consultum*.

Even though our Roman Senate rules the world, in Rome it is - technically speaking - only an advisory body without any constitutional power. The laws are made by gatherings of the people, who vote on bills proposed by the Consuls and Tribunes.

All the Senate can do is 'advise' whether these bills are legal and should be so put forward. That is why it's a *senatus consultum* - to show that the Senate has been consulted about a proposed law.

Of course, in reality, if the Senate allows a bill to be put forward, thereafter it is usually rubber-stamped by a compliant electorate into becoming the law of the land. That would certainly be the case here. If the bill to eject Caepio went forward to a popular vote, Caepio would be fired out of the Senate like a shot from a ballista. The people were indeed furious and were only prepared to go along with voting Caepio (and possibly Mallius) out of the Senate on the understanding that this was the preliminary to yet more severe measures to come.

Sulla gave the crowd a dismissive glance. 'That's Cassius. He's got the mob here to put pressure on the Senate to do the right thing. You can bet they'll be crowding the temple doors and making those meeting inside clearly aware of their opinion of the proceedings.'

'You, on the other hand, have an inside view. Watch Saturninus, everyone's favourite Tribune and demagogue. With Marius still up north with the army, Saturninus is Marius' voice in the Senate. If Saturninus tries to block the moves against Caepio, then Marius and Caepio are still allies. Marius has an excuse, because he can claim to be defending his supporter Mallius. The truth is though, that no-one gives a damn about Mallius. So it depends if Caepio has offered Marius enough to continue their secret deal. On the other hand, if Saturninus joins Cassius getting Caepio expelled from the Senate that means Marius is pandering to popular opinion - won't that be a surprise? - and has thrown Mallius to the wolves. In summary, if Saturninus supports Cassius, then Marius' truce with Caepio is over and you will have to worry about two separate factions trying to kill you instead of one united bloc.'

Most of this politicking I knew already, but it was good to get dinner-time gossip by the Temple's patrons confirmed by a top-level source. There was plenty for me to ponder during the long-winded speeches to come.

'The meeting is starting,' I pointed out.

'Plenty of time yet. Look at the crowd by the doors.' I looked, puzzled. The temple had large doors and the senators were relatively few, even with their retainers taken into account. They should have been streaming into the building.

'No-one likes to be first,' Sulla explained. 'And when the senators do get to the entrance, each one stops for a moment for his eyes to adjust. It's gloomy inside, and it takes a while to work out who's sitting where. Caepio will be on the right as we go in, parked with Scaurus and company in the central row. They'll be calling to 'friends' to come sit with them, and glaring at everyone who turns to sit facing them on the left hand benches. So on entering the meeting, a senator has to make a lightning decision where he's going to sit, based on who's already sitting with whom and who he can least afford to annoy.'

'It's forbidden for senators to sit on the floor between the two factions?'

'Don't be facetious. It is impossible to avoid picking a side, because it's also forbidden to miss the meeting without a good reason, and if a senator is in Rome, being dead is about the only acceptable excuse. So the senators have got to attend, choose a side and make some enemies. Politics is tough.'

'And you?' I wanted to know. 'Officially you and piggy Caepio are, if not friends, at least Optimates, aristocratic allies against the populists. Where will you sit?'

'On the left,' said Sulla cheerfully. 'Caepio went after me when he went after you. I have to be seen to be protecting my clients. I'll be doing that very publicly by voting to get the incompetent half-wit thrown out of the institution he's currently disgracing.

You'll be happy to know that Metellus senior plans on sitting right next to me. You owe him a lot of money and he wants to publicly display his displeasure with Caepio for trying to make it impossible for you to pay it back.'

' Anyway if you had ... ,' Sulla abruptly abandoned me in mid-sentence to turn his charm on some elderly duffer who had come up alongside. Unlike myself, the duffer had a purple stripe on his toga and a vote in the upcoming proceedings, which made him vastly more important than my humble self. I tagged along behind as Sulla oiled his way into the meeting.

'Conscript fathers ... ,' began Cassius. As convenor of the meeting, he had the right to make the opening address and inform the senators why they had been summoned.

'Point of order,' intervened Scaurus loudly. As one of the longest-serving senators, custom allowed him the right to intervene pretty much at will. Sulla had warned me that Scaurus would be using that right a lot. It was one of the reasons he had stocked up on snacks and drink.

'Yes?' Cassius asked politely.

'Closed meeting. This is a private matter among senators. Order the public out, and have the doors closed.' I had the uncomfortable feeling that old Scaurus was looking straight at me as he said this.

Cassius did not change his polite smile one iota. 'No. Res republica res publica sunt.' (The matters of the Republic are public matters.')

Scaurus looked bored. 'Quorum call,' he replied laconically, to a general groan. His remark was senatorial shorthand. Basically Scaurus had demanded that the number of those present had to be checked to ensure that the Senate had sufficient members present for a vote to be legitimate. Since there were quite evidently more than enough senators present, this was a transparent delaying tactic.

'A head count was made on entry,' countered Cassius smugly. 'Including the presence of thirty senior patrician senators such as yourself. We are quorate. Let's get down to business.'

Caepio junior piped up. 'That's not the formal way of doing it. I demand an official head count.'

It was now Cassius' turn to play a procedural card. 'Consule,' he said.

There was a general stirring among the benches. Cassius had called for a consultation. Now each senator would be polled to express his opinion on the matter. This was more than a simple procedural debate on whether a head count could be done at the door. Those who agreed with the Caepiones and Scaurus about the head count were likely to vote with that faction when it came to the crunch, and those who were supporting Cassius would probably also support him later in the more important vote. In short, the Tribune was asking for an early test of strength. This would be interesting.

From my position at the back wall, I could see that Caepio senior was surrounded by a tight clique of friends, family and senatorial clients. However, apart from that tight group, the right-hand benches were relatively sparsely populated until one came to the seats by the door. There, sitting together was a clump of some three dozen men - the Marians. The call for a consult would give the Senate a chance to see which way the Marian faction was leaning, and doubtless not a few senators would shift their seats as a consequence. However, it would take a while before the Marians had their say. Most Marians were relatively junior senators and a consultation went by order of seniority - starting with the most senior member of the Senate, none other than Marcus Aemilius Scaurus himself.

When consulted for an opinion, senators can speak for as long as they wish, about whatever they wish, and Scaurus was prepared to go on for a good stretch of the morning.

'Gentlemen, we must consider the rights and rituals of this house, rights and rituals handed to us by our forefathers ... .' As Scaurus launched into his lengthy peroration, I closed my eyes and filtered him out. Sleeping standing up is a trick you learn quickly in the army. On ceremonial occasions a good sentry can even sleep with his eyes open. It was no secret that the Caepiones hoped to drag out this session with delays, procedural queries and filibusters until the meeting concluded at nightfall before a vote could be taken.

Making sure this did not happen was another reason why Cassius had wanted as public a venue as possible. Senators were not voted into office, but they were voted into magistracies and the magistrates needed popular votes for their laws. This mattered not a bit to patricians like Scaurus, who was replete with honours and military commands. But no aspiring politician could afford to tick off the voters, and there were plenty of voters gathered at the temple doors shouting a running commentary to an even larger crowd further back.

Cassius had made the most of public sentiment against Caepio to make sure the crowd outside was as large as possible, just as he had made sure that the locale for this meeting was as public as possible. About now the booing should start, assuming Cassius had the sense to insert a vocal claque of opinion-shapers into the throng. The boos duly came in on schedule, muffled but very audible within the meeting house. They made no difference to Scaurus, who remained unwaveringly committed to his senatorial faction and anyway possessed an iron hide when it came to public opinion. However, he was elderly and ailing, and eventually lack of puff forced him to re-take his seat while his faction wildly applauded his efforts.

The boos started again when Caepio the Elder rose to speak. This was shortly afterwards, because as a former Consul and proconsul Caepio was himself pretty senior. He was clearly set on personally orating until sunset if need be, yet had barely hit his stride when an elderly senator, the duffer whom Sulla had been courting on the way in, rose from his seat. Ignoring Caepio, whose words faltered at the sight, the senator tucked his cushion under his arm and walked pointedly across the temple to re-seat himself on the left-hand side.

Drawing breath, Caepio prepared to start again from where he had left off. Then one of last year's Tribunes also stood up and crossed the temple floor to sit next to Sulla's new chum. This man was planning to stand for election as Praetor next year, and could not afford to lose popular votes. One of the senators next to Caepio tugged at the speaker's sleeve and whispered to him urgently. Long speeches were costing Caepio's faction votes and supporters that the faction could not afford to lose. Caepio got the hint and scowled. 'I support the motion for a proper head count,' he said with ill grace, and sat down. Ironic cheers filtered in from the crowd outside as word circulated of the curtailed speech.

Thereafter speakers kept their 'consults' short and to the point, and we progressed rapidly to the Marian faction. A speaker linked to the Metellan clan delivered a short speech in Cassius' support and sat down again. Then Cassius called on 'Lucius Appuleius Saturninus', and all eyes turned to Marius' representative at the meeting. Saturninus rose with an ugly grin on his face. Everyone knew that Saturninus loathed Scaurus with a passion. Last year, when Saturninus had a cosy and profitable billet managing the corn supply at Ostia, Scaurus had ejected him from the job, and taken over the position himself. It wasn't that Saturninus had been corrupt or incompetent as a manager, but merely that Scaurus had fancied the position and simply took it, as easily and nastily as a bully steals another child's lunch.

Now, looking directly at Scaurus, Saturninus drawled slowly,

'I concur with the previous speaker. The motion of Caepio should be denied.' Then he sat while members of the Marian faction bobbed up and down like trained puppies barking out different versions of 'I agree'.

Cassius looked politely neutral. 'It appears that the motion is denied. There will be no second head-count. We'll have a short recess while senators consider their positions.'

The Tribune meant that literally. Many of those positioned on the right-hand side of the hall were already standing and drifting across to where Sulla, Metellus and the Tribune-elect Norbanus were grinning broadly, cracking jokes with acquaintances and greeting new friends. I gave a small sigh of relief. It was past the fifth hour of the morning, and so far the Senate had not even started on the business of the day. Yet from here on in it was a formality. The Senate would agree that Cassius had a legitimate law to present to the people, and next month Caepio senior would no longer be a senator. Then Norbanus would begin legal moves to confiscate Caepio's assets and to exile the man himself.

Naturally, despite today's setback, Caepio and friends would go down fighting, and indeed he still had a fighting chance – but only if I was not alive to testify against him.

Liber XIII

'A tisane?' asked the slave girl, raising her voice slightly so as to be heard over the raucous chatter in the tavern. 'You want a tisane? Most customers here complain that their wine is too watery, and all you want is a hot herbal drink?'

I kept my head bowed so that the hood of my cloak obscured most of my face. Not that it mattered, as the waitress was more interested in the coin in my hand. 'Can you do it or not?' I demanded. 'You're bound to have something powerful with, hmmm, say nutmeg, rue and tansy on the boil in the kitchen. That will do nicely.'

The slave girl blinked in surprise. 'That mixture tastes like cat piss,' she informed me. 'And you don't need it.'

As in many back-alley dives, the serving wench was also the house prostitute, and the drink I had described was a known abortifacient. Girls wanting to remain motherless drink the stuff by the gallon every night, much to the detriment of their livers.

'Bring it to my table,' I told the girl's departing back, and shouldered through the crowd toward my destination, a rough wooden trestle against the back wall. The man sitting there stretched out a leg under the table to push out a stool toward me, and waited while I swept back the hood of my cloak and took my seat.

My drinking companion for the night was a slim, dark-haired gent whose disproportionately large arms rested like cudgels on the table before him. Though both well-muscled, the arms had a peculiar lack of balance, a slightly unpleasant asymmetry that was reflected in the set of his shoulders. That's how I knew we had the right man, for only one class of person has that kind of musculature - an experienced archer who has been doing the job since his early teens. With enough practice a man can pull back a bow that a normal human can't even fit the string to, but years of pulling back such a bow and the firing of thousands of arrows cause the body to slowly adapt to its purpose, and this odd-muscled man was the result. He was the archer who had fired at me from the abandoned building opposite the Temple and nearly perforated my gut. It had taken ten days to find him.

Archers are rare in the west. While the Parthian armies might have longbow men, short-bow men, horse archers and every other kind of toxophilite in the lexicon, the legions get by with the occasional slinger. When we really must have archers we tend to import mercenaries from Crete. Cretan archers are as good as you can get, and they are also thoroughly professional. During the Macedonian wars a century ago, it was not uncommon to find that each army had hired their own squads of Cretan archers who cheerfully swapped volleys of arrows with their cousins and in-laws on the other side.

Therefore when we started looking for an archer good enough to take a shot downwards from seventy feet in variable light conditions, we didn't start with a large field. Add that the person should be prepared to kill a total stranger and the field got even smaller. When that person is doing it for money and has probably done it before, you're down to three people. We had eliminated one - literally, due to an unfortunate misunderstanding about our intentions - and another was nowhere to be found, but I had managed to arrange a meeting with the third, a certain Lastares of Gortyna. He was, quite unsurprisingly, a Cretan.

The waitress placed my drink in front of me, and I wrapped my hands around the rough clay mug, trying to ignore the heat. It was a sweaty evening out there, and a long walk to this tavern on the south side of the Aventine Hill where Lastares liked to do his drinking. Lastares regarded me with hooded eyes.

'You're fast,' he told me by way of opening the conversation, 'and your bodyguard is even faster. But even if you dodged my arrow that one time, you are not going to last long. So why should I help you?'

'I have lasted this long. What's to stop me lasting longer?'

'You are an amateur. Look at you. You sit with your back to the room, completely vulnerable, whereas I have my back safely against the wall and can see who comes and who goes. And yes, your bodyguard sitting back there in his silly disguise is fooling no-one. Shall I give him a wave?'

'Please don't. He really doesn't have a sense of humour.'

'And you, with both hands in plain sight. Ever since you sat, I've had one hand on a dagger. You are unarmed and too trusting.'

One sip of the tisane confirmed the waitress' opinion. I imagine cat's piss might even be tastier. But the drink was very hot, and the Cretan was a cretin.

'Well, it's reassuring to know that I am dealing with a professional,' I told him. The Cretan grunted.

'You have an offer for me. What it it?'

I smiled beatifically. 'Oh, it's quite an offer. Life! Yes, Lastares, I'm offering you life. Not in Rome of course,' I leaned forward to squint into his wine cup. 'But the big city doesn't suit you anyway. You're drinking far too much. I understand you come here almost every night. You should go back to Crete. Enjoy the fresh mountain air, raise a family. Take up a hobby. Have you considered the flute?'

Lastares stared incredulously at me for several seconds.

'This is a waste of time,' he announced. 'We're done.' He stood up. As he did so, I leaned back, hooked a foot around his ankle and pulled the Cretan's leg from under him. Lastares sat down again, hard, as I rose in turn to look down at him. My tone was now a lot less friendly.

'We're done when I say we're done. And sitting with your back to the wall? Not so clever when someone can use this table to pin you against that wall like a bug to a board. And don't reach for that dagger. Because if your arm moves just another inch I'll pour this scalding hot tisane over your forehead and watch your eyeballs melt. Clear?'

'You won't get away with this,' the Cretan grated.

'Why not? You've put yourself right next to the door leading to the back courtyard. You probably thought it was a convenient escape route if something went wrong. Well, I can pour this drink over you and duck out before anyone recognizes me. After all, I'm the one with my back to the room. No-one has seen my face.'

There was a thoughtful pause as Lastares worked that out. I helped his train of thought along. 'Yes. I know that out back there is an unsavoury little cubbyhole where the waitress entertains her clients. Two very unkind men are waiting in there. They have instructions to drown you in the - frankly disgusting - latrine on the other side of the courtyard should you leave by the back door. Then they'll do as you were planning to do in an emergency, which is hop over the rear wall and disappear. You're screwed, Lastares. Now sit quietly and let me explain exactly how screwed you are, okay?'

I sat. Lastares watched warily, paying a lot of attention to the mug in my hand where the tisane steamed gently. I told him, 'If I have to burn your face off with this, try to keep your mouth closed. It tastes terrible.'

'Now. To business. You spotted my bodyguard. Well done, though really not that hard. But did you spot that the man tending the wine barrel is new as well?'

Lastares looked across the room. From the corner of my eye I saw Sulla's man give Lastares a friendly wave. The Cretan looked again at his wine cup with a horrible speculation growing in his eyes.

'And now you know why that wine tasted a bit off. It's been poisoned - there's been a lot of that happening lately. Are you developing stomach cramps yet? Contractions of the bowels? It's a very rare poison from North Africa. The main ingredient is scorpion venom.'

I continued reassuringly, 'Don't worry about the intestinal pain. That will go as your gut lining dissolves. By then you'll be paying more attention to the muscle spasms anyway. They're spectacular. Apparently you'll be able to touch the back of your head with your heels - isn't that something? Though you do snap your spine in the process, which some people would consider cheating.'

A fine sweat filmed Lastares' forehead. Judging from the amount of wine he'd drunk, the first effects of the potion should indeed be making themselves felt about now. Of course, his metabolism had speeded up dramatically in the last minute, and that also helped.

I fished a small porphyry bottle from the depths of my cloak and showed it to Lastares.

'The antidote. No, no', I said playfully jerking the bottle back as Lastares made a frantic grab for it. 'We need to talk first. Anyway, this is just the first shot. You'll need purging with one of these bottles per day for a week before the venom clears your system. You'll have truly vicious diarrhoea the whole time, but you'll live.'

My voice and expression were hard. 'You tried to gut-shoot me, Lastares. Now you've cost me a great deal of money for a rare and expensive poison. Perhaps it would be best to just walk out of here now, let you die horribly and save the cost of an equally expensive antidote. Because I really don't like you.'

I looked again at the wine cup. 'At a rough guess, you have fifteen minutes before the effects of the poison become irreversible, antitoxin or not. Why not spend that time trying hard, I mean trying very, very hard, to become my friend? Tell me things I want to hear, and you might get to retire to Crete after all. Don't leave anything out, because you'll want me to send someone around with another bottle tomorrow, and another the day after that. Why not start with how you contact Sabaco, and take it from there? Oh dear. That cramp looked rather nasty. It looks as though you might only have ten minutes, after all. I'll be quiet now and let you do all the talking.'

'Aaaand we're in,' I remarked cheerfully to Tancinus as we made our way back homeward. It was late, because my chat with the Cretan had gone on longer than expected. The streets of the Aventine were quiet, apart from the tap-tap of Tancinus' staff on the cobbles. Though this was a rough part of town I was probably the safest man in Rome. Not only did I have the formidable Tancinus beside me, but Sulla's men were also escorting me home. I knew that because I couldn't see them anywhere.

'You can be plain nasty,' remarked Tancinus. There was a degree of approval and perhaps even reluctant respect in his voice.

I asked, 'Because I doped his wine? Well, that's what they did to me. And you know I didn't use scorpion venom.'

'Only because you couldn't find any in time.'

'No, because it's every bit as expensive as I said, and actually it does not work all that well. I might have oversold it. Anyway, he drank good old hellebore, and that did the job just fine. It's one heck of a laxative.'

'Which was the nasty bit,' commented Tancinus. 'Giving him another bottle of distilled essence of hellebore to take every day while thinking it's the antidote to a poison he didn't really drink.'

'But it's so efficient!' I enthused. 'Getting him to keep dosing himself so that the laxative keeps him incapacitated. It's like having a self-shearing sheep. He was really grateful, too. Now, with Lastares out of action, Sabaco needs a replacement marksman. And we have just the fellow for Lastares to recommend. It was a mistake for Sabaco to use a bowman. They're too easy to track.'

'They've boarded up the windows of that place anyway,' Tancinus remarked. 'Did you speak to the Aediles?'

'It wasn't necessary. The apartment block is under new ownership. There's a lot of building work going on inside now. I'm surprised that you haven't heard it.'

'Building work? The place is a ruin. The only practical thing would be to demolish it and start again from the beginning.'

I shrugged. 'It's no longer a health hazard for us. That's the important thing.'

We walked in silence for a while. 'Pity that Lastares didn't know where Sabaco is hiding out,' Tancinus said. 'Incidentally, I've been thinking. Instead of that whole performance with the fake poison, why not just hand that Cretan a whole lot of gold in the first place? Same information, less bother.'

I kicked thoughtfully at a loose pebble on the paving stones. 'You know, if he takes my advice and goes back to Crete, this whole thing might actually work in his favour. He's not really that good as a hired thug, and I was being completely honest about him drinking far too much.'

'With the bribery, the gold for information thing, that's what he was expecting me to try. He was also expecting to take the money, spin me a load of codswallop and leave quietly over the back wall to share the proceeds with Sabaco. He may not know where the man is, but he knows how to get in touch with him. As do we, now.'

'Those contact details are the sort of thing that Lastares would never have told us, no matter how much we paid him. He would probably have invented whatever he thought could get away with. He thinks - well, he thought - that Sabaco was going to win this thing. So he wouldn't have wanted to upset his employer if he could get me to waste my money on lies instead. Instead, by going the pharmaceutical route we got the plain unvarnished truth, all of it, and cheaply. We also got Lastares to help us place a man in Sabaco's organization. Not a bad deal for ten denarii of herbs.'

'Blame the Tiber Aediles. There used to be a time when this place where we are standing right now was part of the flood plain of the river Tiber, like the Forum Romanum used to be, as well. Every year, this part of Rome turned into a swamp, regular as clockwork. Now I know that the Tiber still overflows on a really wet spring, but the Tiber Aediles have got a grip on the problem. All those embankments and dams. Well, your tax money has been well spent, because since the Aediles started building those things, flooding doesn't happen every year, or that often at all. When is the last time you had to take a boat to the temple of Saturn?

The ground here is drying out. The water table under the building is dropping, and as the ground gets drier, it contracts. An old building like this, there's probably two feet of air between the ground and the foundations in some places. Assuming that this place has foundations, that is. It's a jerry-rigged build if ever I saw one. Surprised it has stayed up as long as it has. But it won't be staying up much longer.'

Aelius Vibianus was an architect. As such, he was accustomed to being patient with both wealthy men and fools - insofar as he distinguished between the two. However, his patience was definitely creaking under the strain I was placing upon it. He went on.

'Look, I told you I can do it. I'll get the men to put concrete piles under the main supports but that's a temporary fix. It will slow the subsidence, won't stop it. You need to tear the place down and start again. You have my guarantee that one way or another these apartments will be a pile of rubble within the next few years. Be realistic. You got the building at a bargain price.

Now put a mortgage on it, and let me do a total rebuild, with proper foundations this time. You'll have an asset worth double your purchase price within five years, and that's taking the building cost into account. What do you say?'

What could I say? Vibianus was correct on all counts. It had not been that hard to trace the owner of the apartment block opposite the Temple - in Rome most of the property is owned by a small percentage of the population. As it happened, the same family which had originally commissioned this building over a century ago still owned it. The current scion of that family had little interest in the apartment block and was currently looking to cash in some assets to pay for his daughter's dowry and a new home for the happy couple somewhere on the Pinician hill. He had leapt at my offer for the place.

Therefore, as my architect had observed, I had got a bargain. Not many people were buying real estate in Rome right now, in case Marius failed to stop the Cimbri and it all got burned down anyway. So the smart bet was to keep assets liquid and wait and see. However, if Rome did stop the invaders, then once this property was rebuilt, it would give a nice return on investment for decades to come. Except I did not want to rebuild it. Not just yet, anyway.

'Can you keep the place standing, more or less at it is, at least until next February? That's all. After that you can wreak your will upon it.'

The architect sucked in air over his teeth, his entire body radiating disapproval. 'I can do it. Shore up the main trusses, stop the cracks spreading, put a joist under that arch. We'll need a buttress, or three ... and danger pay for everyone until we've got the place stabilized. Well, stabilized for the moment. But,' he looked at me with open bewilderment. 'What's the point if it's got to come down anyway? The building is condemned. The city authorities are not going to reverse that decision, nor should

206

they. Why fight it? This place as it stands - and it won't stand much longer no matter what we do - it's a death trap.'

'Have you heard of the Cimbri? Large federation of barbarian tribes, full of ferocious blonde warriors who massacre Roman armies on a regular basis? Those guys?'

'Well, of course. They're having an effect on property values all over town. No one is building, which is why I can get you builders dirt cheap right now. There's outfits that will do the work at cost, just for the cash flow.'

'Well, that's nice. Now go back to the bit about Roman armies getting massacred on a regular basis. It may have escaped your notice, you being focused on the building and all, but I'm by way of being a Roman soldier. Come next campaign, I'll be a military tribune serving with Cornelius Sulla in one of the aforesaid Roman armies. Going by past performance, the average military tribune fighting the Cimbri has a life expectancy that makes the prospects of this building look positively cheerful. This apartment block might or might not be standing this time next year, but the same is very true about me as well.'

'Ah. Yes.' Vibianus looked embarrassed.

'So what I and a bunch of other young military tribunes plan on doing before the campaign kicks off is to party like it's the end of the world. Because when the pointy stuff starts flying about, it is going be the end for a whole bunch of us. Now, it's fallen to me to host the party, being the man best able to lay on wine, women and song in truly Bacchanalian quantities. However, it's a pretty safe bet that our party-goers are going to wreck the joint, so I'd rather start out with a place that's a wreck in the first place, if you see what I mean.'

Vibianus looked doubtful. 'A party venue? I'm not sure ... .'

'Think more of an orgy venue. Right here in the atrium. With those chambers leading off from the upstairs balcony being put to good use by anyone who wants privacy. We're planning on wall-to-wall fornication and regurgitation, drunken brawls and the neighbours calling out the vigiles on an hourly basis. Even with the supporting walls so thick they're almost soundproof, we're budgeting on spending half the party's costs on magistrates' fines afterwards.'

'Well, I can't guarantee the place will be completely safe.'

'Define what you'd call 'completely safe' - when using the term relative to, for example, standing under a medium-heavy drizzle of razor-sharp javelins.'

'Point taken. 'Completely safe' as in a lot safer than that.'

'Remember, you just have to get the place through the party. Thereafter go ahead with the demolition. Venus and the tutelary deities permitting, I'll be back next year to see how the new place is coming along. Can you do that?'

'I can,' said Vibianus with a certain degree of feeling. 'In fact when you put it that way, you can be sure that I'll do the work at cost myself. As you say, the walls are solid.'

The architect glanced up at the balcony. 'I like a thick wall supporting a building. Even at the first floor level, the wall is over four feet thick. See how deep those doorways are set? I can work with that.'

'My only condition is that you commission me as architect and builder for the new apartment block once you and your brave fellow soldiers have finished with this one.'

'Done. Apart from emergency repair work to keep the place standing, I reckon all we need to do is layer the floor with something from which sticky fluids wash off easily, and brick up the downstairs windows to prevent people falling into the street. You wouldn't care for an invite to the party?'

'Not I,' said Vibianus firmly. 'I'm a family man, myself.'

'It's an odd sort of life right now.' I mused. 'Still it does contain Picentine bread, which goes so well with fresh-pressed sheep's cheese and these lovely, fat table olives.'

'And this excellent vintage,' remarked Mucius Scaevola, who had dropped around partly for a social visit and partly to finalise the paperwork of my new property purchase. He sipped from his beaker, and pursed his lips. 'I know you got this wine as a challenge, but there's so shame in confessing oneself defeated when matched against a master. Accept my total surrender. It's light, spicy, and totally suited to our repast. But for the life of me I cannot tell you what it is or where it is from.'

'A matter of regret. Not because you did not know, because there's not many in Rome who would. No, sadly, the regret comes from your brutal candour. Most of my guests would pretend that perhaps they might know, and entertain me with their fumbling failure.'

'And?'

'It's Mysian. Picked up from a Greek merchantman at Ostia where the captain had several small amphorae aboard for his personal use. The advantage of this wine is that it is designed to be mixed with seawater, and this makes it perfectly complementary to dishes which have been slightly under-salted, such as this cheese and the olives.'

Scaevola took a bite out of one of the olives - they were almost large enough to eat like apples - chewed, swallowed, and then took a swig of wine, unconsciously wrinkling up his nose as he considered the combination of flavours. 'Good,' he pronounced. 'I've noticed that you are currently over-staffed with cooks, especially as you like to put in a bit of time in the kitchen yourself. You wouldn't consider releasing one or the other of your surplus staff to my household? If you fancy selling the slave Cyrenicus, just name your price.'

'I might,' I agreed, 'since he'll have to go to a good home eventually. But the man has potential, and he was a pretty darn good cook to begin with. He's training Ava better than I could have done, and I'm making sure that he gets the best possible culinary education himself. He spent last week in the kitchens of Quintus Metellus, learning everything the chef there could teach him about Italian cuisine and taste. North African cookery is my department of course, then he has to learn Persian-style dishes. By the time we're done, he'll be the finest chef in Rome. Then he's yours, in exchange for one of your Sicilian estates.'

Scaevola laughed. 'There are people who would pay a price that high. Invite me to a banquet once his education is complete, and I'll consider it.'

Reminded of the business of the afternoon, Scaevola glanced down at the scrolls that he had pushed aside to make room for his tray of food and drink. 'So now you have the venue, how are preparations for the party going?'

'Well, work on the Death Trap continues apace, and while the work is going on this has the further advantage that it prevents strangers from sneaking into the premises to take pot shots at me from the upstairs windows. I've also made sure that the only entry or exit is by the front door alone. We're commissioning one of the side rooms to hold wines, from rare vintages to kick off each evening to barrels of vicious Gallic stuff to pour into the party-goers when they are too sozzled to care what they're drinking. We've commissioned half the harvest of a vineyard near Baeterrae for the latter purpose. The wine is being shipped in this week. I have also organized the barbarian king of hogs for my chef to turn into hams, bacon, pork pies and every other version of pig known to the human palate.'

'In terms of attendance, we've got some of the best party girls in Rome right here. They're looking forward to the occasion, and the male clientèle are raring to meet them. It should be quite a bash.'

'The Death Trap? Is that what you are calling the place?'

'It's what the builder calls it, and we sort of picked up on the usage. Though in honesty, it will be safe enough to last the next few months at least. Still the name adds a certain ... piquancy to the plans.'

'A collapsing building is certainly the least of your worries right now,' agreed Scaevola. 'Any further attempts on your life this month?'

'All peaceful on that front,' I replied.

All was peaceful because Sabaco had sent to Marius for further instructions asking how blatant he could be in getting me killed. What Sabaco planned was a semi-military action by which he and a squad of mercenaries would storm the Temple on a quiet morning, and then kill me and anyone else who got in his way. The problem with this plan was that that some senator's son or other person of influence might have stayed the night and there was a good chance that these very important people might end up dead in the subsequent fracas. Sabaco was not expecting me to go down quietly. On the other hand, he was also done with trying to be subtle.

Marius, may the Gods rot his foul-smelling scrotum, had agreed to the plan. However Sabaco did not know this. Thanks to the agent we had planted in Sabaco's organization, we had been aware of what my nemesis was up to almost soon as the idea was proposed. Lastares' replacement had alerted us to the sending of the messenger to Marius. We had quietly intercepted the man at Clusium as he carried Marius' reply back to Rome along the via Cassia.

Lastares himself had quietly departed from Rome almost as soon as he was well enough to travel. He had been followed as far as Brundisium, where he had taken passage on an eastbound ship. Rome was indeed very unhealthy for Lastares right now, and he'd had the good sense to realize it. It was my hope that the archer planned to take my advice and retire to the mountains of Crete. Who knows, he might even start playing the flute.

Meanwhile Sabaco would eventually tire of waiting for a messenger who would never arrive, and would send off his query once more. He would not be particularly surprised that the first message had failed. The roads of Italy can be hazardous for travellers, with everything from hungry bears to bandits stocking up for winter. The next messenger might get a bodyguard to accompany him. This was not a problem, for by the time the Sabaco got the signal to go ahead, I would be ready.

'So no developments?' pressed Scaevola.

'Not that I know of,' I lied. 'Maybe Marius and Caepio have given up.'

'Marius maybe, but not Caepio', warned Scaevola. 'At the *contio* in twelve days time, Norbanus gives his big speech to the people to prepare them for Caepio's indictment. You'll be speaking then?'

'No, but I will be standing on the temple steps next to Norbanus when he delivers his speech. That will make it plain that I approve his message, and that what he says about Caepio's murderous incompetence as a general is plain fact and not mere rhetoric.'

Political speeches were often given from the front of temples in Rome, and for the same reason that my newly-purchased Death Trap was subsiding. In early years of Rome, flooding of the Tiber had meant that any God who wanted to keep his feet dry needed his temple in the Forum to be built on a base at least six feet above ground level. This made Forum temples ideal venues for delivering political speeches, being wider than any podium and with the added benefit that vegetables or other missiles were seldom thrown at the speaker. Any that missed would hit the temple behind and incur the wrath of the God within.

'About this speech,' Scaevola paused delicately. 'With the connections my family have, we hear things. I assume you were not expecting an entirely genteel affair?'

I replied, 'Well, at a *contio* the exchange of ideas can certainly happen within a framework of robust debate. Opinions will be expressed forcefully, and the underlying concepts will be both vigorously challenged and defended with equal firmness.'

We both laughed.

'Yes, I have heard that too. It's going to be a full-scale riot. Senatorial retainers versus outraged public with paid thugs weighing in for both sides. Bring your own brickbats and cudgel. Don't worry, Norbanus is going to be Tribune of the Plebs, and the way things are going in Rome these days, as a Tribune you've got to be able to handle that sort of trouble. It's going to be one violent summer storm.'

Liber XIV

Roman temples are extremely blocky edifices, as I had explained to Cyrenicus at the cattle market. The Temple of Castor and Pollux certainly looked an imposing lump of stone as we approached it in the early twilight. The dark building loomed iron-grey against a steel-grey sky. Though it was barely the eleventh hour of the day, the clouds were dark and torches were already guttering and flaring on their brackets in the gloomier corners of the Forum. An impatient, gusty wind tugged at my toga and I hugged its folds closer to me to stop the carefully draped garment from unravelling.

'What these accursed things need are laces, or a good set of toggles holding them all together,' I told Norbanus as we reached the great stone mass of the temple and began to ascend the stairs to the broad pediment. The wind grew stronger as we climbed above street level. This bothered Norbanus not a bit. As Tribune-elect and a member of Rome's governing class he wore a toga almost daily and was as comfortable wearing one as I was in a tunic and slippers.

'Can't have toggles or laces, Lucius,' Norbanus told me. 'The toga is a sacred garment, so it can't have knots, fastening or bindings of any kind. You know that.'

'As a brothel-keeper, I can tell you that a street prostitute wears a toga because once you drop the right arm and shrug, the whole thing goes sliding off your body like a child's blanket. It's the quickest strip there is, and for pretty profane reasons too.'

'Oh, I don't know. There's sacred prostitutes at the temple of Aphrodite in Eryx ... anyway you are hardly naked under your toga.'

'Indeed not. This suede calfskin jerkin you see at the shoulder goes all the way to my waist, and it covers a padded cotton vest.'

'And what do you have between jerkin and vest?' Norbanus

enquired.

'Lamellar scale armour,' I replied promptly. 'It doesn't jingle like chain mail, and also stops arrows better. You?'

We had reached the top of the stairs and several figures gathered around the forest of stone columns in the temple portico detached themselves from the shadows and came forward to meet us. Norbanus had time to throw one sentence at me over his shoulder as he went to confer with the group. 'Me?' he said, half-seriously, 'I'm in the armour of tribunican inviolability. The Gods defend me.'

'Not in everyone's opinion,' remarked Cassius as we joined him. 'Tribune-elects are not sacred. They are merely a pain in the collective backside of Rome until they take up office in January.'

Replied Norbanus sweetly, 'How's it all looking, o sacred official pain?'

The Tribune Cassius frowned across the narrow Forum. 'The space is filling up nicely. You'll have four, maybe five thousand here. Would be more, but it threatens to be a ... vigorous debate. Wives will be keeping their husbands home, count on it.'

'Which is why we're meeting so late in the day.' I can be slow sometimes but eventually catch up. 'It's so the market traders have closed their stalls. Less to get damaged in a riot and less stuff to use as general ammunition if mayhem breaks out.'

'We have no idea this meeting will turn violent,' Cassius reminded me primly. 'We are holding it late so that the craftsmen, builders and other common citizens of Rome can finish their day's work and still attend. What we have to say concerns them all. It would be highly irregular to call a meeting if there was a possibility of public disorder, so naturally we are expecting nothing of the sort.'

'Which is why those bulky servitors who have remained in the shadows of the portico all seem to have walking canes that look like cudgels,' I thought, but diplomatically kept the comment to myself. We were talking for the record here.

'A good idea to put barriers up in front of the steps,' I remarked, keeping in the spirit of the thing. 'Otherwise spectators pushed forward by the pressure of the crowd might stumble and fall.'

'Oh, we have attendants on hand to make sure that nothing like that happens,' Norbanus assured me innocently. I studied the 'attendants' for several seconds.

'They're human, right?'

'Mostly. I think. But they're good to have between us and trouble. The trouble we won't be having, I mean. We would not want to upset the voters.'

The voters were what the meeting was all about, even though there would be no voting at this meeting, which was what we call a *contio*. That's short for a 'convention'. The purpose of a *contio* is to inform voters about forthcoming legislation. Getting a vote together in a matter as drastic as exiling a prominent Roman citizen like Servilius Caepio is a physically demanding process. The people have to form up by rank and class, and then separate into little enclosures that hold the 'yea' and 'nay' voters for each century of each class. The votes of the majority of each century of each class then counts as the single vote of that century.

Trust me, I'm simplifying here. Let's just say that voting is a complex enough business even after the voters have been brought up to speed beforehand on what they are voting about. The *contio* is where that bringing up to speed happens. It's a sort of consultation, where a legislator explains his bill to the people and judges from their reaction what changes he will have to make to get it passed into law. Sometimes a magistrate has to call several *contiones* before he reckons his bill is in good enough shape to pass a vote.

There was no such question here. As soon as Norbanus took up office in the new year, it was his sworn promise to call for a vote to exile Caepio, making it illegal for anyone within five hundred miles of the city to give him fire, water, or the products thereof. Nor did anyone doubt that the voters would enthusiastically back this legislation. However, law and custom required Norbanus to pitch the idea beforehand at least one *contio*, and so that *contio* had been duly called for today. When he was officially turfed from the city, Caepio would not have a legal leg to stand on.

Of course, the *contio* had yet to happen. No one doubted that Caepio and his friends were going to make a determined effort to prevent it. Therefore, Norbanus and his allies might officially deny that they were expecting trouble, but they were also well prepared for trouble if it should happen.

'Not a mixed crowd today,' I remarked to Cassius. *Contiones* were open to all, male and female, slave or free. 'Mostly male.'

'A lot of ex-legionaries in the audience,' Cassius agreed. 'They don't like what Caepio did, because that could have so easily happened to them. They will listen to what Norbanus has to say, and they won't be easily intimidated. The Forum is filling up nicely.'

There was in fact something unsettling about the crowd. The people within did not move around looking for friends and greeting them when they found them. There was little conversation. In fact most people arrived in groups that looked suspiciously like military maniples, and if the groups were not quite standing in ranks, they were not randomly distributed either. I had a suspicion that if I shouted 'Stand To!' the entire crowd would snap into legion formation.

'Stand over here if you would, Lucius,' said Cassius taking my arm. He paused. 'What's this?'

I slipped the fold of my toga back against my forearm. 'It's a leather bracer. Good for archery, but also for blocking blows without breaking my wrist.'

'It won't come to that,' Cassius said reassuringly, but his eyes were darting from me to the crowd. 'Come on, it's time.'

The brassy bawl of a trumpet called the *contio* to order, theoretically silencing the hubbub of a crowd that was not, in fact, hubbubbing. A sea of faces regarded the platform with solemn, intent regard. 'Gods above,' muttered Cassius, as much to himself as to me, 'that lot are a riot waiting to happen. Pray that Caepio shows some sense.'

He then stepped away from me, and raised his voice. It was the voice of a trained orator, heard easily over the gusting of the wind and the background noises of the city.

'Quirites, fellow Romans. Thank you all for gathering here today. As magistrate and your Tribune of the Plebs I have called this meeting. But I now yield my place to today's speaker, Caius Norbanus. Please listen attentively to what he has to say.'

Having said his piece, Cassius stepped back, and indeed stepped back so comprehensively that I did not see him again that day. A shrewd politician, Cassius had little interest in being involved with whatever happened next.

Norbanus stepped up, with me at his elbow, though a pace behind. Gravely, the Tribune stared at the crowd, which stared gravely back. Norbanus closed his eyes for a second, and then began.

'Citizens, I am here to speak for those who cannot and never will speak again. I speak for your brothers, sons and comrades who are not here today, the men who died for Rome on the field at Arausio. I speak for them, for they died who should not have died. You mourn because the barbarians killed them, but I tell you truly that what killed them was the incompetence, pride and folly of their commanders. They would be alive today, your brothers, sons and comrades, but for one man. Servilius Cae... .'

'Halt! Halt! I say.' The shout came from a small knot of men forcing their way through the crowd. It was not easy going, because the people in the crowd mutely resisted the group's progress, with a man stepping forward for each one pushed aside. No one actually resisted, but instead stood firmly, feet planted and body braced, stubbornly facing the platform and looking away from the newcomers. That group were a dishevelled bunch by the time they reached the foot of the temple stairs. The 'attendants' flexed their muscles and looked up to Norbanus for instructions.

'We are Titus Didius and Lucius Cotta,' shouted one of the arrivals. 'We are fellow-Tribunes of the Roman people, and you *will* let us on to the platform.'

'Tribunes of the Senate, more like,' remarked Norbanus to me in a voice that carried easily over the crowd. Turning to the Tribunes he said loudly, 'No-one here would wish to interfere with a colleague in the execution of his duties. You are both welcome to attend this *contio*.' Norbanus gestured to the attendants to let the Tribunes ascend the steps.

As he reached the top of the steps Cotta turned and faced the crowd. Boldly, he announced, 'There will be no *contio*. As a Tribune I forbid it. *Veto*. This gathering is now illegal. You will disperse and go home.'

There came a low, ominous growl from the assembled people, and Cotta glared right back at them with the suicidal stubbornness that only a Roman aristocrat can properly muster. He knew that he had the legal right to act as he did. He also knew that the people had given the Tribunes those legal rights to defend their interests, not to act blatantly against them, as he and Titus Didius were now doing. Smoothly, Norbanus stepped forward again, his servitors from the portico massed in their ranks behind him.

'I'm sorry. I didn't hear that,' said Norbanus into a silence so profound that you could hear a pin drop. 'I could not hear what you just said because of the noise of the crowd.'

He looked significantly at his audience. 'The noise of the crowd,' he repeated emphatically. There was a pause while people figured it out, and then it came - a roar so loud that the pigeons rose in a confused cloud from the roof of the temple of Jupiter on the Capitol; a solid wall of sound from thousands of throats that reminded me of nothing so much as the battle cry of a charging Cimbric barbarian horde.

Cotta tried to speak again, but this time his voice really was drowned out in the tide of noise. Norbanus turned his back to the Tribunes as the chaos of shouts settled into one steady, deafening chant. 'Exile! Exile! Exile!'

'Exile! Exile!' There was scuffling beside me, and I noticed that the servitors of Norbanus had formed a solid wall. The two aristocratic Tribunes were on the other side of that wall of muscular humanity, which was steadily shuffling towards the edge of the pediment. 'Exile! Exile!' the crowd had seen what was happening, and they loved it. The bellow took on a new edge. 'Exile! Exile!'

Apparently not noticing how they had crowded the Tribunes to the very brink of the temple pediment, the servitors turned their backs so that they faced Norbanus, and then shuffled again towards the edge. I saw the mouth of Didius open in furious and futile protest, and then he, Cotta and their retinue were toppled from the platform into the crowd. 'Exile! Exile!'

When last I saw the Tribunes that day, they were in small, struggling clumps of humanity that moved inexorably towards the Forum Holitorum. There, the Tribunes were unceremoniously and quite illegally corralled away from the proceedings of the *contio* by persons unknown and never later discovered. Back at the *contio* Norbanus quietened the crowd. 'Citizens, Quirites! Silence, I beg you! Our Tribunes wish to say something.'

He looked around the platform with exaggerated surprise. 'Oh! It would seem they have wandered off somewhere. How strange. We may never know what they wanted to say. As they are undoubted citizens and patriots, I can only assume that they stopped by to give their endorsement to our cause. Titus Didius and Lucius Cotta, I thank you for your support!'

The Forum rang to ironic cheers, and Norbanus resumed his address.

'Being Romans, we fight. We fight to defend our lands, our homes, our children, the graves of our ancestors and the shrines of our Gods. This is right and proper. When we put our trust in a general to lead us, we trust that this general will lead us in the defence of our homes, our families and our Gods. These are things we will die for.'

'For a general to abuse that trust, for a general to burn Roman lives - the lives of your brothers, sons and comrades - to fuel a petty political feud. That act cannot and should not be forgiven. The sacred dead of Arausio did not die to hold back the Cimbri, they did not die in defence of home and family. They died because Servilius Caepio wanted to save face in a political spat with Mallius Maximus.'

'Those men — men killed through Caepio's political posturing - they lie in their unknown graves, in their hundreds, in their tens of hundreds, in their thousands, in their tens of thousands, all so that Servilius Caepio could look good to his friends in Rome. They died, your comrades, your brothers, and your sons, because Caepio cared that little for their lives. Now the dead call to you from their graves. They ask not that you right the wrong that has been done to them, for so petty a punishment as exile counts not a feather's worth against the enormity, the crushing weight of Caepio's crime. All they ask, the dead of Arausio, all they ask of the living is that you exile Servilius Caepio as an acknowledge-ment of what he has done. That you understand that he betrayed the trust of the men who placed their lives in his hands. That you understand the contempt he felt for that trust, that ... .'

221

Not that I disagreed with a single word Norbanus was saying, but my attention was elsewhere. I looked at the burly freedman who led the servitors and he gave me an enquiring glance. I nodded. Quietly, the servitors lowered themselves from the edge of the platform, this time making no attempt to hide their cudgels. They collected several of the hulking attendants on their way, and pushed briskly through the crowd. They were making their way toward a wedge of some seventy men who had entered the audience from somewhere near the Senate House at the top of the Forum. These men were purposefully bulling their way towards the platform. Having failed to stop Norbanus by legal means, Caepio's faction was seeing what brute force could do.

Mentally I winced. Some of the men in that wedge had the exaggerated musculature unique to trained gladiators, and others were evidently farm labourers shipped in for the occasion. These were rough men, shepherds accustomed to fighting off wolves and rustlers, and they cared little for democratic niceties. If their orders were to break Norbanus' head then that is what they cheerfully do so, counting it as a bargain in exchange for a few days spent enjoying the delights of the capital.

Norbanus' thugs were outnumbered, and in the first surge of the melee, outclassed as well. Cudgels rose and fell and there was the occasional brief shriek. But then the bystanders started to pay attention to what was going on. Some who were standing by the Rostra plucked torches from their brackets, and launched them like flaming spears into the midst of Caepio's wedge. Others turned out to have packed short cudgels and spiked knuckle-dusters about their persons. Fist-sized stones began to fly. Through it all, the Tribune-elect spoke steadily, raising his voice to be heard above the tumult, summing up the charges against Caepio, and presenting the case for exile. As his peroration wound down, so did the melee in the Forum. There remained a degree of turmoil where the wedge had been, but of the men themselves there was no sign - unless you counted the fact that in places some of the crowd appeared to be delivering a vicious kicking to something on the ground.

By now it was harder to see in the gathering gloom, so Norbanus could legitimately appear to have missed the chaos around the Rostra. But with the outline of his proposed legislation delivered to the people, it was time to wrap things up anyway. In terms of what passed for legality in Rome these days, the *contio* had officially taken place. 'This meeting is over,' concluded Norbanus formally.

'Not yet it isn't!' roared a voice from the eastern side of the Forum. Startled I turned, along with almost everyone else present, to behold a small column of men advancing on the platform. They carried torches before them, and at their fore marched Aemilius Scaurus himself.

There was no question of blocking that majestic progress. People who had blocked and tripped the Tribunes fell back to leave a clear path for Scaurus. It was not that they liked the man, but they were swept aside by the sheer arrogance, the total self-belief and the iron-hard certainty of the old senator that they *would* step aside for him. And they did. In silence, we on the temple pediment watched the little torchlight procession make its way to the temple steps. Without consulting Norbanus, the temple attendants pulled back the barriers to allow Scaurus to march up the steps and turn to face the crowd, his attendants pushing the servitors of Norbanus back into darkness of the temple portico.

A pair of torch-bearing attendants tried to do the same with Norbanus and me. Norbanus, though, was no stranger to political theatre and was far less impressed than the crowd. He reached up and violently twisted the ear of the man who tried to shove him back. He snarled. 'Lay one finger on a Tribune of Rome, sonny-boy, and I'll watch as they throw your corpse into the

Tiber.'

The attendant backed off, one hand clamped to his ear, the other still holding his torch. Norbanus looked around for me, and I stared impassively back. I'd gut-punched my man and rolled him off the temple pediment with my foot. Less authoritative, but equally effective. Now I stood holding his torch and daring anyone to ask questions. No one did. All eyes were on Scaurus.

This was the moment when Caepio might have been saved. The audience were mostly ex-military men accustomed to taking orders, and they had an ingrained respect for their 'betters'. If Scaurus had played on that, talked to them as a general to the troops, they might have listened.

But the same arrogance that had brought Scaurus to the platform betrayed him once he was there. To the old senator, the people before him were unruly peasants who needed to be brought to heel with firm words. They had to be reminded of their place. Aemilius Scaurus, Leader of the Senate, patriarch of the Aemilian clan, was the man to do that reminding. After all, his family had been aristocrats in Rome when King Numa took control of that bunch of mud huts from the founder, Romulus. And now Scaurus was genuinely angry.

'You call yourselves Romans?' he blared at the crowd. The faces of the audience turned up to him, shocked and startled. 'You? You who are but the stepchildren of Italy? Oh yes, I see the sly Syrians and little Greeks among you, bringing their violent demagoguery into these meetings - meetings that in the time of my ancestors were affairs of dignity and calm. Dignity and calm, I say. You want to be Romans, you Greeks and Syrians? Then act Roman!'

'And you - I see some of you are soldiers. Well as soldiers, where is your respect? Yes, you men of Aricia, and Arpinum and Milan. Do you think my ancestors did not see your ancestors brought to Rome as slaves and prisoners of war? We took you in, we made Romans of you, and now you share in the glory and the grandeur or Rome. Are you Romans? The Romans of Cannae fought and died in the struggle with cruel Hannibal. Did their families afterwards, like petulant children swarm the Forum seeking scapegoats? They did not. They were Romans, those men of old. They took their losses without flinching, and they stood firm. And you, all of you here, what in Hades do you think you are doing? Do you think you are Romans? Do you think this is how Romans behave? Does this bring anything but shame on our City?'

Being a trained orator, Scaurus knew this was the moment to push his argument home. Being elderly, Scaurus had to pause for breath, and in that pause he lost his audience. A voice shouted from the throng, 'And how much money did you take from Jugurtha, you Roman, you?' Another voice added, 'Bribe-taker!' and, 'You were as incompetent as Caepio!'

'But greedier!' added another. Scaurus had been a general in the war against Jugurtha. His army barely cast a spear against the North African king before they were re-embarked on their ships and returned to Italy. Scaurus had claimed that Jugurtha 'surrendered', but the allegedly defeated Jugurtha had kept this lands, his throne and almost all his wealth - apart from that chunk he had paid Scaurus to leave his kingdom. As models of moral rectitude go, Scaurus was the wrong man to berate this audience.

Suddenly a stone flew from the crowd. It was a well-flung shot, for it hit the old man on the forehead. He reeled and collapsed almost at my feet. Without thinking, I stooped to help him. And as I did, another stone thumped between my shoulder blades. Wool padding and lamellar armour protected my back, so I hardly felt the impact, but it worried me the way things were going. 'Gods,' I muttered, 'they should allow us to wear helmets to these occasions.'

Scaurus' eyes snapped open and he fixed a fierce glare on me.

'Lucius Panderius,' he growled. 'I won't forget this.' Whether 'this' meant my help in sheltering him from missiles, or my presence among his opponents, I never discovered. Scaurus' retainers had recovered from their shock and now they found one of Norbanus' followers bending over their recumbent leader. I was hauled off in a flurry of kicks and punches that made me even more grateful for the protection of my armour. While Norbanus strove with mixed success to calm the crowd in front of him, I was dragged off behind. As I had done to the torch-bearer before me, I was in my turn pitched off the pediment of the temple. My toga was flung contemptuously after me.

I had been ejected off the back, into the alley between the temple base and the Palatine hill. Just a few yards away, the crowd still shouted and milled around the front of the temple. To my left stretched a dank street with the back of the shrine of Vesta on the Forum side, and a series of tawdry market stalls lining the Palatine side. Gathering my toga and my dignity about me, I prepared to slink off into the dark.

'Overall, that went better than it might have,' I muttered to myself. 'I've done my duty, by any account. Time to turn to my own affairs.' Leaving the debate on the future of Rome's ex-general to others, I turned and trudged alongside the hill toward home. It was a good thing I was wearing my high Celtic boots. I was pretty sure I didn't want to know what I was squelching through along the street.

It occurred to me that this was the first time I had been alone outdoors for a while. Usually Tancinus was striding alongside me, and at least one of Sulla's men was lurking somewhere in the background. But Tancinus had other tasks for the evening, and anyway, he expected me to be with Norbanus and protected by his heavies. Sulla's men were occasionally needed for other things apart from protecting me, and this was one of those occasions. Well, there had been no bodyguards in the Numidian wilderness, and I had survived over two decades in Rome without one. The short walk home to the other side of the Palatine hill should present no major challenge.

On reaching the little valley between the Capitoline and Palatine hills, I turned into the Via Labica, the main road between the Forum and the Circus Maximus. To my left, barely visible in the gloom, was the little temple of Minerva Medica, 'Minerva the doctor'. Since I did not want to urinate on the Lady's property I turned right and did my business at the gate of a little courtyard over the road. As my gaze idly wandered over the courtyard I was struck by the number of statues within. These were all of hooded men with their backs to me, staring up the road to where torches glowed in the Forum. They looked almost as though they were expecting someone. Then one of the statues turned and looked over his shoulder at me. Hastily he reached out to shake the arm of another of the shadowy figures standing nearby. It dawned on me that the statues were in fact a party of assassins waiting in ambush for someone coming from the Forum.

His unorthodox expulsion from the temple pediment had resulted in that someone - me - entering the Via Labica a block further down the street than expected. Once aware of the ambush, I might have managed to sneak away unnoticed had not the sound of splashing urine given me away. Now I had the full attention of the group's leader.

'Lucius Pandewius,' lisped Sabaco. 'How nice of you to join us.'

PHILIP MATYSZAK

Liber XV

'What is this?' I asked Sabaco incredulously. 'An assassins' convenion? You need eight people for one simple killing?'

Sabaco sounded defensive. 'Twelve actually,' he said. 'A few of Lucinda's associates wanted to be in on the kill.' He looked up and down the street. 'Where are your men? Oh, Lucius. Don't tell me you are wandewing about, all alone in the city? I expected better of you.'

'Who is Lucinda?' I spoke to buy time as I backed off, bundling my toga in my arms.

'You knew her as the Lady Fadia. If you'd just dwunk her wine, my life would have been so much easier. Now!'

This command was shouted to the man who had been sneaking up on me in the shadows of the courtyard gate. As he pounced, I hurled my bundled-up toga at his knees. The man's feet caught in the garment as he sprang, and the would-be assassin crashed to the ground. The man behind attempted to vault over him, tripped on his cloak and went over as well. That tangle in the gateway was my signal to take off down the road in a flat-out sprint, especially as another four men had come out of an alleyway further up to see what the fuss was about.

If I had come down the via Labica as planned, Sabaco's ambush would have boxed me in, with those four men at my back and the other eight in front. Without my bodyguards or any way to escape, it would have been a downright execution. As it was, I was off a good running start.

'Talk about dying for a piss,' I thought somewhat hysterically as I pounded up the Via Labica, heading for home with Sabaco's pack in hot pursuit.

I threw a quick glance behind me while dodging a startled pedestrian, and decided that I rather liked my chances. The odds might be twelve-to-one, but I had got very fit in the energetic campaigning against the Cimbri after Arausio, and had kept myself in condition since. On the other hand, the average Roman thug is pretty good in a stand-up fight but seldom runs to get there. Rome's criminal class is deplorably out of shape.

As I skidded into a hard left turn on the via Patricus I had a comfortable lead. I was still breathing well, though my woollen vest was getting uncomfortably warm. The pursuit squad with their heavy cloaks must have found the race even more trying, especially as they were also hampered by their swords. All I carried was an aura of pure terror. Whoever had designed the armour beneath my jerkin had factored in that the wearer would be running hard at some point. This might or might not say something about the Libyan infantryman I had got it from seven years ago. Either way, the armour was comfortable in a sprint.

The sight of a high-speed fugitive alarmed a couple walking along the pavement of the via Patricus. The man was already pushing his female companion protectively against the wall before Sabaco and his horde thundered around the corner. Just over a hundred paces ahead, the welcoming torches on either side of the doorway of the Temple of Freya offered sanctuary.

It was too good to be true, naturally. Three silhouettes detached themselves from the shadows, and spread out across the road. They carried an assortment of long swords and short clubs, and represented very bad news.

'Seriously?' I gasped, wondering if Sabaco had recruited half of the Roman criminal class for just one murder. (The other half of the Roman criminal class being in the Senate, of course.) A quick glance over one shoulder confirmed that the pursuit was still coming on, but was now strung out into a ragged line rather than the original disorderly mob.

The door of the apartment block was still open, as it had been when I had left for the *contio* earlier in the afternoon. Tancinus and I had been doing last-minute work, despite Tancinus' protestations that he was a bodyguard, not a builder. Before the men blocking my way to the Temple could work out my intentions, I wheeled on the paving slabs of the road - offering thanks for the good grip of my Celtic boots as I did so. Then I bounded into the apartment block, taking the steps three at a time, and plunged into the welcoming gloom of the old building.

'Gods! It's dark in here!' wheezed one of the first pursuers to enter the atrium. The others spilled in behind him, all in different stages of respiratory distress, bumping into those in front and milling around in some confusion.

'What's that banging noise?'

'Did we wound Panderius? That gasping doesn't even sound human.'

'Hey! The windows are bricked up. We won't get light through them.'

'Anyone see a lantern?'

'Five men! Get outside! One each side of the alley, two at the door. Call out if you find him escaping out of an upstairs window. One to the Temple - get the torches off the wall there and fetch them in here. Then bar the door. Let no-one in or out. Evewyone else, don't move. We can't see who is who until we get some light.' Sabaco took charge with brisk professionalism. He was breathing heavily, but was certainly not as winded as his minions.

I edged along the wall toward the stairs. Fortunately we had already got the polished marble floor in. The marble was to make it easy to wash away sticky fluids after the party, but it also meant that my boots could glide along with just the faintest squeak of leather on stone. There was a smell of sawdust in the air.

What little light filtered into the atrium was suddenly lost as the door slammed shut. In the pitch blackness we could hear the sound of a bar being hammered into place. Sabaco and his gang were now locked in the building with me.

'Fools!' howled Sabaco in the dark. 'Torches! I said get the torches before you bar the door!'

His shout came from uncomfortably near my elbow. It was time to make my move.

'Hello, boys,' I remarked conversationally, and bolted for the stairs. In the dark someone got in my way, but with my shoulder down and charging hard, I simply bowled him down. This slowed me somewhat, and put the pack right on my heels as I fled upstairs. The crudely-rigged staircase swayed alarmingly as it took the weight of a dozen hefty men. Knowing what was coming next, I made a virtue of necessity as my balance went, and flung myself forward at the landing. With a series of bangs and crashes, the staircase collapsed beneath me.

Upstairs was a balcony that ran the length of the downstairs atrium, and behind the balcony were four first-floor apartments with doorways set deep into the wall. The edge of the balcony hit my stomach as I landed, my legs dangling over the drop where the staircase had been. Someone had jumped alongside me. Before he could get set, I dislodged him with a vicious blow from my elbow and he slid backwards, screaming as he landed on the floor below. Scrabbling noises indicated that someone else was desperately hanging on.

I rose quickly, and groped blindly for the sword that should be propped against the wall. Hurriedly grasping this, I swiped savagely at the air where the stairs had been, but hit no-one. Moving as fast as possible, I felt my way along the balcony while sounds of purest chaos arose from the floor below.

That the ramshackle stairs of the ancient building had collapsed should come as no surprise. On the other hand, the sharpened wooden stakes that Tancinus had spent the afternoon wedging under the stairs would have been a shock to the people who landed on them. For everyone else, there was Bocchus. We had designed the narrow pen imprisoning the gigantic pig so that the sides collapsed along with the stairs above it. Now Bocchus was out, and after being whacked by falling planks, he was even more homicidally foul-tempered than usual.

If you've ever seen a boar-hunting spear, you might have wondered at the crossbar set about two feet into the spear's eight-foot length. The crossbar is there so that, once impaled, the boar does not wriggle up the length of the spear and kill the person holding the other end. That detail should tell you all you need to know about hunting boars. Boars are killers. Apart from their diabolical strength, speed and determination, there's the teeth. The upper canine teeth on a pig are are called whetters, because the champing of the boar's jaws causes them to chafe against the lower canines, keeping them razor sharp. The lower canines are called cutters, for obvious reasons. In a large pig the cutters are longer than a man's hand. It takes around a dozen men to kill a boar, assuming they have nets, bows and arrows and spears, horses, and a pack of dogs. Even then, boar hunts are famously perilous.

The main difference between Bocchus and a wild boar was not ferocity or speed, but that Bocchus was farm-fed and therefore larger and more dangerous. Also, instead of well-prepared hunters, the boar was taking on a room full of people who hadn't yet even figured out what had hit them.

All Sabaco's men knew was that in the total darkness there was shouting, screaming and warm, copper-smelling blood flying everywhere. Once they discovered that there was something deadly in the room with them, some men struck out out wildly with their swords. Since no-one could see what he was hitting, others in the room got hurt. These men not unreasonably concluded that they had been ambushed, and counter-attacked with deadly force. Lethal mini-duels broke out in the darkness. The only people who realised that the true threat was moving around at hip height discovered this while being slashed or disembowelled with deadly precision. If that berserker pig had a soul, right now it was in hog heaven.

Fumbling my way along the balcony, I wondered if we had done a good enough job of soundproofing the building. The noise below resembled a small battle, albeit with extra pigs. A prickle of sweat filmed my forehead as I thought how close I had come to falling off the stairs into the room below.

It had seemed so straightforward that morning. That was when the man we had put into Sabaco's organization sent word of the planned ambush by the Forum. My intention all along had been to lure Sabaco and friends into the building to meet Bocchus. After all, I had purchased pig and building for just that purpose. We even called the building the Death Trap, just to make my intentions clear. So when we heard of the ambush planned for after the *contio*, we had spent the rest of the day putting the final touches to this ambush of our own.

A thin red line glowed at the end of the balcony, like the eye of a drowsing dragon. Taking care not to burn my hand, I felt in the darkness for the handle above the red stripe. As I lifted the lid, the charcoal in the brazier that Tancinus had left for me flared back into life. Tancinus and Lastares' replacement - I never did learn the man's name - would be standing guard by the door now, wondering at the muffled sounds from within. Doubtless Sulla's men had disposed of the thugs sent for the torches and to guard the alleyway. Whatever had happened to those outside, they counted as the lucky ones. Bocchus and chaos still raged within. I almost felt guilty about what would happen next.

The fat-saturated cloth of the torch spat and spluttered in the brazier, and then caught fire. Holding the flaming torch high, I walked along the balcony lighting four other torches, one beside each doorway. At the second doorway something rustled behind me, and I whirled, sword outstretched. But it was only the hot charcoal settling in the brazier as the flames consumed it.

In the torchlight, the scene downstairs was something from a nightmare. Blood, black as ink, lay in large pools on a floor littered with bodies. Two men were impaled on Tancinus' wooden stakes over the ruin of the stairs, one still writhing in a vain effort to free himself. That meant my bodyguard owed me three denarii. He'd bet that he would get four victims.

In all, five men were still standing. One did not really count, as he was doubled over clutching at his belly and the intestines which spilled from it in dark coils. Another danced by a bricked-up window desperately trying to find purchase to pull himself up by his fingers. One more was trying to break down the door with this shoulder. Since the door had been reinforced to stop 700 lbs of pig in full charge, the effort was pathetically futile. Two more thugs were backed into a corner holding their swords out before them. I promptly nicknamed the corner Fort Sabaco and turned my attention to the man at the door. This man was now flat against it, looking in horror at Bocchus.

The ferocious Nemean lion, or Cerberus, the doorkeeper hound of hell, could not have looked more fearsome than Bocchus right then. The boar's head was saturated end to end with blood which dribbled off him like an obscene sweat. There must have been wounds on that massive body but I could see none. As I watched, Bocchus lunged, swift as a cobra. A flick of the boar's head literally sent his victim flying. Black blood jetted from the man's thigh as he landed. The artery had been cut through, which was no surprise, as most of the leg had been severed as well. Bocchus' tusks had sliced through flesh like a knife through a melon.

However bad things seem, they can always get worse. That's the lesson for today, lads. There was a short bow next to the brazier, and two quivers of arrows. I had told Tancinus that he had overdone the arrow supply, but the old man had just grunted. 'You are no Nimrod with the bow,' he had told me, 'and an oversupply of arrows is way better than a shortage.'

Exchanging bow for sword, I shot my first arrow at the man trying to scale the wall. The bowstring slapped against the bracer on my forearm, making me glad I had worn it, even though it rather gave away my intentions. Like Lastares a few weeks previously, I was shooting downwards in poor light. I aimed for the chest, but took the man through the neck. He did not drop, but made horrible noises as he staggered from the wall. This attracted the attention of Bocchus. The boar charged in a dark blur to hit my target's hips with a force that snapped bone. I had better luck as the man went down. My next arrow went right through his chest, and thereafter he lay on the floor and did not move.

Back to Fort Sabaco. The men in that group watched as I fitted another arrow to my bow. They had a dilemma. If they stayed together, they were an easy target for my arrows. If they split up to dodge, Bocchus would have them. 'Mercy, for its own sweet sake!' one of the men called. 'We surrender.'

'Is that what you were going to do, back by the Forum? Accept my surrender?' I enquired. 'Anyway, if the pig accepts your surrender. I will too.'

There was no question of the maddened boar giving up. You would think that the sight of two swords held at head level would put a degree of caution into his charge, but Bocchus simply ploughed into the pair at full speed. The man he crushed before his head struck the wall softened the impact, but nevertheless Bocchus staggered back. For a second he sat on his rump with front legs splayed, and then toppled slowly over, for all the world like a drunk after his fifth flagon of wine. That left one man still standing, so I put an arrow into him on general principles. The man threw his sword at me in helpless frustration. It bounced off the bannisters back into the room below as I killed the thrower with my second shot, an arrow to the heart. My aim was improving.

Now only bodies littered the floor. Putting down the bow, I leaned over the bannisters examining the dead and dying. Where was Sabaco? The man holding his intestines lifted his head. Blood was gushing between his clenched fingers.

'Where is Sabaco?' I demanded. The man swore weakly, and then his head flopped down again.

The flicker of a shadow warned me, and I whirled. But Sabaco had already picked my sword from the floor. I sprang backward, but Sabaco was faster. He swept out his foot and sent the short bow skittering down the balcony. There was an intent look on his face as he advanced, holding my sword. A mirthless grin crept over his face as he waggled the blade.

'Look what I found,' he said. 'I let go of mine when the stairs went and I had to jump. It's no fun hiding unarmed in a doorway when someone is looking to kill you.' Sabaco glanced over the balcony, then stopped for a longer look. He whistled. 'Well, well. And they call me a killer without pity. That's quite a number, even for you, Pandewius. You've saved me a fortune in wages.'

'A shame,' he continued. 'I had wanted to kill you with the weapon that killed your father. That would be elegant, would it not? On the other hand, putting you down with your own blade, well, that works for me too. Not quite as good, but okay.' He feinted, then lunged. I spun past the blade and leapt away from the backhand follow-up cut. Behind me, only a few yards of balcony remained before I'd be backed into the brazier.

'Do you want to beg? Sob? Plead with me, and call on the Gods? Your father did all of that before I killed him. Pathetic, weally. How about you? Any final words?'

I let my hands fall to my belt. 'Well sure, do you know that elephants are blue?'

'What?' Processing that total non-sequitur took a half-second of Sabaco's attention, and in that time I palmed the little *sicarius* dagger and threw it at his face. The target was his eyeball, not because the dagger was likely to hit it, but to trigger the most urgent instinctive response.

Sure enough, Sabaco jerked his head violently aside and swatted vainly with his sword. He didn't connect with the flying dagger, but it missed his eye anyway and bounced off his temple into the darkness, leaving a bloody tear in the skin. The miss didn't matter, because I came right behind the blade in a full charge.

We collided chest-to-chest, and with the palm of my hand I connected a solid blow under his chin as we reeled into the bannister. Which broke. In a shower of splintered wood we tumbled to the floor below. I'm pleased to recall that even in free fall I landed a solid punch into Sabaco's face. Then we hit the floor, and pain exploded so violently that the entire world vanished into its vortex. After uncounted time, a sense of urgency forced me to focus. There was danger, and I had to move. Something was desperately wrong with my right leg. Lifting myself on my elbows I wriggled backwards. The agony was so intense that I shrieked aloud, and collapsed with my head and shoulders propped up against the wall.

The shadowy figure of Sabaco moved among the corpses, foraging. Imprisoned by pain I could only watch, unmoving, as he found a sword and took a few experimental swipes with it. He seemed not at all injured, curse him. He walked casually over to look down at me, his face unreadable in the shadows of the torchlight.

'My third blade of the evening,' he remarked. 'Maybe this will be the one to do the job.'

'You can't get away,' I told him through gritted teeth. 'The only way out is ... through that door, and my men are ... the other side ... waiting.' My vision kept fading to black, and it was hard to concentrate even on the mortal danger in front of me. Sabaco regarded me clinically.

'A blow to the head, it looks like. And the hip, hmm, well and twuly dislocated. You must be in total agony. Good.'

'You need me ... hostage.'

Sabaco cocked his head to one side as he considered this. 'No, I don't think that would work. Too clumsy. Better I think, that your men find their employer dead, and me waiting to offer new employment at much higher wages. When your men know who is backing me, and how much I can offer, I'm certain they'll come awound. Why be loyal to the dead? And you, finally, will be dead.' With his free hand, Sabaco touched the remainder of his mutilated ear. 'Jupiter, I've waited a long time for this. No more fooling around, now.'

Sabaco stepped forward. As he drew back his arm to drive the sword into my throat I looked behind him and smiled. Sabaco snarled. 'That old twick?'

His expression changed to shocked horror at the sound of a slow, rasping grunt. Bocchus had lurched to his feet and was woozily looking around the room. The giant boar spotted Sabaco - not difficult, as he was the only person still standing - and that berserker look of hatred swam into his bloodshot eyes.

'Jupiter and Hecate,' breathed Sabaco, only now taking in the size of the animal and the length of bloody tusk on each side of its jaw. Bocchus tensed his muscles, and Sabaco totally forgot about me as he whirled, sword held at shoulder height, to face this new threat.

It seemed that Bocchus did not charge. It happened too fast for that. One moment he was in the middle of the room, a trembling mass of fury and blood-lust, and the next he and Sabaco were right beside me in the air, then a conjoined mass smashing into the wall. There was a sound as though a man had snapped a broomstick over his knee as Sabaco's back broke with the impact. I had not seen Sabaco strike, but as the pair crashed down I saw that his sword was embedded in the pig's forehead, so deeply that only a sliver of its width still showed. Bocchus was finally and definitely dead. Sabaco was still alive – for now.

'Can't ... bweathe,' he gasped.

Turning my head was painful, and made me feel sick, but it provided a clearer picture of the situation. Sabaco lay on his back, so close that one of his arms was thrown over my chest. Apart from his head and shoulders, the rest of Sabaco was hidden by a mass of dead boar. With ten talents of weight on his chest, Sabaco was literally being crushed to death. He rolled his head, and looked me in the eye from two feet away. The tendons in his neck stood out like cords.

'Get him, off. Please!'

I considered this for a second. 'No,' I said. Then I blacked out.

Minutes, or hours later, reality came sweeping back, propelled by a wave of sheer pain. Someone was holding my leg up by the ankle, and Tancinus was saying, 'Now put your foot in his groin and we'll pull back hard. That leg has got to go back in before the tendons tighten up. Ready?'

'Wait,' I said weakly. The pressure on my leg eased, though the pain roared on.

'Oh, you're awake,' Tancinus remarked. 'A pity. You are not going to enjoy this next bit.'

'Before you do that ... one thing. I want completely clear. You got it?'

'What?'

'No-one butchers that pig. No-one. Bocchus ... he gets a hero's funeral, and a warrior's grave. Clear?'

Whatever the reply, it escaped me. Ungentle hands lifted my ankle, and Gods be praised, I passed out again.

Liber XVI

'Well, now you've gone and done it.' For an alleged bearer of bad news Sulla seemed remarkably cheerful. 'Before I give you all the details, do you have to keep these shutters closed? It's remarkably gloomy in here.'

'That bang on the head was harder than it seemed at first. Bright lights hurt my eyes. Loud noises are remarkably painful too, so a lowered voice would be nice. While I'm complaining, did I mention this constant nagging headache?'

'Quite the stoic, aren't you?'

'The only good thing about my health right now is that the dislocated hip is settling right back into place. There's a lot of bruising and the ligaments will need time to heal, but my doctor reckons that, with no other complications, it will all be healed by autumn. However, no more sprinting around Rome with a gang of assassins baying for my blood. The farm looks a good place to rest up for a month or so.'

'I hear your bodyguard's daughter is up there too. Perhaps she can help with your recuperation? Anyway, it's not a bad idea for you to stay out of town for a bit. The authorities are none too pleased with you.'

'Noise, please. Murmur gently, if you would be so kind. Yes, I apologise for the whole Death Trap thing. Who would have thought that Sabaco would invite so many people to a simple murder? Beforehand I was thinking we'd have to quietly dispose of four or five corpses at most.'

Sulla sighed. 'Sixteen actually. My man Quintus died outside. We've kept it hushed up for the most part. It wasn't that hard, persuading the authorities not to make a fuss. The Senate and Aediles don't like reports circulating of wholesale butchery taking place within the city limits. It makes it look as though they don't have a grip on things. There will be no official investigation into what happened that night, because officially nothing happened. None of the friends of the recently deceased are likely to make a fuss about it, so the authorities are holding their noses and looking the other way.'

'The problem is, no matter how one tries to suppress it, word gets around. My men were pulling bodies and bits of bodies out of your Death Trap for most of the evening. People notice.'

I shrugged, then winced. 'At least Sabaco has finally paid his debt to Nemesis. My father's murder is partly avenged.'

My patron clucked sympathetically. 'For the moment 'partly' is where it will have to remain. Word's gone out. Top senators have met, and you and Sabaco were discussed at length. This feud of yours has got to stop. For the past few months bodies have been dropping all over town, and your last little bloodbath put the cap on it. The powers-that-be have had enough. So I came to bring you that fine North African Mulsum to help with your recovery, and to tell you to lay off.'

Reminded of Sulla's gift, I took an appreciative swig of the honeyed wine at my bedside. As I did so I raised my eyebrows.

'Me, lay off?'

Replacing my beaker on the bedside table, I complained indignantly, 'Life in Rome was going fine until Marius and Caepio came after me. They are the ones that need to lay off. All I've been doing is defending myself.'

'Well, your defence has not exactly been passive, has it? Before you say anything, remember there's about two dozen corpses that would like to disagree.'

'I thought you said sixteen'.

'Overall, I mean. Not just your most recent massacre in self-defence.'

'What about Caepio and Marius? If I 'lay off' as you put it, and they don't lay off, then what am I supposed to do?'

'Relax. Some of the recent corpses were Caepio's men. He's

demoralized by this and other recent failures. Our mutual friend Catulus had a word with him this morning. Basically, Caepio is resigned to losing his home, reputation and fortune. His friends have arranged a comfortable exile for him in Smyrna in Asia Minor, and he has come around to understanding he will spend the rest of his life there. Fortunately he still wants to have a life, and so he's agreed to leave you alone.'

'I don't understand.'

'It's simple enough. Apart from that whole Gracchus business, the Roman aristocracy don't kill each other. From time to time - well, all the time actually - we wage nasty feuds in the law-courts and the Senate, or get our agents to run the other fellow into bankruptcy. That's the game; but the actual killing or assassination of a Roman aristocrat is out of bounds. Socially and legally unacceptable.'

'Anyway,' Sulla continued with relish, 'that business at the Death Trap made certain people decide that matters have gone far enough. Your private war has become sufficiently bloody to become the Senate's concern. So Caepio has been told that if he makes another move to harm you, directly or indirectly, the gloves are off. Instead of fighting through proxies, you'll be allowed to take a clear run at Caepio personally. Another attempt at your life, and you're free to go ahead and kill him. Simple, isn't it? Not a judge will hear the case against you afterwards. '

'That's a threat?' I asked incredulously. 'The way my head feels at the moment, I'm incapacitated if a kitten meows too loudly. Do you really think that will scare off Caepio?'

'Well, Caepio still remembers Arausio and that spear you chucked at him. You only just missed, so he has no doubt that you have the will to do the deed. Then there's the matter of the Death Trap. You and a over dozen enemies were locked in there, and only you emerged alive. That makes you all the more terrifying.'

'What? Wait.' I forced my pounding head to do some basic arithmetic. 'Sabaco was expecting me to be with Tancinus and the three bodyguards you lent me. So he had a dozen men at the ambush, and three more guarding the Temple in case anyone escaped.'

'Um ... ,' I was counting on my fingers, 'he sent five outside, I remember him giving the order. Your men ambushed them as they left?'

'Yes, Quintus got unlucky. You weren't the only one with armour under your tunic.'

'Okay, of the ten inside, Tancinus got two with his sharpened stakes. Which reminds me, he still hasn't paid the three denarii he owes. He bet he would get four.'

'Gambling with high stakes, were you?'

I closed my eyes in pain. 'Please, don't. Sabaco made it up the stairs, curse him. But he was unarmed and intent on survival, so that left seven in the atrium. What they and Bocchus got up to in the dark I don't know, but there were basically four effectives left by the time I got the torches lit.'

'Shooting trapped men who have no way of fighting back is not heroic, particularly when a battle-crazed boar is doing most of the killing. I finished off two, I think. I didn't even get Sabaco - that was all Bocchus.'

'But,' countered Sulla, 'it's word of the odds that has been getting around, not the details. In certain circles, they think you did all the killing personally with your teeth and fingernails. Even as I speak, tavern gossip is making you a combination of Achilles and Hercules reborn.'

I groaned, and covered my face with my hands.

'Don't be too discouraged. Caepio's bought into that idea. He believes you are Panderius, the human killing machine. The thought of you appearing at his bedside one night, dripping blood and adorned with the giblets of his bodyguard, has persuaded him to back off. Whether you testify against him or not, Caepio's done. He wants no more of the feud, so you don't have to worry about him any more.'

'Which leaves Marius. He's not going to give up easily. There's the prophecy.'

'Marius also has been told to back off, and in no uncertain terms. Even allies such as Saturninus and Norbanus have put their weight behind it. He might be Consul, yes, but even Marius can't go against the entire Senate alone. I don't think he likes you very much, though.'

'The feeling is mutual. Oh, Gods. How much political capital did you have to spend to get the entire Senate behind you? I'm going to owe you until the tenth generation, aren't I?'

Sulla grinned. 'Oh, relax. I hardly had to do a thing. Marius did it all to himself. When we, well, Norbanus actually, confronted him, Marius denied that he'd had much to do with it all. He blamed Caepio, and Sabaco running out of control. It was nothing to do with him. He was too busy arranging the defence of Italy to be concerned with unimportant little you.'

'Slimy, but typical Marius.'

'That story did not work. Remember what I said about the unofficial rule that senators don't try to kill each other? Even Sabaco knew that some aristocrats would probably get killed in a direct assault on your brothel. That is why he hesitated until Marius gave the go-ahead.'

'It is very probable that some senatorial family members would be at the Temple when Sabaco and his thugs came for you. Norbanus is partial to an evening here. So is young what's-his-name, the grandson of Aemilius Scaurus. Even those aristocrats who don't frequent your establishment took offence at Marius condoning the murder of random Roman aristocrats.'

'No senator likes to think he or his sons might be killed casually, as collateral damage in someone else's vendetta. So when Marius condoned such killings, he was not just breaking the rules, it was plain bad manners. All we had to do was show the correspondence you intercepted from his messenger, and Marius was condemned by his own hand.'

'As a result, Marius has been forced to call off his private war against you and concentrate on his state-sponsored war against the Cimbri. Sabaco did you a favour by inviting everyone and his brother to that ambush by the Forum. Once you had killed the lot, the butcher's bill was too high for the authorities to ignore, and too embarrassing to notice publicly. As I told you earlier, important people have met, and it had been decided that past events did not happen. There will emphatically not be any future events.'

'That is what I am here to inform you. It's all over, Lucius. Furthermore, since you are still alive, it seems that you've won.'

I placed a hand on my throbbing forehead and growled, 'Okay, okay. So long as I don't have to see Marius any time soon, and Caepio is indeed ejected from Rome, we'll count it as a win.'

My patron looked a bit shifty - something very unusual in a man whose expression was famously unreadable. 'Sulla? What is it?'

'You are not going to like it, Lucius.'

'I hate it already.'

'You hate what?'

'Whatever you are not telling me. Come on, out with it.'

'Remember, the official line is that nothing has happened over these past few months. No killings, kidnappings, attempted poisonings, murders, or ambushes. We are all going to act as though everything has been normal. The only mayhem to occur at your Death Trap is that planned for your coming party. Is that going ahead by the way?'

'Of course. We designed the atrium for blood to wash out easily. Why not have the party? The place is cleaned up already.

There is no evidence of the fight.'

'Apart from a shattered bannister and an odd burial along the Appian way. Someone put up an impressive tomb.' Sulla closed his eyes and recited from memory. 'To the spirits of the underworld. Here lies Bocchus of Alba. He died doing what he loved. This memorial was erected by his comrade-in-arms.' A bit bizarre, wouldn't you say?'

'It was a rush job. You had to have been there to understand. In any case, your valiant attempt to change the subject has been noted, as has also your discreet hint about wanting to be invited to the coming party. Please do come. In fact I would be hurt if you did not.'

'Why, thank you, Lucius Panderius. I shall be there. In return, may I invite you to a dinner party of my own? It's in ten days, so you should have recovered by then.'

I regarded Sulla warily. 'And so we arrive at the point. What's the occasion?'

'A meeting of all the officers going with me on campaign in the spring. A sort of bonding, get-to-know you kind of affair.'

'Sounds innocent enough. What's the problem?'

'The guest of honour. Our commanding officer, Caius Marius.'

'What? No, no way!'

Sulla's face was stony. 'Marius is meeting all his officers while he is in town. That is standard practice. I have to meet him with my staff, and that staff includes you. At least by meeting at a dinner party, the occasion will be on my ground with my people.'

'We do not have a choice. If we are pretending nothing has happened, there is no reason for you not to be present. If you stay away that gives the lie to the official line that we all all friends and comrades. We can't do that. Everything has to look normal, so the dinner goes ahead. Start learning how to eat lamprey through gritted teeth. Having got the news earlier, I've already had three days practice.'

'Marius is coming to Rome? Why?'

'He's here. Arrived yesterday. How do you think the big boys on the Senate were able to lean on him so quickly? Orestes, remember?'

I did. Rome always has two Consuls, and Aurelius Orestes had been Marius' fellow-Consul. The old boy had died of a fever, and as the surviving Consul was obliged to do, Marius had come to Rome to organize the election of Orestes' replacement. Obviously, while he was at it, Marius was getting through the bits of the coming campaign that had to be organized in Rome.

Marius would be expected to dine at least once with each of his officers. Since there was no getting out of it, Sulla had decided that Marius should be his guest rather than his host. That allowed Sulla more control of the meeting, but it also meant that Sulla's junior officers would be expected to be at the dinner. Including Sulla's intelligence officer, Lucius Panderius.

'Come on,' urged Sulla.'It won't be so bad. You embrace him at the start of the meal, go to the opposite side of the dining room and recline with your colleagues. As the host, I am the one who has to spend the evening actually talking to the dolt. You just sit quietly in the background. Tell you what. I will even hire your newest clients to do the catering. How's that?'

My 'newest clients' were the team of Ava and Cyrenicus. My mind went back to a morning three days ago.

That was when a rather bashful Ava had approached me for a very large loan. With the money, she proposed to buy the freedom of Cyrenicus and set up her own catering establishment.

'I thought you hated his guts?'

'The swine's guts? Well, no. He stuffs them with a combination of minced venison, spices and meal, then uses egg white as emulsion, and fries them. They're rather good. I don't remember criticizing that dish. I may have mentioned that he's stupidly prissy about the ingredients *and* that he's so annoying about following the recipe to the letter, as though Jupiter would smite him for the slightest deviation. But the results aren't that bad. You had them yourself the other day - stuffed pig intestine with truffles and onion. Remember?'

I sighed, and tried again. 'Are you and Cyrenicus getting along better these days?'

'Gods, no! He's arrogant, inflexible and opinionated. He won't listen to reason, no matter how sweet I try to make it. I came close to braining him with a soup tureen yesterday evening.'

'So what's the deal? Why do you want to free him?'

Ava blushed a pretty shade of bright crimson and looked at the floor. 'I want to marry him.'

'You gave up a slave worth a king's ransom, just to please an employee,' Sulla observed. 'Who would have thought you were that sentimental?'

'Without the quick reflexes of that employee, my skull would have been shattered by a brick a while back. I owe her. Not to mention that she was kidnapped, enslaved and raped because of me. She's due some happiness.'

'There's also a business aspect. Quite a few clients come to the Temple as much for the cuisine as for the sex. Cookery, however, does not pay quite as well as fornication, especially as those two maniacs happily pay over the odds for the best ingredients. They need a wider clientèle to be profitable.'

'I'm buying out the sausage seller who runs his stand in the kiosk built into the Temple's outer wall. We'll combine that with the next door kiosk, and expand the business back through the wall into the Temple. That way, we will have a first-class kitchen, the best courtesans in Rome and the public can pick and mix their indulgences. Everyone's a winner.'

Sulla grunted. 'So, we have a happy ending.'

'For them. I hope so. For me ... there's no way of getting out of this dinner?'

'Not without giving the appearance that you and Marius are still feuding. As it is, it looks as if I'll soon have to call in some favours and get transferred to Catulus' command. Even without you adding grit to the millstones, Marius and I are starting to seriously dislike one another.'

'He sees you as a rival. Marius doesn't like rivals.'

'He doesn't like you either. Your friend Momina has really stirred things up.'

Dinner at the *Domus Sullani*. There were ten of us there, apart from Sulla, our host. The others were military tribunes, mostly aspiring young politicians looking for some military experience with which to impress the electorate. Several were customers at the Temple, and five of them were also friends and invitees to my coming party.

I wore a stylish tunic of Tarentine wool, but several of my colleagues affected the *synthesis*; a special dinner outfit somewhere between a mantle and a woman's dress. The fashion was catching on, but I had gone with the tunic. It allowed me to wear a belt, and my little *sicarius* dagger was tucked into that belt, just in case.

In keeping with our host's mordant sense of humour, the floor of Sulla's atrium was adorned with mosaics of skeletons and funeral wreaths. This made an odd - and deliberate - contrast to the succulent smells wafting in from the kitchen, and the rich taste of the snacks passed around on trays by scantily-clad serving girls. We milled about in the atrium, sipping at a well-watered but nevertheless fair-to-middling vintage Calene wine, and chatted inconsequentially. A flautist provided soothing background music, but despite this the general mood was uneasy. Sulla and

Marius had clashed openly in the Senate that day, and now Marius was late.

A mental picture of the scene in the kitchens came to my mind. Cyrenicus would be pacing up and down expostulating nervously and impatiently. Ava would be stolidly adding water to the meat stock to prevent it congealing, scraping charcoal from the ovens to lower the temperature and periodically turning to snap at Cyrenicus to tell him to shut up and pull himself together.

Out in the atrium Sulla chatted, joked and spun tall tales of his exploits in Africa. He seemed totally unaware of the passing time and the fact that Marius' continued absence was starting to look like a deliberate insult. The guests were starting to throw anxious looks toward the main door. I was not the only one who wanted this dinner eaten and over as soon as possible.

The opening course was to be hot chickpea soup. This showed that Sulla was not exactly trying to appease his guest. Marius was highly sensitive to allegations that his parents had been farm labourers in the mountain town of Arpinum. (They were actually well-off burghers of that town, but a good slander sticks). Therefore serving a peasant dish as the opening course was tactless, and deliberately so. The main course was based on cheeses and meats from the Alpine valleys. This was a reminder that Sulla's main role in the spring campaign would be to provision the army with supplies levied from tribes from these same valleys. The meal would provide a foretaste of what was to come.

After an hour, Marius had still not arrived. I reckoned the soup was still salvageable, but the lamb would be getting dry and stringy. The flautist had run out of tunes and was starting to repeat herself, and the snacks and the conversation had run dry. I was about to sidle over to Sulla and suggest that if dinner was to be saved, we needed to start, with or without our principal guest.

Then Marius chose to make an appearance.

He came on foot, bowling past the doorman who rushed forward to collect his cloak. In the darkness outside the main door I glimpsed shadowy figures taking station by the door with military precision. Marius was without his lictors, but he still had a bodyguard.

Caius Marius stood just below medium height, a stocky man with a pugnacious set to his jaw and disconcertingly merry blue eyes. There was a sprinkling of white in his black curly hair, and his face was lined and reddened. Marius liked to share the same conditions as his common soldiers, and years on campaign had weathered his countenance. Like me, Marius wore a tunic, though his was of coarser wool than my own. His legs were encased in soft leather. Marius suffered from appalling varicose veins, and usually wore high boots to hide them as much as possible. Tonight's boots were custom-made affairs; dining slippers on the sole, but high-cut to simulate a military appearance.

It was immediately clear that our Consul and guest of honour was comprehensively, staggering drunk.

In retrospect, we should have realized that the dinner would be as much, or more, of an ordeal for Marius than for us. Marius disliked subtlety, and no doubt suspected that Sulla's refined urbanite officers would amuse themselves by seeing how many of their digs and insinuations would fly over his tousled head. Nor, as the implied insult of the chickpea soup proved, was Marius wrong in this suspicion.

Furthermore, Sulla's easy mastery of this sort of social situation made Marius both envious and uncomfortable. He was a man known for his poor grasp of etiquette and notorious for his public lapses in taste. Given Marius' large ego and deep-seated feelings of inadequacy among sophisticated Romans, this would have been bad enough. However, at that same dinner, Marius had to meet and appear friendly to his worst enemy. The man whom his infallible prophetess had said would ruin his reputation and legacy, kill him, and throw his dishonoured ashes into the river Aniene.

No wonder Marius had drunk a skinful of courage to prepare himself for the ordeal. Being Marius, he was certainly not going to back down. He was prepared to take the fight to his enemy.

'Hurt yourself, have you?' he sneered, as I was formally presented to him at the pre-meal introductions.

'Indeed,' I responded, looking at the walking cane that supported my still-delicate hip. The cane was of cornelian wood, a joke which Lucius Cornelius Sulla certainly appreciated, and which Marius would have missed entirely even had he been sober.

'Did one of your customers screw you a bit too roughly?' enquired Marius with sweet mock sympathy.

'Oh, no. Here in Rome, brothel owners don't entertain the clients personally. It's rather like the difference between owning gladiators and doing the fighting yourself in the arena. I'm not sure how the brothel business works in Arpinum, though. It may be different there.'

If Marius could fight dirty so could I. By explaining Roman customs, in a slightly patronizing way, I was emphasising to Marius his status as an outsider, the peasant from Arpinum finding his way in the big city.

The Consul's face darkened. 'Are you making fun of me, boy?

'Certainly not, sir. I injured my leg in a fall. At the time I was saying goodbye to one of my *fwiends*.'

At this unsubtle reference to the late Sabaco, the anger in Marius' face deepened to fury. Sulla hastily intervened. Uttering smooth platitudes, he diplomatically took his principal guest by the arm and led him into the dining room. At the entrance to the triclinium Marius wrenched his elbow free and turned to glare back at me. I pretended to be deep in conversation with another guest and paid no attention.

'You have a piss-poor choice of client,' Marius remarked to Sulla in a voice everyone in the room could hear. 'Is that the best class of follower you can find?'

'Well, after the untimely death of his father, poor Lucius has had to to the best he can. In fact, he's done rather well.' Sulla was deftly defending me and at the same time, by his reference to my father, reminding Marius that hostilities in our feud were supposed to be suspended. Regrettably, Marius was too drunk to care. Nor were Sulla's most valiant efforts to distract his guest at all successful. Throughout the soup course, Marius glared at me from across the room.

Then, in a rare misstep, Sulla mentioned that the dinner was being cooked by my staff from the Temple - 'the best cooks in Rome'. Marius responded by glowering at his soup bowl. Doubtless he now considered me the author of the insult implied by the peasant-style food. Deliberately, he tipped his bowl so that it and its contents smashed to the floor. A shocked murmur ran around the room.

'Did you think that was funny, brothel boy?' Marius demanded.

'Sir?' The evening was rapidly going from bad to worse.

'Don't think I'm stupid. Your silly little insinuations and slurs. The way you and your companion have been cuddling up on your dining couch sniggering about me. You think I don't see it?'

In fact the diner with whom I had been sharing a couch had been making rather strained conversation about a play by Aeschylus that we had both seen at the Caelian Odeon. Marius believed otherwise, and would not be persuaded.

'I am your Consul, you whimpering degenerate!' he thundered.

The other diners exchanged stunned looks. This was outrageous behaviour for a Roman dinner party, and since only

253

Sulla and I knew the background to events, Marius' behaviour bordered on the bizarre. The Consul's face was almost scarlet with fury.

'You, Panderius, will show me the respect I deserve!'

It was too much. Before Sulla could intervene, I replied coolly. 'My most sincere apologies, Consul. It was my belief I was showing you exactly the respect you deserve. I shall try to do more in future.'

Drunk as he was, Marius understood what was meant by that. 'I can crush you, Panderius!' he shouted. 'You, with your simpering jokes. I've crushed more important men, senators of Rome. I can wipe you off my sandals like the filthy little turd that you are. And, by Jupiter, I will.'

So much for me keeping out of the way at the dinner party. At this rate, we'd come to blows.

Sulla must have come to the same conclusion. Indeed, for a second it seemed that Sulla was going to hit Marius himself. After all, this was his dinner party. Marius' conduct showed disrespect for his host that went well past the point of open insult. On top of that, Marius was openly and violently attacking one of Sulla's own clients - and Sulla's guest - in front of Sulla in his own home.

'Consul,' Sulla spoke sharply. 'I beg you, please to remember the proprieties of the situation. Such bickering with a junior officer is beneath one of your station. Let us relax and enjoy our meal. If you wish, I shall ask that Panderius be excused from our company.'

Good enough for me. I was already picking up my napkin and preparing to depart, but Marius was not yet done. He turned on Sulla.

'Oh yes, well. Of course you would defend your client. Your dear Panderius. Or is he more than a client? Is he your bum boy too? No, I'll bet you are his.'

There was a shocked gasp from around the room. 'Oh, I say

... ,' someone murmured.

Homosexual relations were not that unusual among Roman men - indeed Sulla was said to indulge himself in that manner occasionally. However, in such cases the paramour was always a boy in his early to mid-teens. For two adult Roman males to have a sexual relationship was scandalous. To allege that one took the receiving, the pathic role, that was a mortal insult.

Sulla's face went sheet-white apart from two ugly red blotches of fury which slowly spread across his cheeks. His grey eyes glittered, but when he spoke his voice was light and controlled.

'Come gentlemen,' he addressed the dinner party. 'Do not look so appalled. Such is the raillery of the tent. If you are going to spend the summer in an army camp, you must get used to rough soldierly humour of this kind. The Consul and I permit ourselves such jests, as we are former comrades-in-arms.'

It sounded almost credible, not that I believed a word of it. Marius might be Consul, but to Sulla he was still an upstart from the countryside. Sulla's Cornelian ancestors had been Consuls of Rome four centuries ago, when Arpinum had been an obscure Samnite town. Sulla's branch of the family might have fallen low before Sulla himself had restored it, but that simply made Sulla all the more sensitive to slights. Nor was this merely a slight. Sulla had been offered a deadly insult, and I knew my patron well enough to know that in his case 'deadly' meant just that. My vendetta was now Sulla's, and it would be to the death.

Marius seemed to realise that he had gone much too far. He offered Sulla a sickly grin, but Sulla was not finished. He told his audience, 'In fact, when this war is over, Marius has an arrangement by which I shall take him swimming in the river Aniene.'

'What?' Marius looked at Sulla incredulously as the words of the prophecy played back in his mind.

Sulla gave the stricken Consul an amiable smile. 'Woof, woof,' he said.

Oh, no. My fellow diners looked curiously from one face to the other in an attempt to work out what was going on. I fought the impulse to bury my face in my hands.

Sulla continued expansively, addressing the dinner party at large. 'Our Consul Marius is a follower of Jupiter, a martial god, and he is therefore occasionally rough in his humour.'

'My Greek friends, on the other hand, call me *Epaphroditus*. Since our Consul here has such poor Greek, let me translate that for him. It means 'Beloved of Aphrodite'. Though the Goddess of Love can be even more cruel than the gods of war, her manner is more gentle. She is kind to her servants.'

Marius looked at Sulla in wild consternation, his mouth agape. 'You?' he asked in a strangled voice.

No priest of the Fetiales delivering a formal declaration of war to Rome's enemies could have done so as precisely and pitilessly as Sulla did now.

Driving each word home like a dagger he said, 'Oh yes. I am a follower of the Goddess. In fact, I consider myself to be the greatest, the foremost, servant of Aphrodite.'

Appendices

The Tolosan Gold
How could you have a craftier crime? ... Consider other cases -
the affair of the Gold of Tolosa.
Cicero *On the Nature of the Gods* 3.74

After the gold was discovered to be missing, there was a huge
enquiry in Rome.
Orosius *Contra Paganos* 5.16

Sertorius
After the Romans had been defeated and put to flight, though he
had lost his horse and had been wounded in the body, he made
his way across the Rhone. So sturdy was his body and so trained
to hardship that he swam the river with his shield and breastplate
and all, and that against a strongly adverse current.

Then ... while Marius was in command, Sertorius undertook to
spy out the enemy. So, putting on a Celtic dress and acquiring
the commonest expressions of that language for such conversation as might be necessary, he mingled with the Barbarians.
Plutarch *Life of Sertorius* 3

Turpillius Panderius
At all this Metellus was evidently displeased. But it was the affair
of Turpillius that most vexed him. This man, Turpillius, was an
hereditary guest-friend of Metellus, and at this time was serving
in the army as chief of engineers. But he was put in charge of
Vaga, a large city, and because he relied for safety on his doing
the inhabitants no wrong, but rather treating them with kindness
and humanity, he unawares came into the power of the enemy;
for they admitted Jugurtha into their city.

Still, they did Turpillius no harm, but obtained his release and sent him away safe and sound. Accordingly, a charge of treachery was brought against him; and Marius, who was a member of the council which tried the case, was himself bitter, and he exasperated most of the others against the accused, so that Metellus was reluctantly forced to pass sentence of death upon him.

After a short time, however, the charge was found to be false, and almost everybody sympathized with Metellus in his grief. But Marius, full of joy, claimed the condemnation as his own work. He was not ashamed to go about saying that he had fastened Nemesis upon the fate of Metellus, who would avenge the murder of a client.

Plutarch *Life of Marius* 8

Mucius Scaevola

As a lawyer Quintus Mucius [Scaevola] was more famous for his knowledge of jurisprudence than, strictly speaking, for eloquence.

Velleius Paterculus *History* 2.9

Quintus Mucius also spoke much for the defence, with his usual accuracy and elegance; but not with that force and reach which the manner of the trial and the importance of the occasion demanded .

Cicero *Brutus* 113

Sabaco

Suspicion was chiefly aroused by the sight of a servant of Cassius Sabaco inside the railings among the voters; for Sabaco was a particular friend of Marius. Sabaco was therefore summoned before the court, and testified ... Sabaco, however, was expelled

from the Senate by the censors of the next year, and it was thought that he deserved this punishment, either because he had given false testimony, or because of his intemperance.
Plutarch *Life of Marius* 5

The Contio of Norbanus

L. Cassius Longinus, Tribune of the plebs in the consulship of C. Marius carried a number of laws ... including this one, namely that anyone who had been condemned by the people or stripped of his command by the people was also to be ejected from the Senate. The main reason for this was his quarrel with Q. Servilius [Caepio].
Asconius 78c

Norbanus' violence was based on the grief of the people, and their hatred of Caepio for the loss of his army. This could not be suppressed, it was justifiable.
Ibid 2.124

You were citing to the Court the violence, the flight, the torch-throwing and the Tribune's ruthlessness that marked the disastrous and lamentable affair of Caepio ; then too it was established that Marcus Aemilius [Sacurus], chief of the Senate and chief man in the State had been struck by a stone, while it was undeniable that Lucius Cotta and Titus Didius, on trying to veto a resolution, had been forcibly driven away.
Cicero *On Oratory* 2.47

Momina/Martha

Marius told his soldiers that certain oracles had told him to wait for the right time and place for his victory. Indeed, he used to ceremoniously carry a woman named Martha about in a litter. She was said to have the gift of prophecy, and he would make sacrifices at her bidding.

She had ... sat at the feet of the wife of Marius when some gladiators were fighting and successfully foretold each time which one was going to be victorious. In consequence of this, the wife sent her to Marius and she was admired by him. She attended the sacrifices clothed in a double purple robe that was fastened with a clasp, and carried a spear that was wreathed with fillets and chaplets.
Plutarch *Life of Marius* 17

Sulla v. Marius
Many wished Sulla to have the glory of [ending the Jugurthan war] because they hated Marius, and Sulla himself had a seal-ring made, which he used to wear, on which was engraved the surrender of Jugurtha to him by King Bocchus. By constantly using this ring Sulla provoked Marius, who was an ambitious man, quarrelsome, and jealous of sharing his glory with another.

And the enemies of Marius gave Sulla most encouragement, by attributing the first and greatest successes of the war to Metellus, but the last, and the termination of it, to Sulla, so that the people would then cease to admire Marius and give to him their chief allegiance.
Plutarch *Life of Marius* 10

But perceiving that Marius was now against him ... and was no longer prepared to give him opportunities for action, but actually opposed his advancement, Sulla attached himself to Catulus, the colleague of Marius in the consulship, a worthy man.
Life of Sulla 4

Of all those who eclipsed him in popular esteem, Marius was

most vexed and annoyed by Sulla, whose rise to power was due to the jealousy which the nobles felt towards Marius, and who was making his quarrels with Marius the basis of his political activity.
Life of Marius 32

But he [Sulla] himself, in writing ... styled himself *Epaphroditus*, or 'Beloved of Venus', and on his trophies in our country [Greece] his name is inscribed as follows: Lucius Cornelius Sulla Epaphroditus.
Life of Sulla 34

AR Denarius (3.86 gm). Diademed head of Venus right; cupid with long palm branch before / Capis and lituus between two trophies. Cr359/2; Syd 761
Coin issued by Sulla in later years.

The Gold of Tolosa
Philip Matyszak

Introducing Lucius Panderius, war hero, connoisseur of fine wines and Germanic prostitutes - and the perpetrator of the biggest gold theft in history. This first novel by well-known writer and historian Philip Matyszak takes us from the mean streets of Rome to the even meaner streets of Gallic Tolosa in a journey filled with ambush, intrigue, battle and double-cross.

In 105 BC Rome is faced with extinction, both from a huge army of invading barbarians and by a dark curse that has been festering for generations. It falls to Lucius Panderius to avert both threats, and incidentally to make himself richer than Croesus. Though fiction, the *Gold of Tolosa* is historically accurate and explains how enough loot to recapitalize a third-world economy was taken in a theft that really did happen.

Whether Lucius is crossing swords with barbarian warriors or Roman magistrates, the pace is never less than frantic, and ancient Rome has never been more fun ...

'Great atmosphere, a good story, and a strong sense of fun all combine to make this a wonderful excursion to the world of Republican Rome.'

Adrian Goldsworthy, author of *'Caesar: Life of a Colossus'*

'Fun jaunt through the bloody landscape of late Republican Rome.'

Ancient Warfare Magazine

ΛΛΛΡ
Monashee Mountain Publishing

CPSIA information can be obtained
at www.ICGtesting.com
Printed in the USA
LVOW01s2342130716
496244LV00036B/1070/P